INFRARED

INFRARED

NANCY HUSTON

GROVE PRESS
New York

Originally published in French in 2010 by Editions Actes Sud , Paris.

This edition first published in 2011 in Australia by
The Text Publishing Company.

Printed in the United States of America

ISBN-13: 978-0-8021-2027-4

Grove Press
an imprint of Grove/Atlantic, Inc.
841 Broadway
New York, NY 10003

Distributed by Publishers Group West

www.groveatlantic.com

12 13 14 15   10 9 8 7 6 5 4 3 2 1

For the Djawara

'...and suddenly the piercing pain of love,
the lost look in the stranger's eyes, expressing all that's missing...'
CLAUDIO MAGRIS

'Take my wound!
Through it, the whole world will flow into you.'
THE BROTHERS GRIMM

CONTENTS

Rena is slanting to the right, slowly sinking farther and farther to the right on the red leather seat of the coffee shop, gradually collapsing against her stepmother's corpulent maternal body. They've been up all night, and it's been a long night indeed. Ingrid puts an arm around her and in the dawn's uncertain light it would be difficult to say which of the two women is hanging onto the other. Though her eyes are closed, Rena is not asleep—far from it. She's conscious of the smells of bleach and frothy milk, the bitter taste of tobacco in her throat, the soft touch of Ingrid's blouse against her cheek, all the reassuring noises in the café—spoons clinking, doors opening and shutting, to say nothing of the numerous overlapping voices, businessmen in a hurry to down a last *ristretto* before boarding the train for Rome, a drunkard ordering his first beer of the day, loud-speaker announcements about arrivals and departures, the chatter of waitresses. I sink therefore I am, Rena says to herself, or rather, I'm sinking towards the right therefore I am in Italy, in italics, all my thoughts are in italics, insisting, repeating, recriminating, accusing, screaming at me, *How is it possible? You claim to be an ultrasensitive film and yet you saw nothing, noticed nothing, detected nothing, guessed at nothing, comprehended nothing?* No, because—not that, you understand, breast yes skin yes stomach yes bronchia yes mediastinum yes, since 1936 infrared photography has been used in all those areas but not in this one not in this one no, no, not at all.

TUESDAY

'I'll go anywhere.'

'So you're the last Greenblatt,' grunts the proprietor of the Hotel Guelfa, in Italian, without looking at her, glancing sullenly instead at the photo in her passport. 'Your parents arrived late last night,' he adds—repeating, in a tone heavily laced with reproach, 'Very late.'

Rena doesn't correct him, doesn't explain that they're not her parents, or rather that one is and that the other isn't; having not the slightest wish to open that can of worms, that Pandora's box, that raft of the Medusa, she holds her tongue in Italian, smiles in Italian, nods in Italian, and strives to radiate the serenity to which she ardently aspires. The truth is that she's been dreading this moment for weeks.

'I know it's absurd,' she murmured to Aziz only a few hours ago as they nosed through the thick fog which for some mysterious reason seems to shroud Roissy-Charles de Gaulle Airport in all seasons and at all hours. 'My trip hasn't even started yet, and already I feel guilty.'

'Hey, the lady exaggerates,' said Aziz teasingly, even as he stroked her left thigh. 'Not only is she treating herself to a week's holiday in Tuscany, but she wants us to feel sorry for her.'

Standing next to the car at the drop-off point, she kissed her man lingeringly. 'Goodbye, love…We'll talk every day, won't we?'

'You bet.' Aziz took her in his arms and gave her a mighty hug. Then, stepping back, looking into her eyes: 'You do look a bit wasted this morning, but I'm not worried. You're armed to the teeth—you'll survive.'

Aziz knows her well. Knows she's planned to keep Simon and Ingrid at a distance by aiming, framing, firing at them with her Canon. 'You'll survive,' he repeated as he climbed back into the car. She leaned down to drown herself in his dark eyes one more time—and then, by way of farewell, slowly drew her index finger along his lower lip.

They'd made love this morning before the alarm clock went off and she'd wanted him to come on her face, it was such a powerful sensation to be holding his sex with both her hands and suddenly feel the semen spurting through, when it had splashed out warm and marvellous she'd spread it over her face and neck and breasts like an elixir of youth, feeling it cool as it dried…Washing this morning, she'd purposely left a bit of her lover's invisible trace beneath her jaw, at the top of her neck—like a thin, translucid mask to protect her, see her through the impending trial…

The man hands her a key and informs her, still grumpily and in Italian, that Room 25 is on the second floor, by which he means the third floor, at the far end of the corridor.

What he doesn't tell her is that the room is in fact the same thing as the corridor; they've simply put up a door and built a tiny shower stall in one corner. Rena sees at once that she mustn't leave anything on the sink, because the sink will be taking its shower at the same time as she does. The room is long and narrow—well, narrow, anyhow—and its window gives onto a charming little garden in the back: flowers, climbing vines, red-tiled roofs. She takes a deep breath. You see? she says inwardly to Subra, the special Friend who accompanies her wherever she goes. It is Florence. I mean, there is beauty.

And why on earth would you feel guilty? Subra asks her. I mean, you're not Beatrice Cenci or anything.

True, Rena nods. In the first place, I wasn't born into an aristocratic family in Rome in the sixteenth century. In the second place, I'm not twenty-one years old. My forty-five-year-old father didn't lock me up in his *palazzo* in the Abruzzi with his second wife Lucrezia, to humiliate and brutalise us. He didn't try to rape me. I didn't plan his murder with the help of my brother and stepmother. I didn't hire professional killers, instruct them to drive an iron peg into his right eye and personally oversee the crime. I didn't go on to push his dead body over the edge of the cliff. I wasn't arrested, brought to trial, and condemned to death. My head didn't get chopped off in 1599 near the Ponte Sant'Angelo on the Tiber. No, no, the whole situation is different—this is Florence, not Rome, my stepmother loves my father, I'm the one who's forty-five, my head is sitting squarely on my shoulders…and everyone is innocent.

Subra chuckles.

Rena walks down the corridor to Room 23 and scratches at the door like a cat. Lengthy silence. So why am I so terrified? There is beauty. I've simply made them the gift of a trip to Italy, a country neither of them has ever visited before, to celebrate my Daddy's seventieth birthday…

Sacco di Firenze

Simon has never looked in a less celebratory mood; as for Ingrid, her eyes are red and puffy from crying.

Though it's past noon, they've just got up. It seems they narrowly escaped a tragedy last night—Ingrid tells Rena about it in detail over breakfast. They'd arrived late from Rotterdam, at one a.m., having travelled all day in a train filled to bursting with rambunctious *ragazzi*. Exhausted, they'd disembarked and tried to get their bearings in this foreign city, foreign country, foreign tongue. They'd wandered endlessly around the Stazione Santa Maria Novella, weighed down by all seven pieces of their luggage, some on wheels, others straining their back and shoulder muscles. Disorientated, they'd got lost and made a huge detour, trudging past wonders and detesting them for not being the Hotel Guelfa. (Santa Maria Novella—not the station but the church, decorated by Domenico Ghirlandaio, the master of Michelangelo himself—right there before their eyes, in the sweet Florentine night...) Bone-tired, they'd stopped on a corner to catch their breath, calm the pounding of their hearts and check the map under a streetlight. When at long last they'd reached their room at the Hotel Guelfa, after waiting at the door, explaining things to the irate proprietor and gasping their way up two steep flights of stairs, Ingrid had automatically counted their bags and... six instead of seven. Re-counted—truly, six. Heart flip. The missing piece of luggage, though the smallest, was also the most precious: a small rucksack containing their money, plane tickets, passports... Simon—dog-tired, wiped-out, septuagenarian, lost—trundled back downstairs, returned to the corner where they'd stopped to rest, and—despite the incessant comings and goings at that spot—found the bag propped up against the streetlight.

'As miraculously intact as the Madonna,' he triumphantly concludes.

The mere memory of last night's panic has reduced Ingrid to tears.

Gee, thinks Rena, we could write an epic poem about this. *The Sack of Florence*, a counterpart to The Sack of Rome. But Ingrid wouldn't want to know that Charles V's armies razed the latter city in 1527, causing twenty thousand deaths and incalculable losses to Italy's artistic heritage: to her mind, the only destruction in the history of humanity is that of her native city of Rotterdam by the Germans, on the fourteenth of May 1940. She was just a month old at the time, her family's house was hit, her mother and three brothers died when it collapsed, her own life was saved by the cast-iron stove next to which her cradle had been set—'I was born in ruins,' she loves to tell people, sobbing; 'I suckled a corpse.'

'Uh…Florence? Did you want to see Florence?'

Bad start.

Angoli del mondo

Whereas the Florentines are already halfway through their day's work, Simon and Ingrid seem in no rush to get up from the breakfast table.

'Won't you have some pastry, Rena?' Ingrid says. 'You've lost weight, haven't you? How much do you weigh now?'

She resents it that my body doesn't change, thinks Rena. So far, at least, neither motherhood nor passing time have managed to fill it out. At forty-five my measurements are the same as they were at age eighteen, when we first met. She thinks poor Toussaint and Thierno must have been horribly squashed in there. She has a hard time with my appearance in general, which she finds morbid—my inordinate taste for dark glasses, dark everything, leather.

That Rena! Subra says, imitating Ingrid's voice in Rena's mind. Still using a backpack instead of a handbag, because she's allergic to ladies' handbags and to everything ladylike in general. Now also sporting a man's fedora, no doubt to protect her head from the sun and rain while leaving her hands free for photography. And her hair's cut so short, you'd think she was a lesbian…Actually that wouldn't surprise me…nothing surprises me, coming from Rena…I mean, why limit yourself to men? If you've got an explorer's soul you explore everything, don't you? Besides which, there's her brother's example…

'You know I abhor scales,' Rena says aloud. 'Even when my kids were babies, I refused to weigh them. I figured if they got too puny, I'd notice it all by myself.'

'But surely they weigh you when you have an appointment at the doctor's?'

'That's one reason I do my best to avoid members of that profession…Um, let me think…Hundred and seven or so, last time I checked.'

'That's not enough for a woman of your height…Right, Dad?'

'Sorry…I'll do my best to shrink.'

Oh, dear, Simon doesn't laugh. He is Rena's father, not Ingrid's, but Ingrid has been calling him Dad since their four daughters were born in the eighties and he doesn't seem to mind.

Poor Simon, Rena thinks. He looks discouraged in advance. Dreads the coming days. Fears I'll be dragging them here and there, pushing them around, impressing and amazing them, overwhelming them with my erudition, my energy and curiosity. Thinks maybe they should have gone straight home to Montreal from Rotterdam. Is afraid of disappointing me. 'Dear daughter, I confess that I am old,' as Lear puts it…Seventy isn't old at all nowadays, but the fact is that he's tired and I weigh on him. No matter how skinny I am…

After ingesting the disgusting cellophane-wrapped pastries and the so-called orange juice, they wonder if they could have a second cup of coffee. Not cappuccino this time round, regular coffee.

Rena moves to the counter to place their order, and when the proprietor mutters that *cappuccino* and *caffè latte* are the *stessa cosa*, she goes into more detail, explaining that what the couple would really like is a pot of weak coffee with a jug of hot milk on the side. This she obtains. The couple is flabbergasted.

'But…you speak Italian!' exclaims Ingrid.

No, not really, it's just that…communication's so much easier between strangers.

'Easy to be a polyglot,' says Ingrid, pursuing her reflection on Rena's linguistic gifts, 'when you've been married to a whole slew of foreigners and travelled to the four corners of the Earth for your profession.'

9

Yeah, Subra snickers, so don't go putting on airs.

Right, Rena sighs. No point in reminding her, as I've already done countless times, that my four husbands—Fabrice the Haitian, Khim the Cambodian, Alioune the Senegalese and Aziz the Algerian—were all, thanks to the unstinting generosity of French colonisation, francophones…as, indeed, were my Québecois lovers—all the professors, truck drivers, waiters, singers and garbage-men whose *t'es belle, fais-moi une 'tite bec, chu tombé en amour avec toué* graced my teenage years…I much preferred them to my anglophone neighbours and classmates—far too healthy for my taste, approaching sex in much the same way as they approached jogging (though usually removing their shoes first), interrogating me in the thick of things as to the nature and intensity of my pleasure, and dashing off to shower the minute they'd climaxed.

Maybe that's when you started thinking of the English language as a cold shower, jokes Subra.

Could be. I'm not a Francophile but a Francophonophile—I have a foible for the French language in all its forms…Still, I get by just fine in Italian.

'Funny expression, when you think about it,' muses Simon, 'the four corners of the Earth.'

'It's a figure of speech!' Ingrid says defensively.

'Yeah, but it must date from before Columbus, don't you think?' insists her husband. 'When people still believed the Earth was flat.'

'Uh…' Rena dares to interject. 'Don't you guys want to go out?'

They can't say no, she adds, in an aside to Subra. I mean, they can't cross their arms and say, To tell you the truth, Rena, we prefer to spend our week in Tuscany locked up in cheap hotel room without a view.

Rena clings to Subra, the imaginary older sister who, these thirty-odd years, has been sharing her opinions, laughing at her jokes, blithely swallowing her lies (feigning, for instance, to credit the idea that she and Aziz are already married) and assuaging her anxieties.

Cro-Magnon

Scarcely half an hour later, they emerge into the Via Guelfa.

When she sees that Simon has donned a bright blue baseball cap and Ingrid a fluorescent pink dufflecoat, Rena swallows her dismay. Okay, I'll go the whole hog, she thinks. I'll drink the bitter cup of tourism to the dregs—why be embarrassed? That's what we are. She gets a hold of herself by gently drawing the back of her hand over the faint trace of Aziz beneath her jaw.

Their first destination is the Basilica of San Lorenzo, but before they've gone half a block, Simon's gaze is drawn by something in an inner courtyard. What is it?

'What did he see?'

'A pair of legs,' says Ingrid.

'Legs?'

'Yes,' cries Simon. 'Come and see!'

The two women have no choice but to cross the courtyard. He's right—beyond the filthy windowpane of some sort of workshop is a pair of human legs.

'Weird, isn't it? What do you think it is?'

I have no idea, Dad— and besides, who cares? *This* isn't Florence...

They approach. There's no denying it's weird. The legs are naked but full of holes, hollow inside, and surrounded by animal furs. Weirder still, they're upside down, spread apart and bent at the knees...

'It almost looks like a woman giving birth, doesn't it, Dad?' says Ingrid.

'Yeah, except that they're men's legs,' Simon points out.

'Don't you want to take a photo, Rena?'

'I don't photograph weird things.'

Oh, I see, says Subra, again imitating Ingrid's voice, you don't photograph weird things. Three hundred and fifty *Whore Sons and Daughters*—there's nothing weird about that, of course. Mafiosi, hooligans, traders, sleeping nudes—just your ordinary, run-of-the-mill stuff.

Rena moves closer to the window and peers beyond the pair of legs inside the workshop, then recoils with a gasp.

'What's wrong?'

There, inches away from her face, lying on his back—a living man. Smouldering dark eyes, slightly yellowed teeth, flaring nostrils, low forehead, reddish beard, hairy arms—a Cro-Magnon male, alive.

No. But for an instant, yes. She receives his presence, the heat of his body. No. But for an instant, yes.

Simon points out a dusty sign tacked to the workshop door, and she translates: 'Taxidermy, Moulding.'

'Must be some sort of wax figure they're making for an installation at the Museum of Natural History,' Simon speculates. 'When they finish with the legs, they'll rotate him through a hundred and eighty degrees and set him on his feet.'

'But he won't be erect,' Ingrid objects.

'Yeah, well, he'll be sort of hunched over—to light a fire, say.'

That mystery more or less satisfactorily solved, they hobble back across the courtyard. The wild man continues to smoulder within her, though. What is it? Like what? A disturbing twinge of some far-off thing...

Simon comes to a halt. 'I wonder what the cavewoman felt,' he says, 'when the caveman grabbed her by the hair and dragged her down the path to shtup her in the cave.'

Rena laughs to be polite, even as she heaves an inward sigh.

'I mean,' her father goes on, 'it can't have been much fun to go bouncing and scraping along on the pebbles and rocks like that. To say nothing of all the thistles and nettles and spiky plants that would have been growing amongst them. After her deflowering, the woman would probably cut her hair real short, to let the other men know—okay you guys, from now on: shtupping yes, dragging no. No more of that dragging crap.'

'What I wonder,' says Rena, joining the game out of habit, 'is why he had to drag her to a cave in the first place. Why wouldn't he just shtup her out in the open? I mean, were the Cro-Magnon as modest as all that? Was shtupping already a private activity back then?'

Ostentatiously, Ingrid holds her tongue. She detests conversations like this between Simon and Rena. Finds it abnormal for a father and daughter to indulge in this sort of banter, as if they were buddies. With her own father…God forbid! Had a single syllable on the theme of sex ever passed her lips in his presence, he would have turned her to stone with a glance. To stone!

Try as she might, Rena can't stop. 'Besides,' she insists, 'why would he have had to grab her by the hair? I don't get it. Didn't she feel like shtupping? The virginity taboo didn't come along until much later, right? In the Neolithic?'

No man ever had to drag you by the hair, that's for sure, says Subra in Ingrid's voice. That Rena is boy-crazy!

True, concedes Rena. All a man needs to do is put his hand on the small of my back and my will dissolves completely, my blood tingles like quicksilver, my skin grows a million small soft glittering scales, my legs become a fishtail and I metamorphose into a mermaid. There's something so hypnotic about a man's desire…its imperiousness…A violent thrill of fright and euphoria goes through you when you sense he's chosen *you*…at this instant…Surely the cavewoman would have felt the same melting, the same tingling…

They start walking again. Some fifty yards along, Simon comes to a halt. 'Maybe the cavewoman didn't mind being dragged by the caveman,' he says. 'Maybe her brain released a bunch of endorphins so she wouldn't feel the pain. A bit like when a fakir walks barefoot on hot coals.'

'That's conceivable,' Rena says.

'But maybe the fakir's pain makes itself felt later on,' suggests Ingrid, in a rare attempt at humour. 'I mean, maybe he nurses his burns in secret after the performance, when no one is looking. Right, Dad?'

'No, no,' says Simon. 'There are plenty of scientific studies on fakirs—the soles of their feet are perfectly smooth and pink at the end of the ordeal. No doubt about that.'

They start walking again.

When did my father lose the ability to talk and walk at the same time? wonders Rena.

She makes every effort not to rush them, telling herself there's no reason to advance at one speed rather than another. ('Why is my little Rena always in such a hurry?' Alioune often asked her, when they were still married…'What Makes Rena Greenblatt Run?'—the title of an article about her in some Parisian magazine, ages ago.) But here, today, her impatience is intransitive. Existential. A solid, flourishing psychic reality, eager to apply itself to any activity that might come along in the course of the day.

Some twenty yards further on, Simon comes to a halt. 'On the other hand,' he muses, 'it's altogether possible that the cavewoman's mother trotted out her herbal pastes and tended to her daughter's back once the caveman had pulled up his pants and trundled off to shoot a mammoth.'

'Cro-Magnon didn't wear pants,' says Ingrid.

'Right,' sighs Rena. 'Shall we have a look at this church?'

Proroga

Before they can even get close to San Lorenzo, though, the couple asks for a break. They want to rest on a bench for a few minutes.

Simon shuts his eyes and Rena studies him: heavy eyelids, age-speckled hands and cheeks, furrowed brow, wispy grey hair...Her Daddy. And such a big belly now. How heavy he's become...Whatever happened to the man she'd worshipped during childhood and adolescence, the Westmount years—that slender, handsome young Jewish scientist with his shock of dark curly hair? You, too, Father, once dreamed of Rinascimento. So many botched rebirths, tufts of hair torn out by the roots, tears shed, screams screamed or repressed, years wasted under the sombre reign of doubt...Hey Daddy, it's a gorgeous day, relax! Sit down, sit back, let this ray of Florentine sunshine warm your face...

When Rena was little, her father would sometimes allow her to creep into his study and watch him read and write. (As for her mother's study, either it was empty because she was off pleading in court or else she was receiving a client there for some top-secret conversation and no one else was allowed in. Ms Lisa Heyward had foreign origins and a man's job—two things Rena was proud of. Whereas other kids' mothers were boringly Canadian and worked as homemakers, schoolteachers or secretaries, hers hailed from Australia and was a lawyer. Not only that, but Ms Lisa Heyward hadn't changed her name when she married, which was almost unheard-of at the time. As mothers went, she was exceptionally independent, not to say unreachable.)

On good days, Simon would let his daughter come and curl up on the couch across from his desk. How she loved those moments! Her daddy looked so handsome, lost in thought…his glasses pushed back on his high forehead, his sensitive hands holding pen and paper… 'Mommy's a lawyer and what are you, Daddy?' 'A researcher.' 'How come? Do you keep losing things?' 'Ha, ha, ha, ha!'

But there were bad days, too, when Simon would stay locked up in his study from dawn to dusk. Silence and absence in the daytime— and at night, spectacular quarrels with Lisa in the course of which Rena would learn new words in spite of herself—pretentious, irresponsible, pseudo-genius, mortgage, immature, castrating princess… Simon would roar and Lisa would shriek. Simon would kick walls and Lisa would slam doors. Simon would overturn tables and Lisa would hurl plates. Rena guessed at this division of labour rather than actually witnessing it, for at such times she had a marked tendency to burrow beneath her blankets, drag a pillow over her head and stick her fingers into her ears…

'I got talking to this American woman on the train yesterday,' says Ingrid. 'She told me two cities were absolute musts for tourists in Italy—Florence and Roma.'

'She's right,' nods Rena. 'Unfortunately, as I told you over the phone, we won't have time to visit Rome this time around. There's plenty to do in Tuscany, don't worry.'

'She didn't say Rome,' Ingrid insists, 'she said Roma—didn't she, Dad?'

Rena glances at her to see if she's joking, but she isn't. Finally Simon leans over and whispers into his wife's ear, 'It's the same thing.'

They attempt to enter the church, but—no such luck. They must first purchase tickets—over there, in the passageway that leads to the Biblioteca Laurenziana. There's a lengthy queue at the booth.

As Simon and Rena settle in for a wait, Ingrid wanders into the courtyard to look at the cloister.

But can she really see it? Rena wonders. Can she feel the beauty of this place? Does she know how to marvel at buildings that date back six hundred years? I do, don't I, oh, yes, I do, no doubt about it...Oh, Aziz, it's only the first day and already I'm floundering, sliding towards hysteria...You told me I was armed to the teeth—was it really only *this morning* you pronounced those words?

Photo. Photo. Photo. In black and white, she captures Ingrid's bleached-blonde hair against a background of the cream-coloured Florentine stone known as *pietra serena*—and, despite the crowds of tourists and her own vile mood, the magic works. The minute she adjusts the focus in the viewfinder, her thoughts settle down and the universe goes still. Always the same elation just before she presses the shutter—the photo may turn well or badly, but whatever happens she will take it, *it will happen*...Same thrill as in department stores at age thirteen when her hand would tense up, preparing to dart and grab and steal, *it will happen*...Or as in seduction, when she can tell that yes, *it will happen*, within an hour or two the man whose gaze has just crossed hers will possess her, rip off her clothes, open her up and bellow...

Through the viewfinder, she can see what escapes her gaze the rest of the time. In the present instance, the distress in Ingrid's eyes. A swirling abyss of distress and insecurity, which vanishes the second Rena lowers her camera.

'You still haven't switched to digital?' asks Ingrid, returning to join them in the queue.

'Nope!'

Rena doesn't even attempt to explain that, seen through a digital camera, reality itself looks unconvincing to her. Or that, in digital, an infuriating fraction of a second elapses between the pressing of the shutter and the recording of the image. Ingrid wouldn't believe her. She wouldn't understand. To her mind, reality is something that can be accurately reflected in a photograph, and a fraction of a second is nothing.

'Doesn't the magazine get on your case about it?' Ingrid insists.

'No, no,' Rena says. 'I scan my photos, that's all—they get their pixels in the end. Besides, they're not about to complain: my name is one of their biggest assets.'

'I see...' says Ingrid.

One of their biggest assets, Subra sniggers softly as the three of them move at last through the portals of San Lorenzo. Schroeder has never given you anything but temporary contracts, and he almost refused to let you take this unpaid holiday—but sure, right, your name is one of their biggest assets...

San Lorenzo Primo

'Designed by Brunelleschi, *the* great Renaissance architect,' Rena hastens to proclaim, having leafed through the *Guide bleu* on her flight this morning. 'Look how the sun's rays light up every square inch of space...'

She can tell Ingrid is disappointed. To her eyes, the church is empty. There's really nothing much to look at—not even any stained-glass windows. Even the Amsterdam Cathedral is more lavishly decorated than this. Yes, thinks Rena, but you don't understand. Here, instead of being dazzled by ostentation, overwhelmed by fancy ornament or intimidated by dark shadows, man himself is writ large. Thanks to the light that comes flooding through the transparent windowpanes, the eye can apprehend the inner space in its entirety. The church's geometrical structure, its sober hues of blue, grey and white, reassure and respect the individual instead of boggling his mind. This is the very essence of humanism.

She spares Ingrid her spiel, though. If her stepmother wants to be disappointed, why deprive her of that pleasure?

So as father and daughter move through the transept, deep in conversation, Ingrid gets bored, allows her mind to wander and waits for the visit to end. This is how it's always been.

Rena holds forth a little longer. 'Lorenzo for Lorenzo the Magnificent, of course—that Medici duke under whose patronage, in the mid-fifteenth century, the arts and sciences blossomed almost miraculously...'

'But also for poor Saint Lawrence,' says Simon, who had picked up a leaflet at the entrance, 'whose martyrdom consisted of being grilled like a hamburger. As the tale goes, he asked to be turned over after a while, saying, "That side's already cooked!"'

Saint Lawrence's flesh sputters on the grill, his fat melts and drips, the flames lick, leap, eat...Rena does her best to banish these images from her mind and force her attention back to Brunelleschi's sober beauty, but no—again and again, grey greasy matter, Saint Lawrence's brain melting, great fat drops dripping and sputtering in the fire, avid flames devouring them, feeding on them, leaping higher and higher...Such a fine brain it once was. Well-lubricated, pulsing, throbbing, palpitating with curiosity...

The brain, she explains to Subra (the only person in the world who is captivated by her stories no matter how often she's heard them before), was my father's passion back in the sensational sixties, when all fields of knowledge—music and biochemistry, poetry and psychology, painting and neurology—were cross-fertilising. Yes, the incredible, unfathomable, untapped potential of human grey matter. The way the human brain contrives to put a self together in the first few years of life, then keep it in place, assign it limits...Even as a child I could sense Simon's enthusiasm for this subject. Sometimes he'd talk to me about the content of his work. I remember how, looking up at me from the book he was reading, he once declared out of the blue: 'A self is neither more nor less than the story of a human body, as told by that body's brain.' I felt proud when he shared this sort of insight with me, even if it was way over my head.

Though only a teaching assistant at the time, Simon was slogging away at his thesis and his future seemed full of promise. His specialty was neuropsychology, but he was determined to throw off artificial shackles and cross borders between disciplines. Freedom, freedom, freedom! One of his heroes was Leonard Cohen: born within a year of each other, raised in Westmount and educated at McGill, both had dabbled in lysergic acid diethylamide—an amazing substance that plunged you into heaven and hell by turn, twisting your memory, splattering unpredictable images—now sublime, now atrocious—onto the screen of your mind, paroxystically heightening all your perceptions, pulverising your sense of self, and imitating the symptoms of psychosis in uncontrollable ways. Also like Cohen (to say nothing of Allen Ginsberg, Abbie Hoffman, Jerry Rubin and many others of the time), Simon Greenblatt had turned away from the Jewish religion of his childhood to explore the arcane concepts of Buddhism, in which the very notions of self, world, and reality were dissolved.

'Challenge authority! Invent yourself! Accept entropy, the only truth of the universe!' My father's other idol was Timothy Leary, one of whose phrases was to become his mantra: 'There is no such thing as mental illness; there are only unknown or imperfectly explored nervous circuits.' After getting himself kicked out of Harvard in 1963 for handing out hallucinogenic drugs to his students, Leary and his colleague Richard Alpert had settled into a mansion in Millbrook, New York and founded the League for Spiritual Discovery or L.S.D. For years Simon Greenblatt had dreamed of going down to work with those pioneers and helping them invent a new paganism. In actual fact, he only set eyes on Leary once. So did I, on May 31, 1969, at age nine. Tim Leary had come to Montreal to support his friends John Lennon and Yoko Ono in their 'Give Peace a Chance' event. Simon dragged my mom and me to the Queen Elizabeth Hotel—where the Beatle, his wife and her young son sprawled stark naked in front of cameras from the world over, to express their disapproval of the Vietnam War. Because of the police cordons in front of the hotel we didn't get to see the bed-in itself, but I did catch a glimpse of Leary's bell-bottomed jeans when, as reporters' cameras flashed and popped, he jumped out of his limousine and dashed into the hotel. 'Look—that's him!' yelled Simon, struggling to pick me up and set me on his shoulders, though I was already far too heavy for those sort of antics. 'One does *not* carry a nine-year-old child around on one's shoulders,' said Mommy. 'Okay, Lisa, keep your cool,' answered Simon, setting me back on my feet. 'That man, darling Rena,' he went on—I can still remember his exact words—'is a true revolutionary in my field of study. But now that he's decided to switch to politics and run for governor of California, the path is clear for me to take up the torch and complete his discoveries. Yes, it's perfectly possible that Professor Simon Greenblatt will some day win the Nobel Prize.' 'They don't give Nobel Prizes in neuropsychology,' my mother pointed out. 'Well, they'll make one just for me,' my father retorted. 'You're not even a professor yet.' 'Not to worry.'

They exit the church.

Stupida

It's only half past three, but Ingrid claims to be hungry. Given the number of pastries she gobbled down at the hotel just a few hours ago, Rena knows this can't be true—what's true is that she's *afraid* of being hungry. She's been in the grip of that fear for the past sixty years—ever since the horrendous winter of 1944-45, when hundreds of Rotterdamers starved to death and the rest were reduced to eating garbage, rats, and grass...Nothing frightens Ingrid more than the prospect of lacking food. Her eyes, like everyone else's, reflect the demons of her childhood.

They spot a perfect-looking café on the far side of the Piazza del Duomo and start to head for it. Oh, but everything is so tedious, so difficult...The throngs on the footpath are stifling. How can my amorous strolls through Florence with Xavier be so very far away? wonders Rena. Was it really the same city? The same life? The same me? How can the past be so irrevocably *past*?

'That's weird,' Ingrid says suddenly. 'All the tourist shops seem to be selling Québecois T-shirts. Now, why would that be?'

Perplexed, Rena glances at one of the shops. Oh, right.

Again Simon undertakes to enlighten his wife. 'No, no,' he tells her gently. 'The fleur-de-lys was the emblem of the Medici family for centuries.'

'You don't need to laugh, Rena,' says Ingrid, turning crimson. 'Anyone can make a mistake.'

'Sorry,' says Rena.

She's right, Subra tells her *in petto*. Why would a Dutchwoman from Montreal be conversant with the history of the Medici court? Who's required to know what about what and why? And who are you to cast stones—you who trot the globe hiding behind your Canon, guzzling down information at random, belonging neither here, there nor anywhere, and whose motto could be the 'Just looking' muttered by people out of pocket in fancy boutiques the world over?

'Hey!' Since they sat down ten minutes ago, Simon has been studying not the menu but a city map. 'This palace here is called

Vecchio, just like the famous bridge. Must be the name of some Tuscan duke or other.'

'No,' Rena says gently, in turn. 'No, Daddy, it just means old. Old palace. Old bridge.'

Those who tourists do become / Must put up with being dumb.

Kodak

After their substantial snack, Simon and Ingrid feel the urgent need to go back to the hotel for a nap. Rena starts leading them in that direction, but in the Via de' Martelli they walk past a Kodak store and Simon comes to a halt. 'Maybe they sell disposable cameras here?'

Rena's heart sinks.

Of course she could wait for them outside, taking advantage of the next fifteen minutes to turn on her mobile phone and call Aziz or Kerstin in Paris, Toussaint in Marseille, Thierno in Dakar...or to take pictures of the Florentine tourists' feet. She decides against it, though. Whether out of masochism or fascination with her own annoyance, she walks into the store with them.

At once, ear-splitting rock music leaps on them and sets about mangling their synapses.

Here goes. 'Would it be better to buy a roll of twelve pictures or sixteen? Maybe even twenty-four?'

'Look—this one's got sixteen pictures for six euros, and this one's got twenty-four for only eight, it's a better bargain.'

'No, twenty-four's too many. I mean, we'll be buying postcards as well—we'll never take twenty-four pictures.'

'Are you sure? If we don't use up the roll, we can always finish it in Montreal.'

'No, ideally we should finish it in Italy and get it developed before we go home—so Rena can tell us which ones she wants copies of.'

Rena wanders through the store, studying the various cameras on sale with a penetrating, professional air, registering nothing.

This, Subra tells her in a solemn voice, is a real moment of your real life. Every bit as real as when, standing in the kitchen doorway, Aziz picks you up and plants you on his cock and you wrap your legs around his waist and toss your head back and start moving on him and moaning...As real as your two childbirths—or a sunrise in Goree—or the war in Iraq. *All these things exist.* Okay, you're uncomfortable being in a Kodak store in Florence with your father and stepmother. Okay, the music is scrambling your brain. But just think, it could be worse. I mean, you're not a pregnant young woman in the Democratic Republic of Congo, faced with a battalion of young militiamen from Burundi who are preparing to gang rape you, then shove sticks or rifles up your womb to cause you to miscarry, then force you to drink your own body's blood and eat your own baby's flesh. That, too, is a possibility of human existence on planet Earth in October 2005. Consider yourself lucky to have nothing worse to complain about than being forced to listen to the hemming and hawing of an elderly couple in one of the most beautiful cities in the world.

Getting a hold of herself, Rena looks over at the young man behind the cash register. Aged eighteen or nineteen and sporting a Bob Marley T-shirt, he flashes a smile at her. Far from cursing them as tourists, he seems to sympathise with her for having to kill time, assuring her that it's no big deal, there's no reason to rush, she's still in the game despite her age and it's a gorgeous day.

Who is this boy? Rena wonders. Who are his parents? What's his goal in life—above and beyond this stultifying job that immerses him eight hours a day in ear-shattering music? What sort of future does he dream of? Our destinies have intersected here—lightly, slightly, it will all be over in a few seconds, this whole event is doomed to oblivion, non-existence, nothing is really happening, yet…What would it be like to stretch out naked on the naked body of this thin, muscular young Florentine, make drops of sweat stand out on his forehead, move my lips over the faint shadow of a moustache on his upper lip, feel his long golden fingers moving between my legs?

Subra encourages her to continue.

Oh, joy of the imaginable, the possible, the conceivable! First and foremost among human rights—the right to fantasise! Not be where you are; be where you are not. Yes, it works both ways—while her husband pumps monotonously away at her, a woman can use her mind to review her shopping list; doing the dishes, on the other hand, she can float off to seventh heaven with the lover of her dreams. In order to concentrate on the Great One's order to Abraham *Go forth and multiply*, a Lubavitch labours his wife through a hole in the sheet that covers her from head to foot; meanwhile, nothing can prevent the wife from imagining that the guy beyond the sheet is Brad Pitt. In a Tokyo nightclub called Lucky Hole photographed by Araki, you see life-sized female figures sketched on a series of tall white plasterboards. Where the woman's head should be they glue a photo of a sexy young film star, and at crotch level there's a hole. The client can slip his member through the hole and, even as he dreams he's possessing the starlet, be brought off by a female employee sitting on the other side of the plasterboard. Though the women hired for this job are usually old and ugly, their technique is unsurpassable. When I told my friend Kerstin about the Lucky Hole, she burst out laughing. 'Just imagine there's an earthquake in Tokyo one day,' she said, 'the nightclub collapses and one of the clients discovers he's just come in his own mommy's hand!' As for me, I can't help wondering what images go floating through the old woman's mind as she deftly, professionally brings off her invisible clients…Yes, women, too, fantasise—thank goodness!

Go on, Subra murmurs, listening to Rena's spiel as intently as if she were hearing it for the first time.

Oh...the day Xavier took me with him to Dublin's National Gallery and we spent a full hour in front of Perugino's sublime *Lamentation Over the Dead Christ*...Sam Beckett was fascinated by this work of art, with its 'lovely cheery Christ full of sperm and the women touching his thighs and mourning his secrets'. And it's true—Christ's fleshly nature is particularly palpable in this painting. Staring at it, I couldn't help wondering why Jesus's experience of humanity had been limited to suffering, why it included bleeding wounds and dark temptations but not erotic swoon, not the marvellous tingling waves of desire that begin in your genitals and flow all the way to your toes and fingertips. The Perugino came back to me that same evening in a pub, as I watched the crablike movements of a musician's left hand on the frets of his banjo. I felt as aroused by the sight of the banjo-player's fingers as Martha and the two Marys must have been by Christ's naked body—and so, with the taste of Guinness on my lips and the sound of words like sperm and chrism in my brain, I began to imagine how those hands would move on my hips, breasts and shoulders...When the set ended and Xavier rose to leave, I motioned to him to wait for me outside and, leaning forward, said to the man in a low voice, 'I love the way your left hand moves on the neck.' His gaze swerved to meet mine and he toppled headfirst into my eyes. As he sat up straight, grabbed my hand and asked me my name, the warmth in his voice told me that he was already rock hard. 'Rena', I replied, delighted to be able to say it in English for once, not retching the *R* the way the French do. 'I'm Michael,' said the man. Then, realising that I was about to walk out of his life as abruptly as I'd walked into it, he asked with frantic hand gestures if I lived close by, if he could get in touch with me, and I answered, also gesturing, that no, I lived far, far away. Then, leaning towards him again until our faces all but touched, I bade him good night.

My blood was fairly simmering with the fire of that brief exchange, the electrically erotic touch of the man's hand on mine. And what caused me to swoon the following morning, when Xavier set me on my knees in our hotel bed and reared up behind me, was not just the view in the mirror of our two bodies gilded by dawn's first light and his member moving in and out of me, but also an intoxicating mixture of Jesus Christ, Sam Beckett, and Michael the banjo-player.

No one can punish us for such joys. Even women who live behind burqas in Afghanistan continue (I hope!) to swing up onto their dream horses and canter off through the clouds, clutching their mount's creamy mane in both hands, feeling the violent shudder of its flanks between their thighs, panting, gasping and crying out in pleasure. Every woman contains a cosmos—and who can prevent her from welcoming into it those male or female guests who know exactly how she needs to be loved, or from loving them back with a vengeance?

The Kodak chapter has come to an end.

Once she has set the couple safely on their way to the hotel, where they've agreed to meet up at eight, Rena heads off on her own. Within the minute, she recovers her body, her rhythm, her elasticity.

Dante

A pocket of calm on the Borgo degli Albizi. Rena photographs the chiaroscuro patterns on the balconies and façades of the buildings: sharply delineated lozenges and triangles of shadow in the slanting rays of the late-afternoon, late-October sun.

Passing in front of a tiny chapel, she reads the sign at the entrance and laughs out loud.

So it was here, on this very spot, in this simple, sober, sombre church with its whitewashed walls, that Dante first laid eyes on Beatrice di Folco Portinari. Electric shock. Love at first lightning-bolt. The year was 1284. He was nineteen and she was eighteen.

Did Beatrice even glance at the young man whose eyes were burning into her? Did she even guess at the tumult in his heart? No one knows. All we know is that he never either touched or spoke to her. The following year he married another woman, who would become the mother of his children…And in 1287, again in this very church, he attended Beatrice's wedding to a wealthy banker (do poor ones exist?). There was nothing between them!

Ah, the fabulous power of male sublimation! Dante's love was entire, intact, immaculate; it had no need of Bea! All it needed was itself, a magic stone that gave off sparks when he rubbed it. 'Beatrice' was an image, an idea, a compact nucleus of energy that eventually exploded into—*La Vita Nuova*! *La Divina Commedia*! All glory to 'Beatrice', who revolutionised not only the Italian language but the history of literature! Bea the woman gave up the ghost at twenty-four, most likely during a difficult childbirth. So what? By that time Dante was far away from Florence, in exile in Ravenna, alone with his masterpiece.

Subra rewards her with a laugh.

And what about me, Daddy? Men must have adored me from afar on countless occasions, don't you think so? Me at twenty, sweet young thing wandering the streets of Naples with my white skin and green eyes, a flowery salmon-pink pantsuit floating on the body you and my mother distractedly made together, eliciting the insults, gropes and pinches of Neapolitan machos…Me at thirty-five, on assignment for a reportage in war-torn ex-Yugoslavia, feeling the

Kosovars' eyes glued to my body like melting, sticky, stinky tar...Me only last year, venturing alone into the casbah in Algiers, hearing *gazelle* at every step and thinking in annoyance that North Africans badly needed to renew their stock of compliments...Who knows how many masterpieces I've given rise to, here, there and everywhere, without knowing it?

In the same street, a little farther down—Dante's house. Ah, yes it is impressive, though of course it's been rebuilt from top to bottom. And now she has the time. She goes inside.

Standing in front of her at the cash register is an obese American couple. 'Isn't it hard to believe,' the woman says, 'that the people who built this house had never even *heard* of the United States?' Her husband nods gravely. (*Those who tourists do become / Must put up with being dumb.*)

The second floor contains a pedagogical display on the famous war between the Guelphs and the Ghibellines, an episode of European history which for some reason never sticks in Rena's mind. She deciphers the explanations. Ah, yes, it all comes back to her. Civil wars in Germany and Italy in the late Middle Ages, spiritual versus secular power, Guelphs for the Pope, Ghibellines for the Emperor, their bang-bang-you're-dead lasting a good two centuries...The usual crap. Infighting, too, naturally. Within the Guelph ranks: moderate Whites versus fundamentalist Blacks, bang-bang-you're-dead...The Blacks of Florence wound up expelling all the Whites, including Dante Alighieri. Banished from the beloved city of his birth, never to return. All glory to exile, all glory to intolerance—were it not for the war of the Guelphs and the Ghibellines, there would have been no *Divine Comedy*!

On the third floor, she finds visitors seated in semi-darkness watching a slideshow of the *Inferno*. Illustrations by Blake and Dürer, recorded excerpts...

'So with our guide we moved on unafraid
By the red bubbles of the scalding ooze
Wherein the boiled their sharp lamenting made.'

Mesmerised, Rena contemplates the tortures of the damned, listens to their screams and blasphemies, feels herself being sucked down into the vortex...

'The soul that had become a reptile fled
With hissing noise along the valley side
And the other sputtered at it as it sped.'

Suddenly, to her left, she senses a man's eyes on her.

Really? She turns her head. Yes. There, by the door. His eyes interrogate, hers acquiesce.

They exit Dante's house together.

Tell me, Subra says.

The man is Turkish. Older than my Aziz—who isn't?—but a few years younger than me. Our only common language is Italian, which both of us speak imperfectly. That's fine with me. Touchingly, lamely, we exchange a few basic facts—true or false, what difference does it make? He tells me his name is Kamal; I'll go along with that. As a private homage to Arbus, I tell him mine is Diane. I gather he works for some sort of import-export business...Then we move away from conversation.

In his hotel elevator, Kamal's eyes move down to my chest. Assuming his curiosity in the area has less to do with my breasts— their exact shape and size, the presence or absence of a bra to enhance their appeal—than with the Canon nesting like a baby's head between them, I say, *'Non sono giornalista, sono artista.'* Having gone that far, I figure I might as well go a bit farther. I ask if he'll allow me to photograph him afterwards, without specifying after what. *'Verramo,'* he answers—making, I think, a slight error in Italian. Then, stroking my cheek, he moves up close. Murmurs something about my *occhi verdi*. When his body grazes mine, I feel he's hard already—and the familiar tingling starts up at once, making me weightless, beautiful, and desirable in my own eyes. As I walk down the worn carpet of the third-floor corridor at the stranger's side, I am floating.

Go on, says Subra.

He opens the door, revealing a room that looks for all the world like a Matisse—shadowy light, deep colours, red-brick wall, a framed picture of flowers, the bedspread striped by the shadows of half-closed shutters…only the fishbowl and the violin are missing. Every detail offers itself up to me, fairly shimmering with beauty and meaning. I move over to the window—red-tiled roofs, swifts wheeling in the air, the murmurs of passers-by in the street below, the occasional roar of a motorbike, the rich resonance of a church-bell. A faintly dank smell in the room, not unpleasant. The firm grip of the stranger's hands on my waist. Oh utter delight. All of this exists—painted flowers, shutters, bell, October afternoon, my father napping a mere stone's throw away. I am in Florence. A man is about to make love to me. Nothing could be more powerful than this anticipation.

No sooner have we settled onto the bed and begun to remove each other's clothes with the clumsy gestures of impatience than I realise Kamal also knows about passivity—yes, he also knows how to remain still, fully awake and attentive, and give himself up to me as a cello gives itself up to the bow. Arching his back, he surrenders his face, shoulders, back and buttocks, waiting for me to play them, and I do—I play them, play with them. Most men are afraid to let go like this—whereas with a little finesse the wonders of passivity can be tasted in even the most violent throes of love-making. In a delirium of restrained desire, I weigh, stroke and lick Kamal's balls, then take his penis in my hands, between my breasts, into my mouth. He sits up, reaches for me and I allow him to explore me in turn. He runs his tongue and lips over my breasts, the back of my neck, my toes, my stomach, the countless treasures between my legs, oh the sheer ecstasy of lips and tongues on genitals, either simultaneously or in alternation, never will I tire of that silvery fluidity, my sex swimming in joy like a fish in water, my self freed of both self and other, the quivering sensation, the carnal pink palpitation that detaches you from all colour and all flesh, making you see only stars, constellations, milky ways, propelling you bodiless and soulless into undulating space where the undulating skies make your non-body undulate… And orgasm—the way a man's face is transformed by orgasm—oh it's not true they all look alike, you have to be either miserable and broke or furiously blasé and sarcastic to say they all look alike—to me, every climax is unique. That's why I love to photograph men when they climax—not the first time but the second—or, better still, the third, when they're completely cut off from their moorings, when they've lost themselves and are wildly grateful to you for the loss…

Speaking slowly in my poor Italian with the assistance of gestures, I explain to Kamal that to take his photo I'll use infrared film, which captures not visible light but heat. I add (not quite truthfully) that this will make his face unrecognisable, even to friends. He consents, as virtually all my lovers have. It takes me a while to arm my camera with the ultrasensitive film: since the least ray of visible light would veil the images, I need to slip my Canon and both my hands into a black lightproof bag. But I've done this hundreds of times before and I work swiftly, still naked, humming a bit and speaking to Kamal in a low voice, preserving the electric arc of desire between us so it will be easy to pick up where we left off. When our bodies unite for the third time we leave all theatres behind. What happens then has as little to do with the libertinage prized by the French (oh the blasphemers, the precious precocious ejaculators, the nasty naughty boys, the cruel *fouteurs* and *fouetteurs*) as with the healthy, egalitarian intercourse championed by Americans (who hand out bachelors degrees in G-points, masters in masturbation and Ph.Ds in endorphines). Kamal and I are totally immersed in flesh, that archaic kingdom that brings forth tears and terrors, nightmares, babies and bedazzlements. The word pleasure is far too weak for what transpires there. So is the word bliss. And it's not even a matter of sharing because, the self having evaporated, you scarcely know whether you're alone or with another person.

This is when I take my picture, from deep inside the loving. The Canon is part of my body. I myself am the ultrasensitive film— capturing invisible reality, capturing heat.

Afterwards, Kamal smothers my hands with kisses. He's happy and so am I. My whole body radiates happiness, from the roots of my hair to the soles of my feet.

A final request. 'One of *your* photos. Could I take a picture of one of your photos, Kamal?' It's not easy to make clear in Italian—no, not a photo of you, but one you carry around with you everywhere, like a talisman. A picture of your wife, your son, your father, whatever—or you, but as a little boy...'Would you have a photo like that in your wallet, Kamal?'

I learned to do this while working on *Whore Sons and Daughters*.

Kamal hesitates. Thinks it over. What are the chances his wife in Gemlik will ever hear about the opening—in Paris, Arles or Berlin— of a show called *My Lovers' Loved Ones* by a weird lady photographer named Diane? None at all.

His wife's dark eyes glint mischievously. Because of the red headscarf she is wearing, she bears a vague resemblance to Monica Vitti in *L'Avventura*. Kamal is showing me this person, whom he loves, to tell me that yes, we've truly been together in this room. I get the photo in my finder. Sense it. Capture it.

Press the shutter. For the rest of my life, the young Turkish woman's face will be imprinted on my retina, my film, and my very being.

'Thanks, Kamal. That was fantastic.'

'Thank you, Diane. I wish you happiness. A long life.'

All this takes place within a quarter of a second on the third floor of Dante's house, as Rena walks past the stranger and heads for the staircase. She doesn't have time to go with him, unfortunately—so she brushes past, lowering her eyes. '*Scusi, Signor.*'

Will he now go off to write his *Comedy*?

Ah. Hopefully, the warmth gleaned from the virtual body of handsome Kamal will last her until bedtime.

Arriving at Hotel Guelfa (hey, Guelfa must mean Guelph, just as Roma means Rome, *Those who tourists do become...*), she climbs the stairs three at a time to her narrow Room 25.

Simon and Ingrid have slipped a note under her door—they bought sandwiches for themselves and decided to retire early, to be in tip-top shape tomorrow morning.

Rena lights a cigarette and goes over to the open window to smoke it. As she stares down at the little garden below, San Lorenzo's melting brain comes back to her—and, on its heels, the scene with her parents in front of the Queen Elizabeth Hotel...

1969, the turning-point.

In 1969 she was playing the little mouse even more zealously than usual because her parents had just decided to kick her older brother Rowan out of the house, packing him off to a Catholic boarding school east of Montreal. Terrified they might reject and expel her, too, she took care never to complain, bother them, ask for anything, or object to having to spend so many evenings alone with Lucille the maid in the big house whose mortgage payments they were finding so difficult to meet.

Good thing you came along, Subra.

Yes…That same year, Rena had been brought up short by Diane Arbus's portrait of an adolescent girl: long, straight blonde hair, heavy fringe all but covering her eyes, white lace dress that looked terribly scratchy, face and body frozen in sadness…If you can do that with a camera, she'd said to herself, I want to be a photographer. Rena had recognised her soul sister in this melancholy girl—and, choosing a name for her by spelling Arbus's own name backwards, resolved to do her best to divert and amuse her. Ever since, the constant rubbing of Subra's mind against her own has been a source of warmth to her; she's eternally grateful to the great American photographer for the gift of this precious alter-ego.

Fatigue suddenly catches up with her and knocks her flat. She undresses, brushes her teeth and crawls into bed with her copy of *Inferno*.

When she falls asleep towards midnight, she is musing about Lethe, the river in Hell whose name means oblivion.

A year from now, she thinks, I'll have again forgotten whether Dante was a Guelph or a Ghibelline. Fifteen years from now, I'll have forgotten what the two sides were fighting over. And it's quite possible that thirty years down the line, my brain will contain no memory at all of this trip to Tuscany…or of Dante.

WEDNESDAY

'I would like to photograph everybody.'

I'm out for a walk with friends in the Buttes Chaumont when suddenly I see, looming up in the middle of the park, a huge white hill made of some unidentifiable substance that looks like wax or chalk. Climbing to the top, I crumble a bit of the substance between my fingers and realise it's artificial snow. A deep crevice appears at the heart of the mountain, I grab onto the walls but they're smooth and slippery, I lose my footing and tumble into the crevice. It's an endless fall, like Alice's in the rabbit hole. Even as I fall, I start worrying about the fragile parts of my body—my sex in particular—that are liable to be damaged when I land. The moment of impact is absent. When I finally catch up with my friends in the Rue Botzaris tearoom, I tell them I left my body behind in the park—it must be badly hurt—will they please come and help me find it? But they just go on with their conversation, paying no attention to me. After a while they get up to leave. 'B-but—what about my body?' I stammer, icy with panic. 'I can't leave without my body!'

How strange, comments Subra when Rena wakes up. If there's one part of a woman's body that can't be damaged when she falls, it's her sex.

Some other kind of 'fall', then? And why would the snow be 'artificial'?

The snow of my childhood…Phony snow…or perhaps…a phony childhood? My lie-riddled childhood come back to haunt my adult life? Sitting there in the middle of my neighbourhood in Paris, as conspicuous as a 'mountain'?

I remember when Simon shoved Rowan's face into the snow. It must have been a Sunday morning, we were out skating in Mount Royal Park—was Lisa with us? probably not—suddenly I turned around and saw my brother waving his legs in the air, gasping for air, and my father laughing as he held his head firmly in the snow with both hands…What had Rowan done? Talked back to him? Refused to obey an order? Broken a skateblade? I don't recall. Simon punished both his children, but his son more often and more harshly than his daughter…Finally he released my brother and acted as if nothing had happened, wanting to pick up our shenanigans where we'd left off—but Rowan sulked for hours, incensed at having been humiliated in front of me.

So many snow games with Rowan and his pals when we were little. Snowball fights that went on for hours…I hated the bite of the cold, like an electric saw the length of my spine, when a boy would shove a snowball down my neck—but the boys themselves I loved. Four, five, six of them—and me, always the only girl. I loved the violent mixing of our bodies when the sled would hit a bump and we'd be ejected, rolling over and over in the snow, elbow on forehead, knee in gut, head slamming nose—it hurt like hell but it warmed me up and turned me on; I wished it would never end.

First a tomboy, then an androgyne, Subra says…Forever hanging out with boys, hankering after a man's life and a man's death…When did that end—when Fabrice died? Or when, scarcely a month later, little Toussaint was born?

Rena stays in bed for a while, eyes closed, breathing in the Florence air and slowly intoning the words Tuscany, Renaissance, beauty.

The laughter of a small child wafts up to her from the street below, bubbling and gurgling like a brook—oh, the word gurgle was invented for that laugh.

Tell me, Subra says.

Toussaint's laughter at age two—his mad joy to be running down the footpath between Alioune and me, left hand in his father's right, right hand in my left—Toussaint the dwarf thrilled to have the undivided attention of two giants, two gods—one, two, *three-ee-ee!*—his feet would leave the ground, he'd go soaring through the air, his laughter would ring out, we'd set him down—'Again!' he'd say—one, two, *three-ee-ee!*—his feet would leave the ground, he'd go soaring through the air, his laughter would ring out, we'd set him down— 'Again!' he'd say—and we'd do it again, five, ten, twenty times—that day, another day, then another—it was infinity, eternity, we wanted it never to end and so did he—'Again!'—the joy of it—'Again!'— his feet leaving the ground, Mommy to his right and Daddy to his left (yes, Daddy: given that Fabrice died before Toussaint was born, Alioune has always been his father)…And then it was over. One day we stopped playing that game with Toussaint and started playing it with Thierno…and then it was over for Thierno as well. Finis. Nevermore. And no one noticed the moment of the ending. Did Simon and Lisa ever play that game with me? With Rowan? If they did, I have no memory of it. Neither, most likely, do my sons. They'll play it with their own children, who will forget it in turn. Invisible connections…

Snow, murmurs Subra.

In infrared photography snow is black, ice cubes are black, people's glasses (even transparent ones) are black, everything cool is black, black, black…But the dark skin of my lovers is subtly shaded, rippling with a thousand nuances of light; sometimes you can even see the veins through it. Infrared reveals what I cherish more than anything else, what I've always longed for, what I lacked most as a child—warmth.

When I'd lose my temper, my mother would call me a 'fury' and send me to my room to calm down. She meant it teasingly, but deep down I liked being called that—I thought the word suited me to a T. In my mind it was connected to fire and I liked the image of myself as flaming and flamboyant…furious, fierce, ferocious—yes, a real Fury—me!

My first memory is of being cold. Can it really have been as cold as all that in our house in Westmount? Carpets in every room, stained-glass windows, wood panelling, book-lined walls…'Shh, your father's working, he's trying to write his thesis.' 'Your mom's with a client. Don't you have any homework?' 'Shh, can't you see I'm reading? I need to concentrate. Please go and play, darling.' 'Rowan, Rena, *please* don't make noise when I'm with a client, all right? They're such unhappy women, you wouldn't believe what they've been through.'

Apart from defending prostitutes, Ms Lisa Heyward's primary concern at the time was the pro-choice movement: her phone would ring off the wall every time a doctor got arrested for having termi-nated an unwanted pregnancy. Henry Morgantaler, for instance, who claimed to have carried out some five thousand abortions single-handedly. The man had a lot in common with France's Simone Veil—born the same year, both were Jewish and had lost their parents in the Nazi death camps; both, moreover, were subjected to revolting slander as they fought for abortion rights (hadn't Jews always ritually killed and eaten Catholic babies?). In 1973, a fifteen-year prison sentence was handed down for Morgantaler, but he was released after only a few weeks, thanks to the efforts of tireless professional feminists like Ms Lisa Heyward.

For me this meant spending long hours alone with Lucille as I waited for Rowan to come home from school. It was Lucille, in fact—a vivacious young black woman from Martinique—who unwit-tingly introduced me to eroticism. Waking up one day from my afternoon nap (I can't have been more than three or four), I heard strange noises coming from the far end of the apartment. I tiptoed across the kitchen and saw that Lucille's bedroom door was ajar and that she was in there with a man. They were naked, their chocolate-coloured skin was smooth and slick and their bodies formed a sort of ebony gondola that rocked swiftly back and forth in the moving waves of blankets and sheets. The man was cupping Lucille's head in his hands, gently holding her neck and staring into her eyes and whispering to her in Creole, I could make out a word here and there but most of them were drowned out by sounds of pure music, pure desire, pure pleasure...

Maybe that's where you acquired your taste for the French language? suggests Subra.

Could be. Definitely it was the first time I ever saw a man's sex erect and in action, and I'll never forget it. As her lover penetrated her simultaneously with his gaze, his voice and his impressive tool, Lucille's eyes sparkled like diamonds, her mouth was half-open in a smile and she kept gasping and letting out these little yelps—no, more like bits of song but always on the same note, staccato—everything about the couple palpitated and vibrated and spoke to me of ecstasy. Yes, that must be when I first realised how much you could ask of life, if only you dared...

Meanwhile there were endless hours of solitude and boredom to be got through. When Rowan finally came home from school, he taught me everything he'd learned there. Day after day—reading, writing, spelling, arithmetic, geography. My brother gradually becoming more than a brother to me—father, mother, god, sole horizon. 'I'm the sun, Rena, and you're the moon.' 'Yes.' 'You have no light of your own; all you do is reflect my light.' 'Yes. We'll stick together forever, won't we, Rowan?' 'Yes.' 'We'll live together when we grow up.' 'Come give me a hug.' Five and nine, at the time. My plump soft body pressed up against his wiry, knotty one. 'I'm a nice girl, aren't I?' 'Sure you're a nice girl.' 'You love me, don't you?' 'Sure I love you.' 'I love *you* more than anything in the world.' 'Damn right you do.' My heart skipping a beat at the swearword. 'But I'm older than you are, so you have to obey me.' 'I know.' 'I'm the master and you're the slave, okay?' 'Okay.' 'Promise?' 'I promise.'

Rowan was warm. And because he was warm, because he was like the sun to me, because I worshipped him, overjoyed by his trust in me and awed by his inside knowledge of the adult world, everything he said and wanted was right. So when he said, 'You know, Rena, it's not enough to be nice, you've got to learn to be bad, too,' I nodded and promised to do my best. And when he slipped his middle fingers inside of me, one from the front and the other from the back, and tried to force them to touch, I winced and squirmed but when he said, 'That doesn't hurt, does it?' I said, 'No.' And when he used his penknife to remove all the twigs and leaves from a thin supple willow branch, then impaled me on it, causing me to bleed, and said, 'Don't worry, Rena, it's only natural, women bleed all the time, you should be grateful to me for making a woman of you,' I said, panting against the pain, 'Thank you, Rowan.' Crying or complaining were out of the question—I had no one to turn to. You weren't around then, Subra; I hadn't invented you yet.

Rowan wept sometimes—when our father, because of the tensions in his marriage or the long hours of fruitless work in his study, would suddenly turn on him, make fun of him, needle and berate him on the pretext of hardening him up, thickening his skin. 'A boy's got to know how to defend himself, hey?' he'd say, flicking the tea towel at Rowan's arm over and over again. Yes, Rowan would weep then, collapsing on the floor in tears. His bedroom was just below my own, and I knew I'd hear him sobbing long into the night…

Basta. Enough—more than enough melancholy for one day.

Rena gets up. Within ten minutes she is washed, dressed, out of there.

Simon and Ingrid are waiting for her in the breakfast room—she, quietly stuffing herself, he, poring over a leaflet about Pico della Mirandola.

'This guy was unbelievable,' he says to her by way of a greeting.

Studying the leaflet as she drinks her coffee, Rena nods. Of course. The philosophical genius who died an untimely death in Florence in 1494 (he was only thirty-one) reminds Simon of himself as a youth.

No doubt about it, Dad. You and Pico were looking for the same thing—'the connections among all the universes, from the lives of ants to the music of the spheres and the dwelling-place of angels.' Though Pico took the high road of religion and philosophy, and you, the low road of brain chemistry and neurology, what both of you hoped to prove was *The Dignity of Man*. 'The only being,' as Pico expressed it, 'in whom the Creator planted the seeds of every sort of life. The only one who has the privilege of shaping himself into angel or beast according to his fancy.' What a thrilling Mirandolian idea!

Simon Greenblatt had exactly the same intuition: that people shaped themselves, fashioned selves for themselves out of the tales they were told, and were freer than they really knew to change their identities. Now, at the breakfast table in Florence, surrounded by the clatter of dishes and the hiss of milk being frothed for cappuccino, he longs to share with his daughter what he's just learned about the great philosopher.

His sentence begins, hesitates at length, turns a corner, goes skidding off track—'Sorry'—begins again. Advances with excruciating slowness. Comes to a halt. Starts over again, after a long pause.

Oh, Daddy, Rena thinks in desperation, you've lost the thread.

Your brain spins dozens of threads that lead you astray, wind themselves round you, trip you up, tie you in knots, immobilise you. Poor Gulliver-on-the-Arno, how will you ever get out of this mess?

Yet your brain throbs with true wisdom and teems with countless facts. No soul could be more generous than yours, no interrogation more genuine, no quest more ardent...it never manages to jell, that's all. What's lacking is...lightness...alacrity...humour...the joy of choosing words, watching them file out on stage, line up, grab hands...and then, to the rhythm of pipes and tambourines, launch into a fabulous farandole!

No. I know.

What's lacking is...self-love. Something Pico probably found at his mother's breast...and that you didn't find at yours?

Granny Rena was a case. You named your eldest daughter after the woman you so desperately wished you could love, so she'd forgive you...for what crime, exactly?

Tell me, Subra says.

My paternal grandparents made a narrow escape from Poland in the early thirties, settling first in France, then in Quebec...But in 1945, upon seeing the photos of the death camps in which every member of her family had perished, from her two grandmothers down to her little second cousin, Rena sank into a permanent stupor. She was thirty-five at the time, and Simon ten.

Whose photos of Dachau and Buchenwald did she see? Very possibly the ones published in *Vogue* and *Life* by that lovely blonde American photographer named Lee Miller. At the age of seven, Lee Miller was so lovely and so blonde that a 'friend of the family' raped her and she contracted gonorrhoea. Over a period of several months, her tiny vagina and uterus had to be subjected to acid baths—an excruciating treatment that made her scream, day after day. Despite the pain inside, her body stayed perfectly lovely and blonde on the outside, so when she was eight her father started photographing her in the nude. As she grew towards adolescence he asked her to strike more and more lascivious poses. Then she left for Paris and was photographed in the same poses, also in the nude, by Man Ray and other Montparnasse artists. Despite her loveliness and her blondeness, Miller thought she might be interested in looking rather than being looked at—so she became a photographer herself. One day, thanks to an accident in her dark room, she discovered solarisation—a technique that consists of very briefly exposing the photograph to light during development—just as she herself had been exposed to male desire during her own development. Solarisation creates weird effects—in photos, halos, and, in little girls, the ability to split off from their bodies and the imperious need to search for meaning…Only in war would Lee Miller find the meaning she was looking for—first the destruction, bombing and ruins of cities in Britain and France, then the death camps, which, in April 1945, she was among the very first journalists to visit. Yes, she must have recognised something in the insane pornography of what she saw in the camps—chaotically exposed nudity, violent effacement of individuality, naked, fragmented, broken Jewish bodies, people turned into objects, non-entities. Unlike the other photographers, Miller approached the corpses without revulsion and photographed them close-up. Instead of framing anonymous heaps, piles, mountains of corpses, she insisted on capturing them as people—one person, another, yet another, each with his and her own history, showing their beauty, their personality, their still-human features, their naked bodies, their living dying bodies, every body a potential *body*, still human, still so very, very human—just as women exhibited in the nude, treated as if they were interchangeable objects, are in fact human individuals. In Buchenwald, Miller finally managed to inject meaning into an existence she had hitherto found, as she puts it, 'extraordinarily empty'…

Once she'd seen those photos and learned what they implied, Granny Rena lost her ability to participate in life. Rena Greenblatt: prostrate, inaccessible. She never talked about her mourning, but it made her indifferent to everything else. Her pain was intimidating. Most days, her room was darkened and off-limits to her two children, Simon and his older sister Deborah. She withdrew her love from them, and her being from the world.

Baruch, on the other hand, poor sweet clumsy Baruch who sold men's suits over on Saint Lawrence Boulevard, was a good dad— present, loving, funny, even erudite in his own way. Though his head was most often up in the clouds with God, his heart was filled with concern for his family. Morning and evening he would tie an apron around his waist and start fussing in the kitchen, trying to cook for you and failing, burning even the fried eggs, forgetting to turn off the gas, tearing the bread when he tried to butter it because the butter was rock hard, straight from the fridge. Oh, your poor pa…Old before his time, forever smiling, overworked, humble and humiliated…You felt sorry for him, Simon. Throughout your teenage years, you were filled with silent rage at your mother for not being like other mothers, and for turning your father into a *nebbish*. No way you could invite friends over to the house: with the invalid woman and the aproned man, your house was far too strange…

A little like yours? Subra whispers.

Yeah, come to think of it, a little like mine…

When you left home at last, at age eighteen, you must have solemnly sworn never to resemble your father, a weakling you loved but pitied. A meek, submissive, altruistic, unmanly man who'd given up all hope of having a great destiny here on Earth.

You, Simon, would be a real man…

Sliding the Mirandola leaflet back across the table, Rena gently pats her father's hand.

They've made big plans for the day ahead: first the History of Science Museum, and then, following their afternoon siesta, the Ponte Vecchio and the Piazza della Signoria…

Haughtily ignoring the hundreds of tourists lined up at the entrance to the Uffizi, they skirt the Palazzo Vecchio and head down to the Piazza dei Giudici, the Judges' Square.

'This is where Savonarola was condemned to death,' Simon solemnly announces.

'Who's that?' Ingrid asks.

'A fanatical priest. In the fifteenth century, right on this spot, he built bonfires of the vanities, burned the works of Pico della Mirandola, and was eventually hanged himself, then burned at the stake. Incredible, to think all this happened five hundred years ago, before the first white man ever set foot in Quebec. Before that part of the world was known as Quebec, in fact,' he adds, savvier than the American lady in Dante's house.

'Right,' Rena nods. 'The Indians didn't do bonfires of the vanities, they just did campfires.'

'And they couldn't burn books,' Ingrid puts in, 'because they were illiterate. Hitler burned books, though…'

Rena hastens to change the subject. She has nothing against Hitler, so to speak, but feels he shouldn't be allowed to invade the whole world.

It's for Simon's sake, of course, that they've chosen to visit the History of Science Museum.

Once they've whisked through the first room, however (wonders of ancient clockwork, tiny crenellated cogs from the workshops of Florence, Geneva and Vienna), Simon decides to peruse the museum pamphlet for a while. No benches—so, oblivious to stares, he sits down on the floor like a tramp, baseball cap on lap, wispy grey hair standing on end.

Ingrid and Rena move on alone—too scared of him to urge him off the floor, too scared of the museum guards to join him there. Astronomy, meteorology, mathematics…but how to discuss these things without Simon? Where to go? What to do? Everything they visit now without him will need to be revisited later with him; the present moment thus becomes absurd.

After a good half hour, they go back to the first room and timorously ask (last thing they'd want to do is offend him, harass him, give him the impression they're bossing him around), 'Don't you want to come and see?'

Rising at last to join them, he strides through one room after another—prisms, magnetism, optical machinery, transmission of energy…

Hey, what's the hurry, Dad?

You the precocious child, forever top of the class, admitted to university at age sixteen…You the brilliant, curious, gifted young thinker, light of foot and heart. You the insomniac, mad with joy, utterly possessed by your vocation: to fathom and describe the origins of consciousness, the fabulous machinery of the human brain. You who, later on, would initiate *me* into these rites—thrilled to see my eyes widening in amazement, the light getting passed on. And it *did* get passed on. Look, Daddy—I inherited all these discoveries! To measure the temperature of the invisible in 1800, Herschel needed both Galileo's thermometer and Newton's prism; these allowed him to demonstrate the prodigious fact that the sun emitted infrared rays. I've been working on that side of the spectrum for twenty years—the spectral side, yes—the ghostlike, dreamlike universe wherein light waves, so short as to be invisible to the naked eye, start turning into heat. I use my camera to slip beneath people's skin and show their veins, the warmth of their blood, the life that pulses within them. I reveal their invisible auras, the traces left by the past on their faces, hands and bodies. In rural and urban landscapes, I explore the ethereal detail of shadows, turning foreground into background and the other way around. I set the motionless into motion as no film could ever do, and show how the different periods of our lives echo one another. Connecting past to present, here to there, young to old, dead to living, I capture the fundamental instability of our lives. I try, in every reportage, to make the acquaintance of *one* person and to do all I can to understand what has shaped them. Leading them away from their official identities, I accompany them home, question them and listen to their answers, play with them and their convictions, watch them change masks, study them in the flow of their existence, love them as they love themselves, leave them freer than I found them…I use infrared to disturb the *hic et nunc* that is the very essence of photography.

Oh, Dad, why are you walking so fast?

'I'm mainly interested in Rooms Six and Seven,' says Simon. 'The ones devoted to Galileo.'

To get to Rooms Six and Seven, though, they must first pass through Room Five—the History of Obstetrics.

Plaster moulds hanging on walls: dozens of life-sized uteruses painted in realistic colours. Nestled amidst the viscera, against the backbones or beneath the ileums: babies babies babies, single or twins, on the verge or in the process of being born, head first, rump first, foot first, arm first, sometimes with the help of forceps.

As they pass through this room, visitors tend to hasten their step.

These gaping wounds are a shock to them. A far cry indeed from the immaculate blue-and-white Virgins of the *Nativities.* Here, bodies teem, glisten and ooze. Flesh is garish, slippery, awful. Piles of intestines. The parturients' legs are chopped off at the thighs, bloody steaks.

Simon, too, hastens his step.

Obscene obstetrical obstacles…It was all those *naissances,* wasn't it, that prevented your own Renaissance? A giant lets out a roar. A jet of sperm shoots from his stiff cock. Year after year, each jet an embryo-clot—cells which, dividing, multiply. The babies grow, come into the world, grow, drink, grow, eat, grow. Horrified, the giant takes to his heels, pursued by his offspring. He trips and falls headlong. His children devour him.

Galileo had only three children, all with the same non-wife, Marina Gamba. The girls were placed in convents; the boy lived with his mother in Padova. No family life of any sort. It was the tradition for erudites to remain unmarried.

Right, Subra nods. Two wives, six kids—far too many, for a man who hopes to think.

Room Six proudly exhibits a framed copy, in both Latin and Italian, of the great scientist's *retractatio*.

At Ingrid's request, Rena translates: 'I have been judged and vehemently suspected of heresy, that is, of having held and believed that the Sun is the centre of the universe and immovable, and that the Earth is not the centre of the same...I hereby abjure with sincere heart and unfeigned faith. I curse and detest the said errors and heresies.'

As she reads, Simon moves on a bit. Suddenly he comes to a halt in front of a glass display case and shouts with laughter, causing dozens of touristic heads to turn.

'What is it?' asks Ingrid in a worried voice.

'Look—oh, no, just look at this!'

Obedient as usual, the two women approach the display case. Ingrid gets there first, and Rena sees her features contract in disgust.

'A finger?' she says.

'And not just any finger,' Simon chuckles.

He goes on chuckling until they get the joke. There, decked out in a lace ribbon and preserved these four centuries under a bell jar, stand the remains of the great man's middle finger. The nail has blackened and the bones are starting to crumble, but the relic proudly declares to the Catholic powers-that-be: *Eppur si muove!*

Oh, Galileo Galilei! If only you and my father could have met, you would have become the best of pals! You'd have spent long hours together, discussing the law of floating bodies. 'Ice: lighter or heavier than water?' 'Heavier,' said scientists of old. 'Why does it float, then?' 'Because of its shape. Large pieces of ice with flat bottoms float, just like boats. Read Aristotle.' 'You're wrong,' said brave Galileo. 'Even if you shove a piece of ice to the bottom and hold it there, it will rise to the surface the minute you let go of it. Lighter than water, then, appearances notwithstanding.'

Yes, Galileo and Greenblatt—thick as thieves, for sure! Alike, as well, in their scorn for all those who prize jaspers and diamonds over fruit and flowers. 'Some men really deserve,' said Galileo, 'to encounter a Medusa's head which would transmute them into statues of jasper or of diamond, and thus make them more perfect than they are.'

Dreadful obstacles were placed in the Italian astronomer's path. Real persecution, real impediments. Harassment, condemnation, destruction of career. At seventy-five—five years *older* than you are now—he was placed under house arrest, and would remain a prisoner of the Inquisition until his death. All this afflicted him at first, yet he recovered and went back to work. Kept at it. So they wouldn't let him speculate about the cosmos anymore? All right, then he'd cast a bell for Siena's cathedral...take up his old treatise on movement... write a few more *Mathematical Demonstrations and Discourses*...In other words, despite all the obstacles, he went on discovering things all his life...because he *wanted* to. Because he could, and would, and had to. Because it gave him joy.

Oh! Had my father only met him! But no...So he spent long years bravely struggling with his colleagues' pragmatism and his employers' indifference, to say nothing of his own doubts. In Montreal circa 1965, where were the Galileos who could have joined him in exploring the farthest reaches of sky and soul?

No one persecuted him. But he used up his time, squandered his energy, and watched his dreams go floating off into the distance. Boats of ice...

Why did Simon Greenblatt never deserve any joy? Why did he let his vocation get bogged down in absurd marital quarrels?

You, of course, Subra teases, would never dream of quarrelling with *your* husbands.

Two subjects and only two spark quarrels between Aziz and me: mothers and God.

Aren't you ashamed of squabbling over such trifles? smiles her Friend.

I am, but there's nothing for it. On the subject of mothers—when I dare tell him I feel asphyxiated by Aicha's hospitality, her endless meals of couscous and sweet pastries, her pathological demand for gratitude, he gets all worked up and yells, 'Basically you think mothers should be unavailable, don't you? The way your mother was with you? Or the way you are with your own kids? Come right down to it, you have no idea what motherhood is all about!' At that point I start beating him up. I enjoy a good tussle now and then—it reminds me of wrestling-matches with Rowan when we were kids, or football games with his friends in Westmount. I adored pile-ups—a dozen male bodies thudding on top of mine as I clutched the precious ball to my stomach—sure, I got hurt, even badly sometimes, but I never cried. Aziz is stronger than I am, and when he gets tired of fending off my punches he grabs me by the wrists and starts twisting my arms; almost invariably we wind up making peace in bed...

On the subject of God, Aziz simply refuses to believe I don't believe in him, though I've explained countless times that in my father's brain there was a place for God but it was empty, whereas in my own brain the place doesn't exist so neither does the emptiness. Those quarrels don't lead to punching or shouting; the air between us simply roils with silence, suspicion and dark misery. Here again, though, the bad feeling usually dissipates when we start tearing off our clothes, panting, soldering our bodies together in the kitchen doorway, in the shower, on the living-room rug, on or under the dining-room table...

Our worst quarrels occur when the two themes converge, for instance when Aziz comes home from a visit to his mother in the projects and I can tell Aicha has been getting on his case again about his girlfriend's age and atheism: 'So you'll never give me a grandson? You'll never have a Muslim son, Aziz? You'll never be a real man?' Those nights, as during the first weeks of our love, my sweetheart's cock stays soft and small...

Still standing next to Simon, Rena stares at Galileo's middle finger.

'Did the Catholic Church ever apologise for its error?' she asks. 'Once they were forced to acknowledge that the Earth revolved around the Sun, I mean?'

'Yes,' Simon replies. 'John Paul II finally admitted Galileo was right, three and a half centuries after the great scientist's death.'

'Did he add that, by the same token, Urban VIII was wrong?'

'Oh, I doubt he went that far. Don't forget, the pope's infallibility didn't become dogma until the nineteenth century.'

'I see. And it's not retroactive?'

'No. So Urban VIII had the right to make a mistake.'

'Well, the museum could at least *mention* the fact that Galileo's story didn't end with his retraction.'

Simon checks to make sure Ingrid is out of earshot. 'Yeah, you see?' he says. 'Only his finger protests.'

And Rena laughs. Even if he's belabouring the point a bit, she laughs. Even if she suspects that, deep down, he's comparing Galileo's persecution to Timothy Leary's, she laughs.

As they sit waiting for lunch in a nearby pizzeria, Rena leafs through the book Simon purchased at the museum gift shop.

Galileo's Daughter. Well, well.

It would seem Virginia and her father shared a deep spiritual communion...just like you and me, hey, Dad? Except that I betrayed you. Virginia entered the convent at age fourteen and took her vows two years later under the name of Suor Maria Celeste; she fervently loved her daddy all her life long—supporting him, doing all she could to protect him from the Inquisition, writing him hundreds of letters, sewing clothes for him, turning his fruit into jams and jellies, running the convent apothecary, concocting remedies, and...dying at age thirty-four, long before he did. Sorry about that, Dad.

Feltro

Their next destination is the siesta—but naturally it would be unthinkable for them to head straight for the Hotel Guelfa and make it there without detours, hesitations, twists, turns or distractions. As they pass a hat stall in the marketplace near San Lorenzo, Simon (who needs to protect his vulnerable pate) decides this is as good a time as any to replace the absurd blue baseball cap he's been wearing since they left Montreal.

He comes to a halt. Rena sighs inwardly.

It's just the opposite of love, she realises in amazement. When you're in love, time expands and boredom is unthinkable; every second is as round, full and juicy as a ripe grape. Your lover needs a pack of Pall Malls? Ah! A thrilling adventure, to spend twenty minutes waiting in line with him in a stinking tobacco shop while fifteen depressing individuals in slow succession scratch their heads over which Lotto ticket to buy. Everything is exciting, simply because the two of you are sharing it. Your love infuses every particle of the universe, even the most trivial and unsightly, with meaning—no, with music...

Simon removes his cap and tries on several hats in front of a cheap hand mirror dangling from a nail. Meanwhile, Ingrid strikes up a conversation with the stallholder. Three minutes later, he opens his wallet to show her a snapshot of his daughter in Sri Lanka.

'Oh, isn't she cute?' Ingrid coos.

'Thank you, madam. Soon I have another child.'

'Really? That's wonderful!'

'God willing, I go to visit them next summer…'

This is October. Rena studies the young hat seller, searching his features for signs of anxiety over his future—money problems, the children not recognising him when he comes home on his annual visit…Objectively, his life seems grim indeed, and yet his face shines with hope.

After trying on some two dozen hats, Simon finally selects a brown fedora almost identical to Rena's.

Ingrid frowns. 'That's not your style,' she says dubiously.

'It can *become* my style,' Simon retorts. And he begins to haggle over the price. But even haggling is something Simon can't do the way other people do.

The young salesman, who had instantly knocked the price down from twenty-five to twenty euros because his merchandise was over-priced to begin with, wants to knock it down some more. 'I'll let you have it for eighteen,' he says, touched by their admiration of his daughter.

'No,' says Simon, digging coins out of his change-purse and laboriously counting them out. 'You said twenty, I'll pay you twenty.'

'No, really, I insist,' says the young man. 'Fifteen, come now, fifteen. You've been so kind.'

'Twenty-three,' Simon says.

This goes on for another five minutes. When at last they move away from the stall, Simon has paid twenty-five euros for his hat and everyone is beaming.

A moment of peace.

Rena showers, puts on fresh clothes and smokes a cigarette, sitting next to the window in her room's only armchair. Down below, the garden is no longer empty: a bare-chested young man stands next to the white plastic picnic table, shouting into a mobile phone.

He looks about twenty—Thierno's age. His authoritarian tone contrasts comically with his fragile body—narrow shoulders, almost hairless chest and tummy. Physically, he reminds her of Khim—the slender, gracious Cambodian she married to do him a favour, shortly after Fabrice's death…

Tell me, murmurs Subra.

Khim was forty at the time but looked twenty. He was a gastro-enterologist and had received his medical degree in Phnom Penh before the Khmer Rouge came to power. After the five years of the genocide, during which he'd been 're-educated' in the rice fields, he'd managed to leave Cambodia following the Vietnamese invasion, thanks to a patient of his who was in the Viet Cong. Once in Paris, Khim discovered that, unless he acquired French nationality, he'd have to start his education all over again, so he set about looking for a French wife. I'd been naturalised thanks to my marriage with Fabrice—who, though Haitian-born, had himself acquired French nationality thanks to his first marriage with a woman from Mada-gascar, who in turn had been previously married to a Basque. That sort of daisy-chain of mutual assistance was easier to bring off in the eighties than it is nowadays…

Subra snickers obligingly.

Anyway, I was happy to be able to help Khim—a lovely, feminine, traumatised, delicate man, Buddhist into the bargain—by wedding him. Our marriage was as light and ephemeral as a butterfly. We lived together for a year, not making love (he was gay) but taking acute pleasure in each other's company. By the time we divorced by mutual consent, I'd taken a thousand photos of him and he'd told me a thousand stories...

Returning to *Inferno*, Rena stumbles on a passage that makes her sit up straight:

> *Per l'argine sinistro volta dienno;*
> *ma prima avea ciascun la lingua stretta*
> *coi denti, verso lor duca, per cenno;*
> *ed elli avea del cul fatto trombetta.*

Incredulous, she checks the English translation. Yes, that's really what it says.

> *Along the left-hand dike they wheeled about;*
> *But first had each one thrust his tongue between*
> *His teeth towards their leader for a signal;*
> *And he had made a trumpet of his rump.*

She laughs out loud at the seven-hundred-year-old fart. At that very second there's a knock on her door and she jumps out of her skin—as if she herself had been caught farting.

Revived by their nap, Simon and Ingrid have come to see her room. Not much to see, but...Simon finds it a pity that she doesn't have a balcony. He goes back out into the hallway, sees a door with the universal no-entry symbol on it—a red circle with a white horizontal line—and opens it at once. Rena represses a flare of anger.

He can't help it, Subra reminds her. That's just the way he is.

I know, sighs Rena. As an adolescent, following Leonard Cohen's example, Simon rebelled against his father Baruch, the sweetest pious Jew who ever lived, and all the restrictions of their milieu. 'Jews are born bargainers, my little Rena,' he told me one day. 'More than anything else, they love to bargain with God. "Listen, YHWH, you don't want us to do *this*, but you don't mind if we do a little of *that*, do you? Will you spare the city of Sodom if we can find fifty good people there? How about if we can only find thirty? How about ten? Hmm, let's see…If there's only *one* good person, will you spare the city then?"…Or else: "All right, you don't want us to use electricity on the Sabbath, but you know how it is in modern-day cities, it's no fun walking up eleven flights of stairs, so listen, YHWH, let's make a deal. Next to the Goy elevator we'll build a Jewish elevator—it'll stop automatically on every floor without our having to press a single button—that all right with you? You won't notice a thing, will you?"… Or again: "You told us not to move stuff from one house to another on the Sabbath, but the fact is that in this Goys' world Saturday's the most convenient day for moving. So we'll just put an Eruv around the neighbourhood—very discreetly running an almost invisible plastic or metal wire through the trees and bushes—that way the whole neighbourhood can be thought of as a single 'house' and we can move as much stuff as we like from one 'room' to another—all right, will you go along with that? You won't notice a thing, will you?" People set limits where they need them, my little Rena. As for my own limits, God and I came to an understanding long ago: I tell him I don't believe in Him, and He says that's fine with Him. That way I can study brain synapses without having to worry about blasphemy.'

Simon thus allowed himself to be carried away by the radical ideas he gleaned from Leary's books (*Start Your Own Religion, The Politics of Ecstasy, Your Brain is God*, and so forth), and was hypnotised by his endlessly repeated order to 'Question authority'. As a result, the minute someone forbids him to do something, he feels compelled to do it—apparently not noticing that this implies unquestioning submission to the authority of Timothy Leary.

The forbidden door opens onto a fire escape, and Simon promptly sits down on it. 'Isn't this terrific?' he says proudly. 'It's almost as good as a balcony.'

The young man in the garden looks up and glowers at them. '*Proprietà privata*,' he says in his booming voice.

'*Scusi, signor*,' says Rena.

She drags her father back inside—gently but firmly, as if he were one of her sons—and shuts the door.

What Simon neglected to explain to me that day, she goes on, mentally addressing Subra, was that there were in fact two ways of being Jewish in Montreal—*on* the mountain and *behind* the mountain (to say nothing of the many nuances in between). Our own family was emphatically *on* the mountain—the affluent, secular neighbourhood of Westmount, inhabited mostly by male Jewish professionals who had married Goys and chosen, among their people's motley and contradictory traditions, to perpetuate only scintillating intelligence and self-irony. Outremont, behind the mountain, was another kettle of fish, and the Saturday morning I first went there with my mother was a real shock to me. I must have been twelve or thirteen, and when I saw the frowning, hard-featured, bearded men striding down the street dressed in black coats and tall, stiff, often sable-trimmed black hats, long ringlets dangling from their temples…and the bewigged women with no make-up, thick black stockings, shapeless skirts hanging to mid-calf, my eyes popped out of my head.

'Who are they?' I asked my mother. 'They're Hasidim,' Lisa answered absent-mindedly, which didn't enlighten me much. 'Hasidim means the very-pious,' she added. 'They're Lubavitches. Orthodox Jews.' Now she'd lost me completely. 'Jews? You mean like Daddy?' 'Yes, but not like him. Daddy's a Jew too, but not an Orthodox Jew.' 'What kind of a Jew is he, then?' 'Well, you see, large groups of people tend to split up into smaller groups, each with its own customs, its own ways of eating and dressing and celebrating feast days…' 'So what are our customs?' 'Oh…nothing special.' 'Why do those men look so angry?' 'They're not angry—they're just not supposed to look at us, that's all.' 'Why?' 'Because we're women.' 'So what?' 'So nothing. So they want to concentrate.' 'On what?' 'How should I know? On what they consider important. The Torah, for example. Especially today, because Saturday's the sacred day they call the Sabbath.' 'What about us? Have we got a Sabbath?' 'No. Yes. Well, not exactly. We rest up a bit on Sunday, which is the Christian Sabbath, but only if we feel like it. Sometimes we work Sundays, too, whereas Orthodox Jews never work Saturdays; they have to obey a whole slew of rules from sunup to sundown. I thought Simon explained it to you.' 'Yeah, he did, a bit, but…but I didn't know what they looked like.'

Impressed by the sullen, scowling faces of the Lubavitches, I conceived the plan of forcing one of them to desire me.

Forbidden? Let's do it, Subra chuckles. Red light? Go for it. Barrier? Plough right through.

I'm not blind, Rena nods. I can see I'm caught in the same double bind as Simon. Not easy to challenge the authority of someone who has ordered you to challenge authority. The more I rebel against my father, the more I resemble him.

Since my parents paid scant attention to my comings and goings, it was no problem for me to jump on my bike the following Saturday and pedal all the way to Outremont. I hid behind a tree on Durocher Street to wait for the ideal victim. The Hasidim men strode past me in their great black fluttering coats, looking for all the world like sinister crows. Finally I saw a young man approaching—mid-twenties or so, tall, thin, angular and nervous-looking, wearing a hat that was too big for him. I made up my mind on the spot: *he'd be the one*. Carefully concealed behind my tree, I let him go by, then leapt on my bike and zoomed past him, hitting him just hard enough to knock off his hat. As the man was picking up his rolling hat and clamping it back on his head, I braked and turned at the same time, let out a yell and tumbled painlessly to the ground. There I was at the poor man's feet, spread-eagled on the footpath with my skirt awry. 'Ow, ow, I'm sorry, sir,' I moaned. 'I'm terribly sorry, but a bee stung me…and now I think I must have sprained my ankle. Oh, it hurts, it hurts…'

Torn between the instinct to help a fellow human being and the impulse to flee, the man froze. Taking advantage of his momentary paralysis, I caught his gaze and hung on to it. That was when I first learned the technique of breaking and entering a man's soul through his eyes, swimming in deeper and deeper until I could tell he was mesmerised by my green gaze…Ah. Yes.

I was inside. I'd captured and captivated him. He was at my mercy.

The man knelt by my side, glancing nervously left and right to make sure no one was watching us. I noticed he was wearing a thin gold wedding band. In tears, I reached up and flung my pretty arms around his neck, so that he had no choice but to rise to his feet with me in his embrace, his body and ringlets fairly trembling with desire. 'Thank you, sir,' I whispered into his ear. 'I'm so sorry…I just need to rest for a few minutes, I'm sure I'll be all right…It's probably not even a real sprain. I'm just a bit shaken up, that's all…'

Clutching me to him, convulsively now, the way a thief clutches a just-stolen wallet or a tiger its prey, he carried me to his home in a blind trance of desire. I could tell that laws were toppling like dominos in his heart, and that he was firmly convinced he had some important things to reveal to me…but I decided to leave it at that. I'd achieved my goal and that was enough; I didn't want to plunge the poor man into the throes of eternal guilt. And so, after a few delicate caresses, as light as they were intoxicating, after the delight of watching the young man's lips part in a joyful smile, his eyes shine with gratitude, his hands run over my naked thighs, and his tongue play with my nipples—I tore myself out of his arms, thanked him profusely and saved us both.

I'm a sin for him, I said to myself as I moved away from his house, heart pounding.

It's weird to be a sin for someone, comments Subra.

Yes. I was to discover this on countless occasions in my adult life, always with the same incredulity—whether in Gaza, Istanbul, the Vatican, Mount Athos, or at the entrance to an ordinary café in one of Paris's impoverished suburbs. I, Rena Greenblatt, without moving or speaking or misbehaving or taking off my clothes or baring my bottom or sticking out my tongue or brandishing a gun or selling Kalashnikovs or heroin or child porn, just by standing here, calm, smiling, motionless, with my face visible and my genitals invisible— am a sin for the men who are looking at me right now.

It's not their fault they get hard-ons, the poor guys. Since Cro-Magnon days, their pecker has been programmed to stiffen whenever they set eyes on a shtuppable lady; their gonads are plugged directly into their retinas. Actually, they'd just as soon dispense with this reflex because it's painful to them. I'll never forget the day Alioune taught me that, during a Fela Kuti concert in Dijon in 1993. As Fela's sublime dancers filed out on stage (to avoid jealousy amongst them he'd married them all, so there were no fewer than twenty-seven gorgeous young Madame Kutis; later on, as punishment for the singer's virulent political lyrics, the Nigerian government would arrange to have all his sweet wives raped and his elderly mother tossed out of a window, but on the night of the Dijon concert none of that had happened yet), Alioune leaned over to me and moaned softly into my ear, 'It hurts,'—I've never forgotten it. Seen from the front, the dancers hardly seemed to be moving at all, their hips and shoulders barely undulating—but when they spun around you saw their bead-fringed rear ends jouncing wildly up and down in synch with the wild Afro beat. Of course men find this painful. They can control the world but they can't control that crucial part of their anatomy. It has this maddening way of standing to attention when they don't want it to and refusing to budge when they most desperately need it to perform. Whence their tendency to cling to things whose firmness is reliable—guns, medals, briefcases, honours, doctrines…They can't stand the fact that females hold the remote control to their cocks. It scares them, their fear makes them angry, and the effects of that anger are apparent everywhere. Since they can't control their own bodies, they control ours by declaring them taboo…

'Shall we hit the old bridge?' asks Ingrid.

'An excellent idea,' Simon says.

Ponte Vecchio

Unfortunately, dozens of tourists have had the same excellent idea at the same moment—to stand on the Ponte alla Carraia and take each other's pictures with the Ponte Vecchio in the background, tinged blood-colour by the dying sun.

We no doubt look grotesque to the Florentines, thinks Rena. 'What a cliché…' Yet each of us integrates this cliché into a specific history. That young Asian man, for instance, clambering over the parapet of the Ponte alla Carraia to set his Nikon up on one of the pylons, then dangerously backing up to be in the frame and smiling as he takes his own picture with the famous bridge behind him—where's he from? Who is he?

How sad, Subra nods, to have such a sophisticated camera and no one to smile at...

They walk back to the Lungo Corsini and begin to wend their way along the river. The temperature is delightfully mild, and an all-but-full moon is rising beyond the Ponte Vecchio. Impossible, however, to savour the instant: no boardwalk to stroll along, no bench to sit down on, no way to be together. Squashed between the flow of cars and the flow of pedestrians, they're forced to advance in Indian file.

'Hey!' Simon suddenly exclaims. 'Doesn't that look like a satyr's knees?'

Hubbub cars pedestrians jostling crowd commotion...

Rena stops, turns, looks at what he's pointing to—the wrought-iron balustrade is studded with a decorative motif. 'I suppose so,' she nods vaguely. 'Very stylised, though.' She sets off again.

'And if those are his knees,' her father insists, 'what's this, in your opinion?'

Hubbub cars pedestrians jostling crowd commotion...

Stopping, turning, looking again, Rena sees a protuberance between the 'knees'.

'Dad!' Ingrid protests.

What does he want them to say?

'Wow.'

All right? That make you happy? You got one, too?

Rena turns away. Sets off again, jaws clenched. Stares up, beyond the sunset-gilded bridge, at the moon. Almost full, yes, almost pure.

They reach the Ponte Vecchio at last—'the only one of Florence's bridges,' the *Guide bleu* informs Rena, 'to have escaped destruction by the Germans.'

Having no wish to get Ingrid started on the subject of the Second

World War, Rena refrains from translating this passage for them.

'Isn't it magnificent, Dad?' Ingrid exclaims.

'The ancient neighbourhoods on either side of the river,' the *Guide bleu* goes on, 'were destroyed by landmines. Though reconstructed, they delude no one.'

Oh, yes, they do. They delude us just fine, thanks.

The elderly couple stands there, entranced.

Delusion is a many-splendoured thing...right, Dante?

Piazza della Signoria

Simon is impressed.

'Incredible. To think Savonarola held sway on this very spot.'

'Who?' Ingrid asks.

'You know, the fanatical monk we talked about this morning.'

'Oh, yes, right...'

It's nearly time for dinner. Why not have a real meal this time, in a real restaurant?

They find a place. White tablecloths, ancient wood panelling, grey-haired waiters.

'Do you prefer red wine or white?'

'I don't drink anymore,' Simon says.

'Oh? You mean not at all?'

'Not at all.'

Rather than leaving it at that, he launches into an explanation. Alcohol, Rena learns, is incompatible with the drugs he now takes to steady his heartbeat, soothe his soul, calm his nerves and keep despair at bay. With Ingrid's assistance, he runs through the list of his current medications, counting them off on his fingers, explaining dosages and proportions, chemical interactions and adjustments, experimentations and side effects (drowsiness versus insomnia; stupor

versus restlessness; blinding light versus darkness; vertigo, palpita-
tions, panic attacks).

'I see,' Rena says. 'Just water, then?'

'Just water.'

She orders a bottle of Valpolicella for Ingrid and herself.

Can this really be the man who used to drop acid with me when I
was seventeen or eighteen, ostensibly to cure me of my migraine
headaches?

Tell me, Subra says.

'You'll see, it's pretty amazing,' he'd say, putting Bach's *Sonatas for
Solo Violin* on my record player, carefully extracting from his wallet
the tiny squares of blotter paper he called Timothy Leary tickets and
slipping them under our tongues, then calmly sitting down next to
me on the couch to await the first effects. After about forty minutes,
the patterns in my wallpaper would start to swirl gently in time to
the music.

Now, three decades later, only a few scattered memories remain
of our trips together. How excited we were, for instance, to discover—
familiar, yet exponentially enhanced—the miraculous combination
of tastes, colours and textures that went into the making of a ham
sandwich. Ham…butter…bread…mustard…lettuce…Each ingre-
dient a quintessence, an absolute. Explosion of saliva. 'How is it
possible,' we'd say to each other, 'that we usually gobble this down
without noticing, after muttering, Hm, I'm feeling a bit hungry,
why don't I slap together a ham sandwich?' Yes…'slap together'…
Following which we'd spend another twenty minutes admiring—as
if it were a precious gem—the various facets of the expression 'to
slap together'.

Once, I recall, as I stood at the window marvelling at the beauty
of the sky, Simon came up to me and announced, 'Blue does not

exist.' 'What?' 'The colour blue. It doesn't exist objectively in the universe. Only in the brains of certain mammals whose retina happens to capture a particular wavelength of light emitted by the sun.' 'Wow!' I answered. 'For something that doesn't exist, the colour of that there sky sure is gorgeous.'

We laughed and laughed.

The expression *I'm feeling blue* was suddenly imbued with tragedy.

'Maybe the same goes for God?' I suggested a while later. 'Huh?' 'Maybe God's like blue—He exists only in the eye of the beholder.' 'Magnificent!' Simon said, applauding in delight, and pleasure flooded through me.

Und so weiter. Every detail of the world, whether sensory or mental, would get blown up out of all proportion the minute we brought our attention to it, and we'd tumble into it head over heels, losing ourselves in its contemplation and exhausting ourselves in its commentary. When a silence came, each of us would wander through it separately, heading off on a solitary path through the forest of our own thoughts and memories, often winding up in dark thickets rife with danger. Sometimes my father would come upon me huddled in a corner of the room, convulsed with sobs and shaking in fear—in which case he'd take me by the hand, help me up, lead me over to some image, smell or sound into which I could plunge with delight. Other times, I'd come over and sit down next to him, lay his dark curly head gently on my thighs, dry his tears, stroke his forehead and sing him a lullaby to calm him down...

The bottle of Valpolicella is empty, and Ingrid has drunk only one glass.

Lurching over to the cash register to pay the bill, Rena realises her mind is a blur.

They emerge into the white floating ineffable beauty of the

square by moonlight—ancient façades, Arnolfo Tower, giant statues of David, Perseus, Hercules. All is still. Perfection petrified as in a dream. They stand there staring at it in silence.

'Takes your breath away,' murmurs Simon.

Rena glances at him. Which of us is better able to receive this beauty, she wonders—Simon drugged, or me drunk? Which of us is happier, right now?

Davide

Ruthlessly, she whips out her *Guide bleu*. She can tell her stepmother resents it.

Why can't Rena just experience the beauty? Subra says, mimicking Ingrid again. Why does she have to obfuscate it with facts and dates, darken it with ancient wars, smother it under dusty erudition?

But she *does* have to.

Come on, wake up, get a hold of yourself—do you realise we're standing in front of Michelangelo's *David*? Genius, great man, amazing feats of courage, are you listening? Remember David, thirty centuries ago—the little Jewboy who felled Goliath the giant with nothing but a slingshot? The young musician who appeased King Saul's melancholy with nothing but a harp? The young warrior who defeated the Philistines and took over the city of Jerusalem with nothing but an army? O, intrepid hero! Artist and soldier, king and composer, peerless creator and destroyer! Admire him! And then… Buonarotti, at age thirty (he, too, a genius) received a block of marble another sculptor had damaged and turned it into a sheer masterpiece. The young, perfect, muscular naked body: symbol of the soul, in the loftiest neo-Platonic tradition. Stunned by the statue's beauty, Florence's greatest artists met to decide where it should be erected. It took four days, forty men and fourteen wooden cylinders to move the cage from the Duomo workshops to the Palazzo de la Signoria—and here it stands, before our very eyes, its perfection intact these four centuries! The acme, nay, the very *epitome* of the Renaissance! Twelve feet high, the kid with the slingshot! Admire him!

She doesn't tell them this statue is in fact a copy. Who knows if they'll have the time and energy to visit the original at the Accademia?

A young man goes by, selling postcards. One is a close-up of *David*'s genitals.

Ingrid giggles. 'I promised to buy a postcard of this statue for our friend David in Montreal,' she says. 'But being a minister, he probably wouldn't appreciate this one, tee, hee, hee! Right, Dad? Oh, no, I'm pretty sure we shouldn't bring this card home to our David, aren't you, Dad?'

Finding her own joke irresistible, she repeats it several times. Inwardly, Rena rolls her eyes heavenward.

Then she finds herself tormented by questions again. How do I know my approach to *David* is right and Ingrid's wrong? Who has the ability to judge? Based on what criteria?

One thing's for sure, Subra says. Ingrid's having more fun in Florence than you are.

Il Duce

They drift back through the Centro Storico in silence. Approaching the Piazza della Repubblica, they hear festive noises—drum roll, circus music, salvos of laughter—what's going on?

They decide to check it out.

It's a clown. A clown who, though imitating Charlie Chaplin, is missing Chaplin's humility, self-irony and truculence (missing Chaplin, in other words).

With imperious gestures—'You! Come here!'—the clown picks a young boy out of the crowd.

The boy shakes his head, trying to resist, but his mother gives him a little shove. 'Go ahead, little one. Don't be shy.' Reluctantly, the child enters the arena.

The clown gives him orders, punctuated by deafening blows of his whistle. By obeying every time, the child makes a fool of himself.

'Come here!' the clown says, again and again, his tone of voice more furious by the minute. 'Sit down! No, stand up! Turn around!'

The boy does his desperate best to comply.

'Go away, I told you—are you deaf or what? Come back here!'

The child reels. 'Fine, son,' his mother beams. 'You did just fine.'

The clown struts and swaggers. Ingrid joins the crowd in applauding him.

Rena is nauseous. 'Let's get out of here,' she says.

'What's wrong?' asks Ingrid.

'I never liked Mussolini.'

'Come off it, Rena. This has nothing to do with fascism.'

'It does so.'

'It's getting late, maybe we should be on our way?' says Simon, who can't bear any form of conflict between his daughter and his wife.

The true source of Rena's nausea, though, is in her brain, her distant memories, much too close for comfort.

'Do you remember Matthew Varick?' she asks her father as they head for the Hotel Guelfa.

'Sure,' he replies. 'What reminded you of him?'

'No, nothing, he just flitted through my brain, I don't know why.'

You do, though, Subra says. *Tell me...*

Dr Varick was a colleague of my father's at the university. He had an autistic son named Matthew; the boy's mother had either died or flown the coop, in any case she wasn't in the picture. Dr Varick had been offered a sabbatical in Europe, and since hospitality was one of the values of Simon's Jewish upbringing he cared about preserving, he suggested Matthew come and live with us for a few months, under his scientific observation and Lucille's care.

How did the rest of the family feel about the idea? Well, Ms Lisa Heyward gave her consent, provided that it didn't keep her from putting in her seventy-hour week at court; my brother was already off at boarding-school and didn't care a whit; as for me…no one asked my opinion. And so it was that in September 1973, Matthew Varick moved in with us. I hated his guts from the minute I saw him. He was twelve, just a year younger than I was. He was a plump albino with ginger-coloured hair and eyelashes. Unnaturally pale beneath a thick sprinkle of freckles, his face and neck flamed crimson whenever he blushed, which was often. For no good reason I could see, he walked on tiptoe. Matthew was an unusually gifted autistic child, virtually an extraterrestrial—he had an IQ of 180, was obsessed with astronomy, and did mathematical calculations at lightning speed. He spoke incessantly in a high, thin voice, making the same exclamations over and over again, blinking his pale lashes, waving and flicking his fingers in the air—especially when he was scared, which was often. Over breakfast, the only meal the Greenblatt family took together, his excitement and volubility made conversation next to impossible, but Lisa's mind was elsewhere and Simon found Matthew's behaviour fascinating. I was the one who had to put up with him day after day, from after school till bedtime. Since his room was directly beneath mine, I'd hear him chattering to himself as I tried to concentrate on my homework and it would drive me up the wall.

One evening when everyone else was out, I strode into Matthew's bedroom, grabbed him by the collar and dragged him up to my room. Fuming with rage, I brandished my skipping rope under his nose, pointed to a roll of Scotch tape on my desk, and said, 'If you don't shut up right this minute, I'll bind you hand and foot and tape your mouth shut. Do you hear me?' Matthew blushed and gulped and started shaking like a leaf.

Never had my words had such a powerful effect on another person. I found it thrilling. I wanted more. 'S.T.A.R.,' I went on. 'Scotch Tape And Rope. That's what's in store for you if you don't shut up. Now get out of here!'—and, so saying, I shoved him out into the hallway. He stood there gesticulating and blushing, so frightened he couldn't budge. Then he peed his pants. The piss puddled around his feet on the hardwood floor and I told him to clean it up...But just as he was filling a basin with water at the kitchen sink, Lucille burst in and gave him the dressing-down of his life.

In the course of the ensuing months, I whispered the word S.T.A.R. to Matthew on an almost daily basis and it never failed to scare him out of his wits. I got a huge kick out of watching his cheeks go from white to red in the space of a...

Rena retches.

Remembering this story in detail between the Piazza della Repubblica and the Via Guelfa has brought her to the verge of vomiting.

Piccoli problemi

Alone at last in Room 25, she listens to the messages that have accumulated on her mobile since the day before—a good dozen of them, including two from Patrice Schroeder, her employer at *On the Fringe*, and three (the only ones she cares about) from Aziz.

'Call me back.' 'Rena, please call me back.' 'Rena, what the hell is going on? Will you call me back, please? Make it snappy.'

She puts the call through, undressing as she does so. 'My love.'

'About time!'

There's something odd about Aziz's voice, a tone she's never heard before. Inwardly, she steels herself to hear bad news.

'Is anything wrong? You're shaking, love.'

Often, as he approaches orgasm, Aziz's whole body starts to shake. But she can tell that right now he's trembling not with pleasure but with rage, reactivating the stammer that had plagued him throughout childhood.

'All hell is b-b-b-breaking loose here, Rena. Have you been following what's going on?'

'No, I haven't had a second to watch the news.'

Spluttering and stuttering, Aziz quotes to her the French government's latest outrageous remarks about the projects north of Paris, a neighbourhood they both know well since Aziz was born there, his mother and sisters still live there, and Rena has done numerous reportages in the area. Rena listens closely, but finds it hard to connect his words with what she's currently enduring in Florence.

'Don't they have TV in Italy?' Aziz says at last. 'Everybody's talking about it.'

'Of course they've got TV! But the Italians don't care about France's little problems.'

'Little problems? You think this is a little problem?'

'No, *I* think it's a big problem, but that's because I'm French. Maybe they'll mention it on the news tomorrow morning—I'll look out for it. Meanwhile, how's my man doing?'

'He's eating his heart away.'

'Hey, love, why is that?' (She doesn't tell Aziz you can't eat your heart away, only out.)

'Cause his lady's a thousand miles away and his heart is wasted.'

'So why doesn't he play his lady a song on the guitar?'

'Oh, Rena, this week will last a year! I can't help imagining things…'

'Seriously…get your guitar and sing me a lullaby. I need it.'

'Why? Are the old folks giving you a hard time of it?'

'Not exactly, but…Oh, please, Aziz…Sing to me.'

'All right, hold on…'

Before long she hears chords being strummed, before long she hears her beloved Aziz singing songs that revive and enhance the folktales his mother Aicha told him as a child, in Arabic, a language that to Rena's ears is as sensuous as it is opaque, before long her cheeks are bathed in tears, before long she thanks Aziz in a low voice and before long she is sound asleep.

THURSDAY

'I see the divineness in ordinary things.'

Two young adults, a brother and a sister. They're in some foreign country—Israel, perhaps—where the political tension is palpable and intimidating. Two circles have been drawn on the ground, one for believers, the other for non-believers. Saying he's a believer, the boy walks over to stand inside that circle. The girl announces that she believes only in her love for her brother. To punish her, the authorities give her a gun and order her to kill him. As he slumps lifeless to the ground, her brother falls into the circle of non-believers.

No idea why my brain would suggest *that* version of my relationship with Rowan.

Still in bed, Rena grabs the remote control and surfs channels for a while—but there are only half a dozen of them, all in Italian, and she learns nothing of what's been going on in the projects around Paris.

When she knocks at the door to Room 23, Ingrid, still in her night-gown, sticks out her head and whispers to her that Simon spent most of the night reading *Galileo's Daughter* and didn't get to sleep until about an hour ago. It would probably be best for Rena to do some visiting by herself, and for them to meet up at noon. Where? The Ponte Vecchio? Right.

Filled with evil delight at this new prospect of freedom, Rena runs all the way to the Piazza del Duomo, enters the Museum of the Works of Santa Maria dei Fiori, buys a ticket and draws up short, heart thumping, in front of Michelangelo's *Pietà*.

A sign explains that this actually isn't a *Pietà* but a *Descent from the Cross*, and that the old man standing behind Christ's body—bearded, hooded, his face twisted in pain—is actually not Nicodemus but the artist himself. 'Aged eighty at the time,' the sign goes on, 'suffering from increasingly acute bouts of depression, Michelangelo was obsessed with death; the statue was meant to decorate his tomb.'

Oh, all these moping, miserable men, Rena sighs. Jesus, Nicodemus, Michelangelo, my dad...If only I could pick them up and bounce them on my knees! 'Come to me, one and all!' Rocking them and singing to them...*Lullaby and good-night, With old age bedight*...La, la, la, I'd hum and croon to them, time is but a lullaby...Mary knew this well, having held her son on her lap first as a baby, then as a corpse...But men insist on pursuing lofty goals. Each wants to make his mark—God by creating the world, Jesus by saving it, Nicodemus by carrying Christ's dead body, Michelangelo by sculpting the whole mess, my father by understanding it. They all try so hard! None will achieve his goal. Instead of complying with their wishes, reality resists. Buonarotti worked on this statue for eight years and winded up hating it. The poor-quality marble gave off sparks when his chisel bit into it. Furious, Buonarotti struck out at his creation, mutilated it, and turned away. God, too—strikes out, mutilates, turns away. My father too—strikes out, mutilates, turns away.

Subra laughs in appreciation.

Seriously, insists Rena. Michelangelo and Simon Greenblatt have all sorts of things in common. Grand ambitions, high hopes, woefully inadequate accomplishments, self-castigation. Indifference towards food, sleep, and clothing. Refusal to take care of their bodies. Fits of anger and despair. Unstinting generosity. My father could have echoed each and every word of the artist's poem:

Woe! Woe is me!
In all my past I can find
Not a day that belongs to me!

Oh! Above all, I pray
Not to return to myself!

Before he died, Buonarotti burned all the drawings, sketches, cartoons and poems that betrayed his fumbling and uncertainty; my father will probably do the same with his own 'scribblings'. Only difference: however much he wept and lamented (*'Painting and sculpture have been my downfall'*) Buonarotti was sufficiently arrogant—or vulgar?—to leave a few rough drafts lying around for terrestrial judgment. *Pietà, Moses, David,* Sistine Chapel, Capitol Square, *Night, Day, Slaves, Last Judgment,* Dome of Saint Paul, and so forth. Not my Dad. Oh, no, not that! Either wait for the right moment—the ripening, the glorious culmination, or...nothing.

So...nothing, echoes Subra with a sigh.

'After Michelangelo's death,' the sign concludes, 'this statue was completed by a certain Tiberio Calcagni. He added a Mary Magdalene to conceal the mutilation.' Who—oh, who will come to complete my father's absence-of-works?

Never have I been impressed by great men, or considered they were a species unto themselves.

Maybe, whispers Subra, because so many men who were powerful in the outside world turned out to be powerless in your bed?

True, Rena agrees. Yes—a fact to be stated without the least mockery or bitterness. In fact it's rather moving when a man wants to make love to you and can't. The child is there at once. And I don't mean only older men—no, I mean men in their prime, who block, stress, seize up, freak out and freeze. It happens all the time. I've known at least as many too slow to start as too fast to end.

Tell me, Subra says.

Kerstin and I were talking about it just the other day. 'Men have so much less fun in bed than they claim,' I said. 'It's tough for them,' she nodded. 'They've got so much responsibility in love-making—the whole thing rests on their...' 'Shoulders,' I put in. 'Ah, yes, those poor shoulders of theirs—so exposed, so vulnerable. They have to keep proving they're up to par, and if they're not...' 'If they're not,' Kerstin said, 'they feel pathetic, ridiculous, unmanly...And if their lover takes advantage of their weakness to make fun of them, all they yearn for is the void.' 'Yeah,' I nodded. 'Times like that, there's not much difference between homicide and suicide.'

Aziz, too, at first. It took him months to learn to give himself up to my caresses. His mother had done everything in her power to keep him from reaching manhood, including taking him to the Turkish baths with her until he was fourteen. 'But madame,' the cashier finally protested, 'he's not a child anymore. At fourteen, he should be going with the men.' 'Not at all, not at all,' Aicha replied, pressing and squeezing him against her body, squashing his face between her breasts, 'what are you talking about? He's my baby —look, he's still a little boy, my darling son!' And so, week after week, Aziz found himself surrounded by frightening mountains of female flesh—blue-veined breasts with giant nipples that looked like repulsive brown suns, quivering marbled thighs and buttocks, stomachs whose rills and ripples jiggled at every step, bloated backs and necks dripping with henna...an experience all the more traumatising that these same bodies were ferociously concealed the rest of the time, hidden scalp to sole behind long dresses, scarves and veils, so that no one could glimpse as much as an ankle or a strand of hair...

I know what I'm talking about because Aicha once dragged *me* along with her to the Turkish baths. It was an unusual gesture of inclusion on her part—proof of the huge effort she was making to accept this new daughter-in-law of hers, whose age (fifteen years older than Aziz), appearance (androgynous), origins (Judeo-Christian), and morals (loose to say the least) made her the antithesis of the wife Aicha had always dreamed of for her next-to-eldest son...even if she still secretly hoped I'd magically vanish some day soon and Aziz would go to find himself a sweet, submissive virgin in Algeria. Anyway, one Sunday when we were over at her place for lunch, Aicha announced that she planned to go to the baths, then added, turning to me, 'Would you like to come along?' And how could I refuse how could I refuse how could I refuse?

What an expedition! Worse than an outing to Disneyworld with a group of preschoolers. Just making preparations took us nearly an hour: Aicha filled three huge plastic bags to overflowing with towels, robes, hijabs, thongs, horsehair washcloths, leather slippers, boxes of henna, combs, brushes, creams, shampoo, nail files, pumice stones...'Okay, are we all set?' 'No.' We needed oranges, for our after-*hammam* snack. 'Really, Aicha, we can dispense with oranges...' 'Out of the question...' So, as we drove to the baths (yes, yes, she has her licence), she stopped in front of a fruit stand. I saw her hesitate, make as if to get out of the car, then decide against it. 'Is something wrong?' I asked. Aicha told me she couldn't purchase the oranges herself because there was 'a whole tableful of Arabs' on the café terrace across from the fruit stand. I was floored. 'She's a widow,' Aziz explained to me later, 'and widows mustn't allow men to look at them.' I managed not to retort: Listen, what kind of bullshit is it that turns a man's eyes into a man's cock and a fully-dressed woman into a naked woman, so that the gaze of any man on any woman, even from a distance, even if she's clothed from head to foot, is tantamount to rape? What kind of bullshit is it that makes women lower their eyes, avert their eyes, abdicate their vision, pretend they can't and don't see anything, so men can go on thinking they're the only ones with eyes in their heads? Just what are men afraid we might see? I, for one, refuse to lower my gaze. I insist on looking. It was the first decision I ever took on my own—to steal a camera and learn to frame, zoom, print, study, reprint…

In the end, Aicha sent *me* to buy the oranges (given that I was already an infidel, *id est* practically a whore)—but with her money, of course; after all, I was her guest. We got to the baths at last, and to me it was a foray into hell. The hot steam clogged up my nose and throat until I could hardly breathe; even more stifling was the sight of so many women endlessly rubbing and scrubbing their bodies, working themselves over with soaps and creams—how can you spend four hours just getting *clean*? As always happens when I can't take photographs, I gradually felt myself being overcome by nausea. I kept thinking about the odalisques, all those nineteenth- and twentieth-century images depicting the voluptuous mysteries of women in the baths…Why do we never see *men* in the baths? I wondered. Why has no painter or photographer ever deemed it worthwhile to show us what *male* bodies look like as they lie around sweating and chatting? Hmm, that's what I should do—disguise myself as a man, put some infrared film in my camera and do a series of photos in the Turkish baths on men's day.

A hitch, Subra puts in. Not easy to disguise yourself as a naked man…

Even now, on women's day, I wasn't exactly blending in. Abnormally white and skinny in this context, my body elicited an embarrassing number of stares. Despite my polite refusals—'No, thanks. Really, there's no need.' 'Yes, yes,'—Aicha plastered henna all over my hair because she had some left over and didn't want to waste it. Then, still under the pretext that I was her guest and that hospitality is sacred, she made me the gift of a peeling. So it was that I found myself in the fleshy claws of another ogress—who slammed me down on my back and scrubbed me sadistically with a bar of rough black soap, literally tearing the skin off my poor little breasts, back, thighs and ass…When she released me some ten minutes later,

I was flayed, scarlet, and incensed. Realising I'd go berserk if I stayed there one more minute, I told Aicha I was late for an appointment, skipped the last two stages of the inexorable ritual—donning *djellabas* and eating oranges—and went back to the foyer.

There, a group of young women were chattering up a storm in a mixture of French and Arabic, indulging all the while in mutual eyebrow-plucking, cream-rubbing, back-massaging, make-up-applying, hair-brushing and toenail-painting. A pert young mom in her early twenties tugged at her four- or five-year-old son. 'Hey, you! Come over here.' The boy stiffened, refusing to cuddle up against her body. 'Oh, so you're a big boy, now, is that it? You're acting proud? Well, then I won't be your friend anymore…What? What did you say? Ha-ha-ha-ha-ha!' She amplified her son's whisper for her friends' benefit: 'I tell him I won't be his friend anymore, and he says that's fine with him!' Cascades of shrill laughter. Glancing down at her son's crotch, the young mother giggled. 'Look! He loves me in spite of himself!' And she started fooling around with his penis, setting off fresh gales of laughter. That'll make one more macho for the crop of 2020, I said to myself. Yet another young man who'll be incapable of making love to women…

Subra nods gravely.

'It's the old story of Achilles' heel,' I remember saying to Aziz, after our second or third fiasco in bed. 'Whose heel?' 'In the *Iliad*. When Achilles was a baby, his mother grabbed him by the heel and dipped him in a bath of immortality. His whole body was immersed except the heel, and he ended up dying when an arrow struck him there. Moral of the story: all men are vulnerable where their mother once held them—in your case, by the weenie.' 'Weird place for a heel,' laughed Aziz. 'Oh, it's much more common than you think,' I told him as I went about covering the said heel with all sorts of naughty kisses and caresses. 'Plenty of men have heels between their

84

legs.' Still, it was months before Aziz was finally able to enter me, stay inside me, bloom and blossom there.

Turning away from the pseudo-*Pietà*, Rena finds herself face to face with Donatello's *Maria Maddalena*.

Maddalena

Pretty piece of wood, this wild woman, her voluptuous naked body concealed behind a rippling curtain of long hair.

Clasping her hands, Mary Magdalene weeps and supplicates. Tears stream down her face. She regrets her former life, no doubt about that. She falls to her knees and weeps. She washes Christ's feet with her tears and dries them with her hair. Her tears gush forth, splashing all over the handsome young Jew's feet. Hair on feet, tears on feet, lips on feet, perfume on feet. 'Her sins, which are many, are forgiven,' Jesus says, 'for she loved much.'

My favourite quote by that cute bearded guy who died young, Subra murmurs.

I've always preferred Mary Magdalene to the Virgin Mary. In fact I'm allergic to adult virgins in general—from the goddess Athena to Mother Theresa, and from Joan of Arc to the Pope. Every time I think of the innumerable streets, buildings, neighbourhoods, towns and cities all over the world that have been named after Christian saints, *id est* virgins, *id est* individuals who deemed physical love to be dirty and vile, who dirtied and vilified physical love—every time I think of the millions of children including my brother who've been diddled or worse by priests who were starved for tenderness, and the millions of deaths inflicted by chaste and gallant knights of all persuasions, I pale and tremble with rage. That Saint Paul was a real catastrophe!

All my friends crack up when I tell them the apartment Aziz and I moved into last summer is on the Rue des Envierges, Envirgins Street. So far, I haven't been able to find out where the name comes from. 'You can devirginate people, but can you envirginate them?' I asked Aziz on the day we signed the lease, and he reminded me that such a medical specialty indeed exists in Europe today—certain doctors skilfully sew up the ruptured hymens of young Muslim girls to make them marriageable.

Really? Subra says, feigning surprise. I didn't know Aziz co-signed the lease for the Rue des Envierges.

He will, don't worry, Rena replies. And she hastens to pursue her train of thought.

'Tell me, Aziz,' I crooned to my sweetheart one evening as he went about covering my face with droll little kisses and gently rolling my clitoris between his fingers as he's learned to do so well, 'faithful Muslims who die as martyrs are supposed to be rewarded with ninety-two virgins when they get to heaven…But what do women get? What's heaven like for Muslim women?' 'When a woman gets to heaven,' Aziz murmured between kisses, 'she can't see her husband's other wives anymore. That's it—no more jealousy.' 'Oh, I see. That's a woman's paradise: no more jealousy. You mean she can't even see the ninety-two virgins?' '*Especially* not them.' That made me laugh so hard I was unable to come.

Being a whore, Mary Magdalene reminds me of my mother.

Not that my mother was a whore, no, but people called her that because she frequently invited prostitutes into our home and defended them in court. Little wonder that, thirty years later, I did the reportage called *Whore Sons and Daughters*—visiting two dozen different countries, using hundreds of rolls of film, asking thousands of questions…What the hookers emphasised more than anything else was…their clients' vulnerability and need to talk. Eventually I came to see prostitution as akin to psychoanalysis. Short but repeatable encounters whose terms were fixed in advance—one person paying the other not to talk, the horizontal position relaxing inhibitions... 'Basically,' a gorgeous African-American call-girl once told me in New York, 'the john pays you for the right to be a little boy again. A little tyrant is more like it. Talking without listening, taking without giving...But afterwards, if he's not in too much of a hurry, he'll sometimes tell you things he tells no one else...You'd be surprised. It can be very moving. Sometimes they start to cry and you can sense the kid they used to be...Can't get too close, though, or they'll switch back to scorn.'

The whole tentacular, wildly lucrative prostitution and pornography industry, which makes billions of dollars by portraying fertile young females as being sterile and infinitely cooperative, reflects not men's irrepressible desire for women but just the opposite: their need to keep them at bay. Whether the anonymous woman is in a luxury hotel room, a sordid dive or on screen, the message is the same: *Do as I say. Desire me, adore me and admire me but don't threaten to devour me, don't bleed, above all, don't make babies.*

Asked how they chose their profession, few hookers mentioned anything vaguely synonymous with desire or pleasure; all, on the other hand, mentioned money. That's why so many of my photos included close-ups of cash—bills changing hands, being slipped into pockets and wallets, stashed, checked and rechecked, even kissed. Yes, whether for good reasons or bad, prostitutes care deeply about money; nine times out of ten that's what they think about when they squander their intimacy, when the client is on them and in them, seeking oblivion. The stranger's congested face is almost invariably replaced by the faces of their parents, their children, or else the sweetheart they hope to return to once they've earned enough money. For some women, cash gets caught up in a vicious circle between pimp and coke and fuck; the coke helps them survive the fuck that brings in the cash that pays the pimp that keeps them in coke—those women are *really* lost.

My project was more than a challenge, it was a contradiction in terms: to use photography, the art of the present moment, to activate the women's pasts and futures. That's why I took photos of them with their kids. Virtually all of them carry around snapshots of the person they love more than anything in the world, the child for whose future's sake they initially agreed to rent out its former home, their bodies. First I'd photograph the women, then I'd photograph the snapshot of their child, blowing it up and framing the two faces together—the same size, but one rendered blurry and ghostlike by the enlargement.

Throughout my childhood I had seen whores go traipsing through our home with one or several kids in tow, so when I heard about the antinomy between mother and whore, in an Introduction to Psychology lecture my first year at Concordia, I burst out laughing in the middle of the auditorium.

Tearing herself away from Magdalene, Rena moves on to the next room.

Cantoria

Luckily there aren't too many visitors in the museum and she can stare at the next wonder to her heart's content—Della Robbia's *Cantoria*, stone made music. A group of choirboys in high relief, some singing, others playing instruments. They're neither angels nor cherubim but real teenagers, with individualised features. This one has a protuberant Adam's apple, that one's eyes are glittering, the other one's nose is too long, and look over here—this one's trying to grow a moustache...

The violinist reminds her of her brother Rowan.

The words they're singing may be pure, but Della Robbia gives us to understand that their voices have already broken and that their balls are thrilling to the first thralls of pleasure. They praise the Lord on High while fantasising about the baker-lady's buttocks—what could be more normal at their age? Looking down at them from the pulpit, the priest swallows hard. Though he, too, is aroused, he's compelled to hide it. Same goes for God, who's following the scene by satellite.

Right, Subra chuckles. Ball-less: God for priest, priest for choirboys, father for daughter. *Tell me...*

It all began with a commendable solicitude. Worried to see his adolescent daughter increasingly introverted and withdrawn, Simon Greenblatt set up an appointment for her with his friend Dr Joshua Walters, the great gangly manitou of the psychiatry wing in one of Montreal's most prestigious hospitals. Though chronically overbooked, Walters agreed to see Greenblatt's neurotic daughter in therapy, at least until a diagnosis could be made. The daughter presented—I presented, that is—with the following symptoms: nervousness, kleptomania, insomnia, agoraphilia, and episodes of derealisation.

Agoraphilia? Subra queries.

Yes. I felt comfortable only outside the home, in crowded places.

I took an instant liking to Dr Walters. He was my dad's age, forty or so. He had big hands and feet, wheat-coloured hair, and an excellent sense of humour. Also he was a man, with a man's body; no way around it. At the first session he complimented me on my intelligence, and at the second expressed his admiration of my beauty, and at the third took me in his arms and stroked my back, shoulders and forehead, gluing his trembling lips to mine by way of a farewell, and at the fourth, taking advantage of the fact that I was already supine on his couch, stretched out on top of me and rubbed his body against mine, moaning, his face red and congested with desire, and at the fifth removed a sufficient amount of my clothing so that, using our hands and mouths—for, such is the naiveté of great scientists, Dr Walters was convinced I was a virgin and didn't want to end up desperately scrubbing bloodstains off the light beige upholstery of the couch in his hospital office—we could bring each other to bliss. Following which, running his hands again and again through his bristly, wheat-coloured hair, he explained to me that he no longer loved his wife (she bored him now, he said; she never talked to him about anything but the value of their stocks and bonds and their children's progress at school), that he'd never done anything like this in his life before but had simply been unable to resist my charms, that he'd been obsessed with me since I'd first floated 'wraithlike' into his office (yes, such is the picayune vocabulary of certain scientists), that he sincerely hoped I wouldn't hold it against him but he was obliged to ask me not to come in again—no, never—I'd have to find myself another therapist, preferably a woman, for he was sure that no man in his right mind would be able resist feverishly tearing off every piece of my clothing. 'Can you forgive me, Rena, my angel, my marvel? I have nothing to say in my defence except that I got carried away. I'm just a poor, defenceless male animal and *you*, as I'm sure you know, are an irresistibly sensuous young woman.'

Any fifteen-year-old girl, Subra murmurs, would be flattered to hear herself called a woman, to say nothing of a sensuous woman.

'I shouldn't have touched you—oh, you naughty hands!' And he started slapping his own hands, making me laugh and leap to stop him—'No, don't do that. I forbid you to hurt the hands that just gave me so much pleasure!' I thought the doctor looked cute as hell, all deprofessionalised like that, with his hair tousled, his jacket off, his tie askew, his shirt wrinkled, his cheeks fairly flaming with embarrassment and arousal. I was still lying on the couch, and he was on his knees between my thighs. 'Well, if I can't come to any more appointments with you,' I added, gently running my index finger along the three parallel lines on his forehead, 'I hope I can at least see you outside of the office now and then.'

A silence ensued. The good doctor's eyes were riveted to mine. 'Do you mean that seriously?' he asked me. 'Do you really want to see me again?' 'My father holds you in high esteem,' I told him disarmingly, in a clever reversal of roles. 'So I mean, maybe we could just get together downtown every once in a while and chat over coffee?' 'Maybe we could, little one,' said Dr Walters. 'Just maybe I'd be able to handle myself a little better in a coffee shop. But I'm not making any promises.' 'Oh, I wouldn't want you to handle yourself *too* well,' I said, pouting up at him sweetly. And so, laughing, elated, in cahoots, the great specialist of neurosis and the little madwoman buttoned and zipped themselves up, kissed each other on the lips, and parted ways.

Thus ended my first experience with psychotherapy. I was careful, though, to say nothing to my parents about its termination; that way I could go on staying away from home every Thursday after school, wandering around the eastern part of the city, watching life, devouring life, drinking life in through my eyes, stealing make-up, clothes, records, books, a transistor radio, and finally—my crowning glory—a Canon. I brought that off, I remember, in an under-protected camera shop at the corner of Saint Lawrence and Saint Catherine…Hmm. Turns out the guy who got grilled like a hamburger has been part of my destiny for a long time! As for lovely Saint Catherine, her body was reduced to bloody mush by a four-wheeled machine bristling with spikes and saws that revolved in opposite directions. (When I think some critics dare to call *me* perverse…I who so ardently cherish the human body!) That's how, from the ruins of my therapy, my vocation was born.

Josh Walters and I continued to see one another and enjoy each other's company. We stuck to cafés, but what went on in the bathrooms of those cafés was memorable. Memorable. Joshua taught me any number of positions, the most apparently awkward of which were not the least arousing. True, I could have noticed certain things…For example the way he'd sometimes jerk my arms behind my back when he was about to climax, brutally handcuffing my wrists with his own hands. I didn't find that significant until much later. But I took pleasure in our conversations and actually started feeling something like love for this man.

It's almost impossible, murmurs Subra, not to love someone who has told you about the pain of his childhood.

The following year Dr Walters got a divorce and, to celebrate, invited all his friends and acquaintances to a party on the roof of his building. My mother refused to attend—she was friends with Joshua's ex-wife, and found the idea in poor taste. So my father and I went to the party together. My therapy with the good doctor now being officially and successfully terminated, Simon must have figured it wouldn't do any harm for me to go along. Is that logical? I'm not quite sure. Maybe he wanted me there so as not to arouse Lisa's suspicions? I'm trying to understand.

Josh was already half-soused when he welcomed us at the door. Seeing the Canon hanging around my neck, he burst out laughing: 'Hey, that's a terrific idea, young lady. You could make a fortune specialising in divorce photos. I mean, why does everybody take wedding photos? Weddings are banal. All weddings are alike, whereas every divorce is unique, unforgettable…and so much more dramatic! Let me do your Divorce Album! Marital quarrels with flying crockery! Tug-of-wars over children, books, furniture, household appliances! Gloomy hours spent in judges' waiting rooms! Astronomical checks for legal advice…'

Simon and I laughed until we wept.

Up on the roof, the party was going full blast—Brazilian music, eighty people intent on having a good time, barrels of sangria, the late-June sky an abstract painting of pink and purple swirls. And when Simon saw his colleague clap his hand onto his daughter's ass as they glued their bodies together to dance the samba, he held his tongue, and when I saw my father do the same with a girl I'd never seen before, I held mine. Blonde and buxom, the girl was wearing stiletto sandals and a fuchsia miniskirt; each of her fingernails was painted a different colour and her hands moved incessantly over my father's back, now on his shirt, now under it. All that. All that, that night. An unending flow of sangria and saliva and sap. My excitement at being suddenly acknowledged by my father as an adult. My discomfort at seeing him blithely betraying my mother before my very eyes.

'The human species still has a long way to go,' he said to me gravely in the car, as we headed back towards Westmount at four a.m. 'Possessiveness and jealousy are really nothing but vestiges of our ancient past. They date back to the Neolithic, when men first co-opted women's fertility and invented the nuclear family to keep track of lineage and property rights. Jealousy serves no purpose at all in our day and age. Between women's lib, the high divorce rate and contraception…Speaking of which, I hope you're taking precautions?' 'Yes, Daddy.' 'Good. That's good.' 'What's her name?' 'Sylvie.' 'Is she Québecoise?' 'Yes, but perfectly bilingual. She works as a secretary at the university and takes night classes in theatre. She's an amazing person.' 'I see.' 'Let's leave it at that, okay? You agree we should leave it at that?' 'Yes, Daddy.'

To Lisa, Sylvie was neither more nor less than a vague colleague of her husband's who occasionally phoned him at home to discuss administrative issues. It was both thrilling and guilt-inducing to share this secret with my father—concealing from my mother, by tacit agreement, such a crucial part of our lives. A bit like mutual blackmail—*I'll keep your secret if you keep mine*—each of us holding the card which, slapped down, could ruin the other's game in an instant. The incredible thing was how easy we found it to be duplicitous, week after week and month after month for nearly a year. I even made friends with Sylvie. We compared our methods of contraception. I was on the Pill, and Sylvie, to make sure she didn't give me a half-brother or -sister, used a diaphragm. How did we convince ourselves that the situation could lead to anything but disaster?

What's going on? Subra asks. Why are all these old stories coming back to haunt you this morning?

Rena has no idea. Photography's not allowed in the museum, so her Canon is of no avail. She's at the mercy of every memory her brain chooses to dredge up. No matter what work of art she chooses to look at, the floodgates open and it seems that nothing can shut them again.

She moves on to the next room.

La Scultura

Here, aptly enough, are the different art forms as sculpted by Andrea Pisano. Chiselled in small marble panels: *La Musica, La Pittura, La Scultura*. The latter brings her up short.

Burned into her retina: the primal scene, the primordial scene, the primitive scene.

The marble sculptor holds the marble body. The living sculptor holds the marble body. The living sculptor holds the living body.

Furious, the sculptor strikes the marble body. Pygmalion dances with Galatea. I dance with your friend. Donatello kisses Mary Magdalene. You kiss my friend. Mary Magdalene weeps at Jesus's feet. Camille Claudel weeps at Rodin's feet. Rodin sculpts Camille Claudel. Your friend kisses me. Your friend strikes the marble body. I weep at your friend's feet. Furious, you strike your friend.

I was sixteen now, and Sylvie must have been pushing twenty. Simon Greenblatt—who, though he hadn't yet completed his thesis, had managed to publish a couple of valid articles on the medical uses of LSD—and Joshua Walters, who now ran the psychiatric ward of his hospital, had been invited to London for a conference on *Mind and Brain*. It so happened the dates of the conference coincided with my Easter holiday.

Why didn't I go with them? 'It would be a great chance for our Rena to discover Europe!' Simon exclaimed. And Lisa walked right into his trap. I don't really know how to explain my mother's blindness except by saying that she was preoccupied with her work, her struggle, the daunting problems of all the Québecoises who filed into her office seven days a week, fifty-two weeks a year, knocked up, drugged, infected with syphilis, abused by family members or raped by strangers. Simon told his wife only as much of the truth as he figured she could digest: the conference organisers had reserved two hotel rooms for him and Joshua, each of which contained a double and a single bed; they could easily share one of the rooms and leave me the other one; the only remaining expense would be my plane ticket—it was well worth it! Absent-mindedly, Lisa must have given her consent. She must have smiled, written out a cheque for the plane ticket, and trotted off to plead at court.

Sylvie met up with us at Mirabel Airport. The money for her ticket had been forked out by Joshua (a detail we all, for some reason, found hilarious). Standing together at a counter in the airport bar, we raised our glasses in a toast—my, weren't we clever!

While the men attended and delivered lectures, Sylvie and I spent two euphoric days criss-crossing the city of London in search of bargains. And at night…Well, under cover of night-time, many things come to pass that no one can judge or comprehend…I have no idea what went on between Simon and Sylvie in Room 418, nor do I recall the exact progression of events between Joshua and myself in Room 416; it must have been fairly swift, though, because by the morning of the third day I found myself strapped to the bed with ropes brought especially from Montreal—naked, naturally, spread-eagled and blindfolded—while, standing behind me, also naked, Joshua whipped me with his belt. I knew quite well why the good doctor was treating me like this, knew it was nothing personal—he'd told me all about his childhood…

Right, Subra puts in. Mommy's always running off, so we have to tie her up to force her to hold still.

…and I'd given my consent. 'You're insatiable,' he said—and I nodded, for it was true. I had a consuming desire to know the adult world in all its unadulterated splendour. The intervals between blows varied in length, lasting anywhere from a few seconds to a few minutes—and since I never knew when they'd fall I couldn't prepare for them and they kept taking me by surprise. Usually Josh aimed fairly well and the lashes fell on my buttocks, where they didn't hurt too much, but sometimes they fell on my upper thighs or lower back and the pain was excruciating. It must have been after one of those poorly aimed blows that I let out a scream that changed my life forever.

In other words, it's all my fault.

Of course, Subra says. What isn't?

Everything that ensued was the result of that one scream. Disturbed by what he thought he'd heard, my father detached himself from his mistress's body in Room 418, burst through the connecting door into Room 416, registered the scene at a glance and went berserk. Striding over to poor, disoriented, detumescent Joshua, he grabbed the belt from his hands and started using it to deliver wild blows to the psychiatrist's head and body, all the while shouting at the top of his lungs, thereby drawing the attention of the chambermaids appointed to clean the fourth floor of our three-star hotel, who rang the reception, who called the police. Because I was wearing a blindfold, I didn't actually see any of this, merely grasped it thanks to my acute sense of hearing and my gift for deduction. Charged with statutory rape, the two scientists spent the day in police custody, while Sylvie and I were transferred to a facility for juvenile delinquents. Thanks to the intervention of the prestigious *Mind and Brain* conference organisers, we all got released the next day—but that didn't prevent the British government from kicking us out of the country the day after that. By the time we landed in Montreal, our story was on the front page of the *Gazette*. The publicity was to have two dire consequences—it destroyed my father's last remaining hopes of having a successful career, and precipitated my mother's decision to return to her native Australia.

You don't say, murmurs Subra almost inaudibly. The front page of the *Gazette*!

Rena leaves the museum, shattered.

Belvedere

Nightmarish crossing of the Ponte Vecchio. Ingrid and Simon cling to one another; the crowd is so dense that she loses sight of them for a few minutes and fears that one of them must have fainted.

Why, in Simon's eyes, was it not all right for Josh to hit me with his belt but all right for him to hit Rowan with his? I mean, maybe there's something intrinsically edifying and instructive about having one's naked bottom strapped, maybe it teaches bad little boys not to set fire to the curtains in their bedroom, what it teaches pretty young girls I don't know yet but I'm sure I'll find out someday—maybe we should all just spend our time whipping each other to prove our love?

Having reached the far side of the Arno safe and sound, they order sandwiches in a snack-bar on the Borgo San Jacopo.

Ingrid wonders why all the stalls on the bridge sell exactly the same thing—silver jewellery. 'I don't get it,' she says. 'Such close competition just doesn't seem like a good idea—that way none of them can make a profit!'

Rack her brains as she might, Rena is unable to come up with an answer to this important question.

'How about a little digestive rest?' Simon suggests.

They find a perfect bench in the sun to rest on in the Giardini di Boboli, but then Simon and Ingrid decide to use this moment to bring Rena up to date on the medical history of one of their friends in Montreal. The woman's illness spreads, gradually infecting the landscape in front of them; Rena knows that in her memory, every detail of this magical moment—the pond, the water-lilies, the bronze statue of Neptune bursting up from the fountain brandishing his trident, his body greened with age and moisture but still magnificently muscular and manly—will forever be tainted by the symptoms of multiple sclerosis.

She can take no more. On the improbable pretext of wishing to photograph the flowerbeds, she gets up and heads for the Forte de Belvedere, ascending the hill alone in long, swift strides.

Why am I so averse to talking about illness? It's not illness itself I object to (Fabrice's kidney failure taught me to respect the body, and its countless forms of strength and weakness, once and for all)— no, what sets my teeth on edge is making illness the main topic of conversation, forcing people to listen to tales of woe they can neither respond to nor escape from. That's why I never talk about my own health problems. In fact I have none...

Apart from insomnia, Subra interrupts.

True. The bane of my existence, these past few years. After I hit forty, it started getting so bad I couldn't hide it anymore. When Thierno spent nights at my place, it worried him to see me get up at noon, pale and haggard, with purple rings beneath my eyes. 'You know, Mom,' he said at last, 'there are cures for insomnia.' 'Thanks but no thanks. Seen enough shrinks to last me a lifetime.' 'I'm not talking about analysis, I'm talking about acupuncture.' 'Wha...?' 'You heard me.'

He went on to tell me that the mother of his piano teacher Pierre Matheron had studied acupuncture in Indonesia. Her fees were reasonable, he said, her office close by, and her talent considerable. 'Seriously,' he wound up, laying a hand on mine, 'you should give it a try.'

Touched by my son's solicitude, telling myself it wouldn't hurt to try, I called Dr Matheron's office and set up an appointment.

One of the best decisions you ever made, whispers Subra.

The doctor shook my hand warmly as she ushered me into her office. In her mid-fifties at the time, she was a smallish woman with a reassuringly sturdy build and laughing hazel eyes. But it was her face that set me instantly at ease—a broad face framed in blonde hair liberally mixed with white; a good, crinkly face with high cheekbones and a surprisingly pointed nose; a face that freely admitted to having smiled and frowned millions of times.

Taking out a form, she asked me the usual questions: medical history, date and place of birth...'Ah, you're Canadian.' I was bracing myself for the inevitable That's funny, you don't have a Canadian accent—such a charming accent it is, too!—a double insult for the Québecois, who prefer not to be called Canadian and consider (as do many French provincials) that if anyone has an accent, and a ridiculous one at that, it's the Parisians—but Dr Matheron said nothing of the sort. I deduced that she wasn't a native French speaker herself, which endeared her to me even more. I have a marked preference for people who are split—bi's and ambi's of all sorts. That's why I live in the neighbourhood of Belleville, where bilingualism is the rule and not the exception, where you know that behind every face in the street is a brain teeming with sentences, quotes, expressions, songs and proverbs in French *and* another language, whether Chinese or Arabic, Turkish or Kurdish, German, English or Cambodian. I have no patience for people who think they know who they are just because they were born somewhere. 'What about yourself?' I asked Kerstin Matheron with my usual impertinence. 'Swedish,' she replied.

As she took my pulse, holding two fingers against the inside of my wrist and looking at her watch, I began to feel suddenly and unexpectedly euphoric. 'Thirteen/eight—that's fine. Now...How long have you been finding it hard to sleep?'

I told her about my nights—my addiction to working at night, whether out of doors or in my own dark room at home. My clinging to wakefulness. Wanting never to let go. My pleasure in feeling the neighbourhood asleep around me, its inhabitants' dreams floating in the air. I go back and forth from printer to baths and from baths to printer, always on my feet, turning the lights on and off, at once excited and focused. On the dry side, I love studying the grains through the grain magnifier—they have an organic feel to them that reflects the nature of light, something pixels can't achieve. (Pixels are real Germans: *Alles ist immer in Ordnung!*) On the wet side: the same awe every time an image appears, even when there's something wrong with it. It's like making love—stirring no matter what happens. When I take the paper out of the first bath, slick and shiny as a fish's stomach, it seems to be alive. I slide it into the other two baths, spend long minutes washing it, slap it up on the wall, study it, and start over, printing a bit differently, using a masking card to bring out detail in one part of the image without overexposing the rest...I can remain on my feet twelve hours straight without even noticing fatigue. Night hours are flexible and generous—they have no minutes—whereas day hours go marching past like soldiers, in serried ranks...These last few months, though, nightmares have been tearing me out of slumber and washing me up on the shore of the day dead beat, broken.

I lay down on Dr Matheron's medical bed, wearing nothing but my blue silk lace panties. She exclaimed at how thin I was. When she asked if I ate normally, I said, 'As a rule, yes, but my sons are living with their dad right now and I find it hard to cook just for myself.' With swift, deft, gentle motions, dabbing each spot in advance with a bit of alcohol-soaked cotton, she went about screwing thin needles into my ankles, hips, and collarbone, talking to me all the while in her warm, musical voice. 'Everyone finds it hard to cook just for themselves,' she said. 'I myself have been eating like a barbarian even since my husband's death. I just take some salmon out of the freezer, slap it into a Pyrex dish, add a bit of white wine and stick it in the microwave for ninety seconds.' 'I doubt the barbarians used microwaves to cook their salmon,' I said. 'You're right, we have no idea what they used their microwaves for,' she said without missing a beat.

Rena laughs out loud, remembering. Thanks to that witticism, the tendrils of friendship that had been sprouting in her heart since she'd first entered Kerstin's office burst into bloom. Now, five years later, the two women are inseparable.

Exhilarated by the panoramic view, Rena phones Aziz and gets his answering machine. 'Aziz I love you I miss you I want you I desire you I wish I had your gorgeous cock in my mouth this very minute. When you're not around I feel I'm going mad, I lose my sense of humour, my bearings—my *self*. Just now I was looking at a statue of Neptune and I thought it had multiple sclerosis, can you believe that? Oh, baby, if only you were here with me…At least we could fool around together, sneak off into dark corners and do all sorts of naughty things to each other…I adore you. I can't stop thinking about you. Catch you later.'

Their branches waving gently in the wind, their foliage rusted by autumn nights, the trees look like wild-haired witches. Rena crouches down, takes out her black bag (a sort of sweater with no neck opening), and loads her camera with a roll of infrared film. Instantly elated, she moves slowly back down the hill, concentrating passionately on every object in her viewfinder.

The extraordinary thing about infrared, the voice in her head tells Subra, is that it happens *elsewhere*, in an alternate reality. What you photograph is not what you see. You have to imagine what the photo will look like once you develop it, taking all sorts of factors into account—the reds in the landscape, the angle of sunlight, the filters you use or don't use. You have to dream each tree individually and try to guess at its secret, knowing the foliage will end up looking like an explosion of white lace. Infrared reveals a delicately deformed light that seems to come from a forgotten past. It is not, as many people think, a gimmick. The eyes of some animals capture infrared light rays; ours happen not to—but those rays are emitted whether we see them or not.

It all depends on who's looking at what, with what, from where. Close up, a cloud is a mass of water droplets in suspension; from far away it's a purple mountain against a blue sky—and even the blueness vanishes, as Simon pointed out to me under LSD, if you get too close to it. Photography is relative: when you slip the negative into the enlarger and beam light through it, tiny black spots get projected onto the Barite paper below but those spots are not the photograph, they're only a network of possibilities; you can move in closer until all you see are tiny filaments dancing in the void, or move away until the whole image is one black dot; you can drown the spots in light or lose them in shadow...People, too are relative: seen from too close up or too far away, they lose their meaning. Instinctively, you learn to manipulate distance, framing, exposure, contrast, searching for what is meaningful...'They want to be paid that much attention,' as Diane Arbus once put it, 'and that's a reasonable kind of attention to be paid.'

What a lovely thing to say, Subra breathes...

When her ex-husband and best friend Allan Arbus went off to live in California, Diane started hanging out with fringe groups— dwarfs, giants, hermaphrodites, twins and mental patients...She said her camera lens protected her, opened doors for her, helped her forage in forbidden territory...Did she use people to get the pictures she wanted, or did she use her camera to get close to people? Probably both. Later, after her father's death, while continuing to work and to take care of daughters during the daytime, she started going on sexual sprees at night, giving a new slant to that 'reasonable kind of attention'...

I, too, use my Canon to convince men I'm interested in them— and I *am* interested in them, *very* interested. For whatever reason, the theatre of masculinity, with its spectacular rituals, games, contests and costumes, has been studied far less than the theatre of femininity.

I slip into soccer stadiums and take photographs of hooligans, big bad boys, young and not-so-young supporters. Men blind drunk on beer and testosterone, high on collective emotion, floating on the anonymity of the pack, bawling out the names of their favourite players and insulting those of the opposite team, ecstatic to be part of a group. On the surface, the supporters of Paris-Saint-Germain may seem potent and frightening, but in infrarouge you can see they're frightened as well. Close-ups of young men's faces twisted with hatred. Moving in...closer and closer...oh the sweet dizziness of blowing up images until you enter matter itself...slipping beneath the skin...down, down...passing through layer after layer of memory, all the way to childhood. It's overwhelming when that starts to show up in the revealing bath...

Misteries has been my most successful show to date. It travelled to a dozen cities and was made into a book. Juxtaposed images of male behaviour the world over—military marches in front of Moscow's Kremlin, meetings of the Camorra in Naples, welcoming speeches at the French Academy, complete with swords and green uniforms, Hell's Angels gatherings in California, initiation rites of Brazil's Bororo Indians, pimps in Tel Aviv, traders in Tokyo, soccer fans in Manchester, right-wing militiamen in Montana, senators, freemasons, prisoners—oh, such posturing! Such strutting and swaggering! Men, men, men! As anxious as they are arrogant, their arrogance being merely the flip side of their anxiety *because they're so much more mortal than we are.* It moves me to see the way these womb-less higher primates clench their jaws, march up and down, do everything in their power to attract attention and remind the world that they, too, exist, count, matter.

I longed to understand what went on in men's bodies, why danger turned them on...Some stories on the subject had made a powerful impression on me. The one my Cambodian husband Khim had told me, for instance, about the Viet Cong who'd received a dozen fragments of shrapnel in his crotch. Khim had operated—successfully, he had thought—but the man had come back to the hospital two days after his release. 'What's the matter?' Khim had asked him. 'You told me you were fine.' 'Yes, Doctor,' the man said. 'I felt fine when I was released...But every evening when I go out to fight, excuse me, but...I get a hard-on and the pain comes back again.' Khim checked and found a tiny piece of shrapnel embedded in the man's penis, so he reoperated...Or the stories Aziz's uncle told me about his military service in Algeria in the seventies: 'The intellect is soluble in weapons, my dear Rena,' he told me once. 'The minute a friend got promoted, even if you'd been hanging out with him since grade school, he suddenly started looking down his nose at you and insisting you salute him every time you ran into him. His Kalashnikov made him forget everything else; he *became* that intoxicating power...'

Working on *Misteries*, I sometimes felt like relieving the planet of nine-tenths of its phallophores—who, by their constant insecurity, the uncertainty of their being (*Who do you think you are?*: the male question par excellence), their passion for weapons and power, their scheming and rivalry, their scuffles and brawls of all sorts, are driving the human species towards extinction; at other times, on the contrary, I wanted to fall to my knees in gratitude because they'd invented the wheel and the canoe, the alphabet and the camera, to say nothing of developing sciences, composing music, writing books, painting paintings, building palaces churches mosques bridges dams and roads, working hard and selflessly, giving unstintingly of their strength and patience and energy and know-how, century after century, in fields, mines, factories, workshops, libraries, universities and laboratories the world over...Oh, men! Wonderful, anonymous, myriad men, suffering and sacrificing yourselves day after day so we can live a little better, with a little more comfort and beauty and meaning...how I love you!

Whenever possible, I would drag one man away from the pack, shower my attentions on him...and remunerate him. Yes: whereas men pay prostitutes to forget their individuality and play the generic Female, I paid men to renounce the comfort of the group and usher me into their privacy. Having gone home with them from stadium, colloquium, stock exchange, parade or training field, I'd ask them to talk to me, take out their photo albums, and show me the teen-ager, toddler and infant they'd once been. As they did so, they often wept—and I consoled them. Men are so grateful when you shower 'that much attention' on them. I learned to sense where they needed loving, go straight there and give it to them. I learned to take their faces in both my hands, smooth away the lines of worry between their eyebrows and on their foreheads, graze their noses with my lips and draw my fingertips over their cheekbones, ever-aware of the skull with its black eyeholes and gaping grin, right there behind the skin. I learned to slip into their souls, lick and suck them, drive them mad with my caresses, allowing them to arch their backs and discover the incomparable pleasure of passivity, calming them down so their true strengths could surge forth, instead of the phony ones they trot out for display the rest of the time. Gradually their defences would crumble and melt. I can't even look at a man anymore without wondering how, under the onslaught of my love, his face and body would relax, fill up with light, be transfigured...

Subra sighs contentedly.

Putting her Canon back in its case, Rena returns to where her father and stepmother are sitting on the bench across from poor sick Neptune. She finds them slumped against each other, snoozing. A moment later, they head slowly for the Palazzo Pitti.

This may be our only chance, Rena tells herself, to spend a little
time with Italian Renaissance painters. I must, oh I simply must get
Ingrid and Simon to fully appreciate their works.

Just what do you mean by fully appreciate? Subra asks.

Well, the way I do. Or the way I would, if...

If what?

Er...if I weren't quite so nervous. Or if Aziz were here...

Aziz can't stand museums.

Okay, not Aziz. Someone else...

Kerstin?

Kerstin, right. Titian, Tintoretto, Rubens, Veronese, Van Dyck,
Andrea del Sarto, Velasquéz, Raphael...*Some* of this greatness has
to rub off on their souls!

But her father, made groggy by his nap in the sun, takes every chance
he can to sit down and nod off again. And Ingrid is oblivious to the
technical feats of the Italian masters (perspective, shadows, shading,
nuance, trompe-l'œil). With disarming naiveté, she responds only to
the content of their paintings.

Saint Agatha, for instance. Any number of paintings depict the
lovely Sicilian maid carrying her breasts on a tray. Great are the
masters who have taken up this theme; subtle are their colours; skilful
is their arrangement of forms and hues on the canvas. But every
time she sees one, Ingrid cries, 'Isn't that *dreadful?*', forcing Rena to
wonder whom she hates most—the Christian virgins or the Roman
monsters who martyred them.

According to the guidebook, Agatha was a sweet young thing
born in Catania, Sicily in the third century A.D. When the Roman
prefect Quintianus started cutting off her breasts to punish her for

her conversion to Christianity, she cried out, 'Oh, cruel man, how can you mutilate me like this? Have you forgotten your mother and the breasts that fed you?'

Bad mistake, Rena says to herself. The last thing you should do when threatened by a macho is to mention his mother. That's rubbing salt in the wound. If you want to escape alive, you should talk to him about the weather, politics, sports—anything *but* his mother. In a macho's brain, the word mother is a raw nerve; I know of no exceptions to this rule. Whenever a man boasts to me that mothers are sacred in his culture, I know for sure that women get the short end of the stick there. Anyway, Quintianus freaked out and ordered that Agatha be dragged over hot coals until death ensued.

'Isn't that *dreadful?*' says Ingrid.

How can people not notice, Rena goes on (Subra hanging as usual on her every word), that the accoutrements of érotisme noir, from de Sade to Madame Robbe-Grillet, from Réage to Bataille, come straight out of Christian martyrology? Whips and chains, hairshirts, blasphemy and transgression, pleasure derived from punishment and pain, Saint Theresa swooning as she is pierced by the angel's 'arrow'...

'Not my cup of tea,' said Fabrice, laughing, as, during a visit to him in hospital, I described a few of my libertine misadventures—for instance the evening when, rigged out in black stiletto heels, a basque and a garter-belt, my thighs sheathed in fishnet stockings, a padlock dangling from my clitoris, gagged and bound yet at the same time armed with a whip, I walked upon, nay, trampled Jean-Christophe's swollen testicles as he writhed in pleasure and shouted, Fuck God, Madame! Oh, would that I had sodomised you with the barrel of my Kalashnikov! Would that I had pissed into your left ear! Would that I had scattered holy wafers all over your alabaster breasts!... 'Not *our* cup of tea, in fact,' Fabrice corrected himself as he laughed and clapped at my parody. 'Haitians think highly of French literature in general, but they draw the line at érotisme noir. They just can't get off on whips and chains—the memory of slavery is too recent.'

Kerstin once told me how nonplussed she'd been, arriving in Paris to pursue her medical studies in 1967, at the mixture of Gothic eroticism and dogmatic Marxism in the French intellectual milieu. Aged twenty-four, she'd already undergone a fair number of sexual initiations in the hippy communes of Stockholm, and had had to repress her laughter when a Leftist high school teacher announced his intention of showing her what was what, sex-wise.

'Alain-Marie, his name was,' she told me as we ate out together for the first time, washing our food down with liberal amounts of wine. (Our relationship had swiftly moved from professional to personal and the acupuncture sessions had had no effect on my insomnia.) 'Alain-Marie took The Revolution very seriously. To show his support for the future dictatorship of the proletariat, he wore a red neckerchief. The son of a Catholic family from the provinces, he got a big kick out of blasphemy: his favourite book was Nietzsche's *The Antichrist*, and when he saw a nun or a priest walk down the street he couldn't refrain from going "Bang-bang, you're dead!" For weeks on end, though I was dying to make love with him, he gave me lectures on Bataille's theory of transgression.' '"You bitch in heat, you dare to want," that sort of thing?' I asked. 'Exactly. To my Swedish mind, all this was fascinating but also terribly frustrating.' 'Yet you desired him in spite of it?' 'Well, he was a Frenchman, right?' Kerstin answered. 'I mean, he spoke such beautiful French! I was turned on by the mere idea of making love with a Frenchman, given their worldwide reputation in the field.' 'It's an overrated one, wouldn't you say?' 'Unfortunately, my sample is too small to do the statistics.' 'Well, from my experience, intellectuals are the worst by far. Same problem as with French novels. They spend so much time holding forth on literature and eroticism that they've forgotten how to tell stories and make love. Hyperintellectualism is an STD specific to France.'

Having endured an entire semester of lectures on the subject of desire *qua* transgression, Kerstin had all but given up on getting laid by this man. At long last, however, Alain-Marie decided she was ready to move on from theory to practice. They were walking side by side down the Rue Mouffetard, it was a gorgeous spring day, a market day, she was wearing a flimsy dress, and suddenly Alain-Marie caught her by the hand and dragged her into Saint-Médard Church. 'What's up?' she asked him. 'Shhh!' he said, putting a finger to his lips. And then, gluing his body to Kerstin's, he started caressing her through the silky material of her dress. Apart from a few little old ladies kneeling in prayer and an organist doggedly practising Bach, the church was empty. 'Come with me, I want you,' Alain-Marie whispered into Kerstin's ear (fortunately one of her erogenous zones)—and, so saying, he pulled her into one of the small side chapels, where the confessionals were.

Though she knows this story off by heart, Subra is in seventh heaven.

The confessional turned out to be locked, foiling what must have been Alain-Marie's plan—but they slipped behind it, into the furthermost corner of the chapel. Glancing up, Kerstin noticed that the painting on the wall across from them (chosen in advance or just surrealistic coincidence?) was none other than an *Education of the Virgin*. 'I'm going to look after your education today, little one,' the Marxist-Leninist muttered. Kerstin found this a bit ludicrous, given her age—but if it could help him, who cared? Turning her around and pressing up against her from behind, he lifted her pretty dress and pushed aside her panties with his fingers. 'What sins have you committed this week?' he asked. 'You must tell me every one of them without exception…Sins in thought, word and deed…' Sensing that something was about to happen at long last, Kerstin repressed a titter and blurted out, 'Yes, Father, yes, Father…' And he: 'So you've been naughty? Very naughty?' And she: 'Yes, Father, very, very naughty.' She wracked her brain in search of a nice juicy sin, but her imagination always failed her at critical moments like this, and she drew a blank. Luckily, though, she saw that Alain-Marie didn't need it anymore, the *Education of the Virgin* would be enough—and since she herself was slippery with desire, things went smoothly from there on in. He continued to berate her in time with the organ music: 'Ah, ah! You naughty little girl, here's your punishment, here's what you deserve, and if you go on sinning it'll be worse next time, yes, much worse, I'll take a candle and shove it…*aaaaah!*'—within a few seconds the inundation took place. 'And you never enlightened him on the subject of your virginity?' I asked Kerstin. 'Of course not. If we spoil their pleasure we spoil our own, don't we?'…

'Yes,' Rena acquiesces, nodding. 'It *is* dreadful.'

Putti

There are limits to her spinelessness, though. She's got to draw the line somewhere. Here in the Pitti Palace, she decides to draw it at the putti. Where the putti are concerned, she'll refuse to go along with her stepmother. She'll speak her mind.

Catching sight of a group of plump, ruddy, naked cherubim, Ingrid begins to coo. 'Look, Rena—aren't they sweet?'

'No,' snarls Rena.

'What?'

'I'm sorry, Ingrid, but I can't stand putti. They make me sick. They embody everything I abhor. Vapid smiles, smooth pink skin...'

'Rena! How can you *say* such a thing? You're a mother! Don't they remind you of your own boys when they were little?' Ingrid bites her tongue, trying to take her question back—but it's too late. The words are out; they hang there in the air between the two women...

'No.'

'Sorry.'

'My kids are black.'

'I know. I apologise. Well, they're not black, really...More like *café-au-lait*. Anyway, I wasn't talking about skin colour...'

Rena decides to go no further in that direction, though words of fury are stampeding in her brain. *Well, let's talk about it! Let's talk about skin colour! Why do all those cute little angels have white skin? Why do Jesus, Mary, Joseph and the apostles all have white skin? Weren't they Palestinians? Swarthy-skinned Semites, in other words? It's a scandal! It's racist propaganda, that's what it is!* She says none of this because it's certainly not Ingrid's fault if European painters hired local girls to pose for them, rather than importing more plausible-looking models from the East.

'I meant the kids themselves,' Ingrid goes on. 'The babies themselves. All babies are cute, aren't they? Don't you find them irresistible?'

'No, not those ones. Not babies with harps and wings. They make me want to puke.'

'Rena!'

Seeing her stepmother's eyes fill with horror, Rena breaks off, blushing.

Why do you have to make sure Ingrid knows how much you detest putti? queries Subra. You're spoiling her pleasure, dragging her over the hot coals of your rage, as sadistically as Quintianus dragged Agatha...

112

To Rena's surprise, Ingrid fulminates in turn. 'Would you mind telling me,' she says, raising her voice, 'why it's unthinkable for you to take an interest in pretty things? Why, to your mind, pretty can only mean insipid and despicable? Not just the cherubim and seraphim but flowers...landscapes...You haven't even been taking pictures of our holiday! It's not worth your while, is it? To you, anything that's merely nice is a waste of time, isn't it? You claim your photos tell the truth, and yet you intentionally leave out half the truth—the pleasant half. As far as you're concerned, pleasant things are a load of...crap!'

To use that sort of vocabulary, Ingrid must be really mad.

'Sorry,' Rena says, contrite. 'It's silly to stand here fighting over putti. I'm just...allergic to innocence, that's all. I don't know why.'

Silence. Her head is spinning. Whatever happened to Renaissance painting?

Simon is sitting there snoring in a corner...

Might as well give up on the Palazzo Pitti.

Fuoco

All of a sudden the world is heavy. Everything they set their eyes on is heavy. The heavy sky seems clamped like an iron lid onto the heavy city of Florence. They go plodding heavily past the souvenir stands along the wall across from the museum, oppressed by the sight of the vendors sitting on their little stools looking bored to death.

Not exactly a thrilling existence, Rena thinks, to sit there from morning to night trying to convince tourists to buy your postcards and calendars, cups and various bits of junk embossed with reproductions of fifteenth- and sixteenth-century masterpieces, then take a two-hour bus ride home to an ugly distant suburb, catch up on the world's bad news on TV while bolting down a plateful of spaghetti at a table covered with a wine-stained oilcloth, and fall into bed with your wife. Would you still have the modicum of energy and optimism you need to make love to the little lady? And what has *her* day been like? Did she tear her slip? Snap a heel off one of her sandals? Scream at the kids for getting on her nerves? Why doesn't Aziz call me back?

Leaden thoughts, weighing her down. She feels like sinking to the ground in the middle of the Via Guicciardini and never getting up again.

Gee, what a fun holiday, Subra says.

Seeing a colourful sign advertising ice-cream cones, Ingrid realises she wouldn't mind having one—her stomach is growling. What do they think? Ah, a plan at last!

They file into the café to choose their flavours. Simon insists on paying for the cones—but when the bill arrives it horrifies him. 'You can get a *quart* of ice cream for that price at the local supermarket!' And that's just for take-away—if they eat their cones here they'll be even more expensive. Humiliated at the rip-off, they file back out of the café.

A few yards down the street, Rena finds a charming little court-yard for them to sit down in. Perched on a low cement wall graced with flowerpots, they can admire the gay blue-and-yellow crockery in the nearby store window and slurp their cones to their hearts' content. Okay, she doesn't want to die anymore, for now.

Inferno, Purgatorio, Paradiso—oh, Dante, Dante! They're inside of us—you knew that, didn't you?

Suddenly they hear a commotion in the street behind them. They all get up, then rush to see what's going on. A building is on fire, directly across from the little courtyard. Up and down the Via Guic-ciardini, crowds of people shout and jostle one another. A chaos of cars, sirens, fire engines, fumes of black smoke, panic-stricken faces. No way they can walk back across the Ponte Vecchio.

The hubbub reminds Rena of May 1968 in Paris as described by Kerstin. Simon would probably get a kick out of those stories, but Ingrid definitely would not.

Tell me, Subra suggests.

'The funny thing about my Maoist lover—no, the sad thing, really,' Kerstin told me, 'was that in private he just couldn't get it up. We were lucky, though—the lovely uproar of May '68 came to our assistance. Barricades, street battles, riot police—all that worked just fine, so when June rolled around I discovered I was pregnant. Naturally, fatherhood was out of the question for my handsome Trotskyite. While libertines endlessly repeat the platitude that eroticism is connected to death, they refuse to entertain the notion that it might be connected to birth. Anathema, for the bellows of transgressive orgasms to give rise to the gurgling of babies! So their charming libertine girlfriends frequently wound up on their backs with their feet in stirrups, having their entrails mauled by metallic instruments that gave them internal hæmorrhages and horrifying nightmares...A couple of my closest friends had been rendered sterile and depressive by that sort of butchery, so I was scared stiff of abortionists and had no intention of putting my life in their hands. My handsome, red-neckerchiefed revolutionary vanished into thin air. After the birth of our child, Pierre, I'd sometimes call Alain-Marie in the middle of the night—"Here, your son wants to talk to you"—and hold the receiver to the baby's screaming mouth.'

I nodded, imagining the scene. 'And did you ever tell Pierre he'd been conceived at Saint-Médard's?' 'Not in the church. In the middle of the Rue Gay-Lussac at five in the morning.' 'Did you ever tell him?' 'Are you kidding?' 'And did he see his father, growing up?' 'No, virtually never. But I married Edmond five years later, and he was a father to Pierre—a marvellous one—until his death last year...' 'I'm

sorry, Kerstin, forgive me for prying but…what about Alain-Marie?'
'Listen, Rena. Get this through your head. Alain-Marie has hated his
son at every stage of his existence. Disgusting fœtus, bawling baby,
mumbling toddler, pimply teenager, and now—by far the worst—tall,
dark, handsome young rival!'

I couldn't help laughing. The idea of an ageing libertine devoured
by jealousy of his own son was irresistibly funny.

Paradiso

Night is falling by the time they get back to the Piazza San Giovanni;
the tourists have dispersed and the Baptistery stands deserted. Here's
their chance to study the famous gilded *Doors of Paradise*. But…do
they feel like it?

Putting on her reading glasses, Rena holds the guidebook up
under a streetlight. 'Ghiberti, 1425,' she reads. 'This door is his
masterpiece. It took him twenty-five years to complete.'

Silence.

'Before becoming a sculptor,' she goes on, 'he was a goldsmith.'

More silence.

'His techniques'—one last try—'range from high relief to a mere
shiver on the chiselled surface of cast metal.'

Hm, that's not half bad. Not easy to translate, though. Can gold
shiver in English?

No, it isn't working. They don't know how to look at this door.
Don't have the strength to identify the ten Biblical scenes—this
one's Noah, that one's Esau, and over there must be Abraham's
philoxenia…

What the hell is philoxenia, anyway? wonders Rena.

Maybe it's like xenophilia, Subra suggests. People who, like yourself, are keen on foreigners? Sorry.

Ingrid, however, still has the strength to talk about World War Two. She tells them how the Wehrmacht soldiers marched down the streets of Rotterdam singing at the tops of their lungs in German, giving her a permanent allergy to that language. Obligingly, Rena denounces the Third Reich's cult of obedience. Simon chimes in, wondering why people are so often happy to abdicate their will… *nicht wahr*, Abraham?

Sorry, dear Ghiberti. Yet I assure you, we're not betraying your masterpiece. Past, present and future: same abdication, same stupidity, same massacres.

Once Ingrid gets started there's no stopping her, so the war rages on throughout their evening meal. It's surreal.

A terrace restaurant on a little square near San Lorenzo market—*the Winter of Hunger*—they order grilled fish—*the atrocious famine of January 1945*—it'll take a little while—*we waited for days, for weeks*—they're in a good mood—*there was nothing to eat, no supplies coming into Rotterdam*—no matter, we've got good wine—*we were starving, overcome with anguish*—glad to be together—*we stole lumps of coal down by the train tracks*—this squid is scrumptious!—*we melted snow for drinking water*—the mullet, the bass, the gilt-head!—*and then my father's mad decision*—lovely, everything's just lovely—*to travel to Aalten on foot*—a bit of lemon?—*185 kilometres of cold, hunger and illness*—another drop of wine?—*I was the youngest, sent to beg at farmhouse doors*—dolce, dolce vita—*the bombing of Arnhem, huge holes in the ground*—the air so mellow—*bomb shelters in Baarlo, rockets, sirens*—the perfection of this square—*a bomb fell right on top of the shelter*—its lamplit terraces bubbling with laughter and conversation—*everyone was killed*—If only life could—*women were mummified as they sat with their children on their laps*—be like this—*poisoned by toxic gases, their bodies intact…*

The third day is over.

Back in her room at last, Rena calls Aziz, Toussaint and Kerstin, then three or four other friends…

She gets nothing but answering machines. What on earth is going on in France?

FRIDAY

'I think I must have been brought up to be a sort of magic mirror…'

In the offices of On the Fringe, Schroeder is showing me the mock-up of the cover for the next issue. To my surprise, it's a frontal portrait of a voluptuous nude, her legs cut off at mid-thigh, her head tossed back. 'What's this?' I ask. 'Have we decided to sell ass like everyone else?' Schroeder looks a bit uncomfortable. 'It's because we're in the red just now,' he says. 'Still, it's a good photo, isn't it?' As I look again, the cover suddenly comes to life. The photo turns into a film and a baby bursts out of the dark triangle at the woman's crotch. It's violent and magnificent. A few seconds later, a geyser comes gushing from the same spot, literally inundating the child. Schroeder is stunned speechless, but I assure him this sort of flooding is fairly common in the aftermath of a delivery, adding that I experienced it myself when I gave birth to Thierno.

I wonder why I said *that* in the dream? Rena muses. It's not true at all—I experienced no flooding of any kind after my deliveries. Only before, when my waters broke…

Not only that, Subra points out, but Schroeder never consults you about cover illustrations.

Another dream about whores *qua* madonnas…Reminds me of the pin-ups in all the trucks that picked me up hitch-hiking when I was fifteen or sixteen. When the drivers noticed my eyes glued to the photos of those broads with siliconed boobs, dumb looks on their faces, eyes half-shut and pointy pink tongues between their teeth, they would blush and apologise. 'Sorry,' they'd say, in French or in English, to the skinny adolescent they mistook for an innocent child.

Heavens, how often did *that* happen? Subra says, with the faintest trace of irony in her voice.

Oh, dozens of times, Rena answers airily. Er, would you believe… ten? How about…three? Anyway, all the truck drivers said the same thing: 'What are you doing hitch-hiking around all by yourself? Don't you know how dangerous it is? You're lucky I came along, you could have been picked up by some pervert, I picked you up to protect you from perverts…' But as we moved from coffee to sandwiches and from conversation to jokes, they invariably wound up pleading with me to climb in the back with them, into the bed behind the cab, with its stained wrinkly sheets, reeking of the tobacco, sweat, and sperm of their solitary nights. I saw no reason to decline, for I'd never believed in God, was on the Pill, and passionately longed to know what adults knew and to do what adults did. So, time and again, I revelled in the sensation of their scrapy cheeks against my neck, their impatient cocks seeking out my cunt, their groans of climax, and their surprised embarrassment, afterwards, to find themselves with a minor. 'Sorry,' they'd mutter. And I'd forgive them, because I knew, had known for a long time already (ever since the garage event) how helpless men are in the face of this mystery, how much it scares and stupefies them, how ardently they respond *Yes* and *No* simultaneously when confronted with the simple fact, as self-evident as it is unfathomable, that all of us come out of a cunt, owe our presence on this Earth to a cunt…

Never have I forgotten the valuable lesson Rowan taught me that day. Scared stiff—not only pubescent boys in garages and tenement basements but also Hasidim and Taliban, pure hard men of every religious war and gang bang in history, Sadean libertines who bind and lacerate, desperate militiamen who rape and mutilate—all, all—fear and trembling and sickness unto death.

Tell me, Subra says.

'Meet you in the garage at five,' Rowan said to me, and when I showed up at five on the dot I wasn't even surprised to discover that I was yet again the only girl, a diminutive seven-year-old girl surrounded by half a dozen eleven-year-old boys…'You know how to play spin-the-bottle, Rena?' 'No…' 'Look.' We got into a circle, kneeling on the cement floor, and set an empty glass Coke bottle at its centre. One kid set the bottle spinning (I can still hear the scrape of thick glass on cement); the child it pointed to when it stopped had to remove a piece of clothing. But after a few rounds and the indifferent shedding of their shoes and socks, the boys began to cheat, shoving and jostling one another and re-spinning the bottle so that it pointed always and only to me, and Rowan insisted I comply, reminding me I'd sworn obedience, and saying, 'Come on now, Rena, don't be a sissy, take it off.' And since I dreaded nothing in the world more than being deemed a sissy by my brother, I kept my eyes trained on him as my hands peeled away the final shreds of clothing—hair ribbons, undershirt, finally my flower-printed pink cotton undies. Seeing the other boys' eyes fill with apprehension, I realised that Rowan had selected those of his schoolmates who'd never before seen a girl in the nude. At first they stood there and gawked in disbelief; then they muttered and mumbled and averted their eyes. 'Show them, Rena,' Rowan said. 'Go on, show them all you've got!'

And because my brother and I were so powerfully together, because I felt his confidence and his love, I stepped daintily out of my panties and thrust my tiny hips forward, reaching down to part the lips of my vagina with my fingers. Several of the boys drew back in fear. I felt a thrill of pride go through me, flushing upwards from chest to brow. Made euphoric by my power and their fear, I moved towards them, brandishing my sex at them, and Rowan snorted with laughter as his friends rose hastily to their feet, stammering and blushing and stumbling backwards, breaking up the circle, blurting out excuses, urgent matters they had to attend to, things they'd just remembered now, important reasons for which they had to get home lickety-split.

It's a gesture you see in thousands of Japanese photographs, a gesture that's become banal in nightclubs in Tokyo's Shinjuku neighbourhood. The stripper walks up to the edge of the stage, her body ferociously protected and contained by her black and strass costume (fishnet stockings, basque, stiletto heels). The clients swarm up to her and, using her long varnished fingernails, she parts the lips of her vagina—Yes, dear children, this is where you come from. As incredible as it may seem, each and every one of you entered the world through here. Araki claims the first thing he did when his mother gave birth to him was to turn around and photograph her cunt. His own beloved wife had no children; she died young of uterine cancer. After her death he began taking pictures of nude women— thousands of them, some prostitutes, others not, but virtually all of them young, with vapid smiles on their faces. Again and again he zoomed in on their cunts. Seen by Araki, flowers, too, become vaginas, their petals labia majora and minora, their pistils clitorises. He captures them in close-up—'because, quite simply,' he says, 'I love vaginas. I wish my eyes could travel inside the womb. In spirit I keep getting closer and closer.' Yes—if men have drawn and filmed and painted and photographed the female body from time immemorial, if they've devoted so much time and energy to scrutinising, imagining, projecting, fantasising, veiling, unveiling, hiding, revealing, reworking, decorating and banishing it, it's because everything revolves around *that*, the vortex both boys and girls burst out of, the opening that bespeaks…not castration, as Freud stupidly claimed, but rather the void that precedes and follows being.

Precious few women, on the other hand, have painted or photographed male genitals, despite their reputation for being so much more visible! Even I who specialise in the invisible world of heat— night scenes, the hidden face of reality—even I who have always been insatiably curious about the wonders men carry around down there, so different from each other in shape and colour, smell and size—even I, who love to pay the most attentive homage to those wonders with my hands, eyes, lips, and tongue—even I, who relish every micro-stage of undressing a man, figuring out what sort of trousers he's wearing and how they open, undoing the button or the hook or both, feeling his member's soft hardness already beginning to swell, trying to guess which direction it's pointing, undoing the fly and slipping my hand through the opening, still outside of the underpants for the time being, that's one of my favourite stages—pressing my hand, cheeks, and nose into his crotch, feeling him harden against my face, finally slipping one hand behind the elastic waistband or through the opening of his underpants, sometimes gently removing with my finger or tongue the single pearly drop that oozes from the tip, then circling the stiffened organ itself with my warm and avid hand—even I don't photograph these things I so adore.

For Fabrice I regret it—I'm sure he would have given his consent. My beloved Haitian husband complied with all my wishes. I was a few weeks shy of nineteen when we married. I'd just arrived in Paris with a scholarship to pursue my studies in photography, and turned my back on the hip neighbourhoods, like Saint-Germain-des-Prés or the Marais, in favour of the city's northern and eastern edges, where immigrants tend to gravitate because the rents are lower. Fabrice and I were both living in Montreuil when we met at the flea market there. Entranced by the sight of his long fingers on the red Moroccan leather case he'd just purchased for his manuscripts, and with the white pants he was wearing in mid-winter, I entered his bed that same afternoon. He read his poems out loud to me and allowed me to photograph him. That was in December 1978; I became his wife in January; in February we celebrated my naturalisation with a bottle of Asti Spumante; and in April my husband was diagnosed with acute kidney failure. Fabrice and I didn't have time to disappoint each other.

Oh, the abysmal anguish of that diagnosis. 'Come off it, doctor.

What are you talking about? I've just married the most wonderful man in the world and you're telling me he's going to *die*? Come on. You can't be serious.' I remember that nephrologist very clearly. His name was Dujardin and he had a salt-and-pepper beard. One day he came in to check the fistula he'd created in Fabrice's left arm for dialysis. 'Are you okay?' he asked the patient. 'You're looking a bit pale'—and Fabrice burst out laughing because he was just as black as usual.

Another day, mad with fear, I got down on my knees in Dr Dujardin's office, feverishly begging him to allow me to give Fabrice one of my kidneys (we had the same blood type, a rare one)—but the answer was no. The law stipulated that donors had to be either newly dead, the patient's blood relatives, or both. 'Besides,' Dr Dujardin said, walking me to the door of his office with an arm nonchalantly thrown around my shoulders, 'there's no way I'm going to carve up such a lovely body. Out of the question.'

I managed to smile back at him, but not too much, just enough so that he'd allow me to take photos of Fabrice anywhere in the hospital including the dialysis centre, and to declare his room off-limits to the nurses during my visits. The imminence of death seemed to make Fabrice's whole body as swollen and hypersensitive as his sex. I came to see him every day but only dared slip into bed with him on the days midway between his sessions with 'The Machine'. Then, no longer exhausted by the previous session and not yet exhausted by the impurities accumulated in his blood, he had energy and could stay inside me for hours on end, hard and happy. We'd fuck calmly, casually, talking and teasing each other even as we fucked; now and then our passion would suddenly burst into flames, and when that happened he'd give himself up to me, tossing his head back and saying, 'Yes, yes, fuck me, my love, fuck me, baby' the way a woman might say to a man—'Yes my love, take me, take me'—and, acutely aware that the illness was destroying his beauty (his hair was greying by the day and he was putting on weight), I photographed him a few times like that—naked and totally abandoned beneath me, yes, while he was still inside of me and I was fucking him so to speak with his own cock, I'd get him in the viewfinder and press the shutter again and again, moved to tears by Fabrice's wild beauty when he came. 'More, my love,' he'd say, 'more, more, take me, yes, fuck me, give me your syrup…' Looking at him through the viewfinder I'd see him as a child, an adolescent, a youth, an old man, I was insanely in love with this poet and I was about to lose him, and so, even as I fucked him, I took pictures of him in that position of utter abandonment, his head tossed back, his neck offered up to me and his lips moving, murmuring—until the explosion of light made me release the camera, arch up, then collapse, laughing and weeping myself to sleep upon his chest.

My, my, says Subra. Are you sure all that happened in the *hospital?*

Well, it might have been at our place, between hospitalisations. But what I wanted to say was, why would I have taken photos of his cock? The upright peckers immortalised with maniacal symmetry by Mapplethorpe leave me cold. Body parts in general bore me, and the only time I ever made pornographic photos, with Yasu my Japanese 'twin' (polaroids of our organs in close-up, intensely involved in this or that), I threw them out afterwards because they'd lost their meaning. What I care about are stories. Faces always tell stories, bodies sometimes do, body parts, rarely. Flashing—an exhibitionist who gets off on the shock in a girl's eyes when he suddenly, unexpectedly shows her his penis—is the exact equivalent of peepshows, where men pay to spend a few seconds watching flesh in movement…Furtive, transgressive, breathtaking bits of image, fragmentary as hallucinations—infra-meaning, infra-syntax, flash, flash, flash! Nothing could be more at odds with my own æsthetics. My gaze insists on moving slowly and deeply, so I never use flash. I put a filter over my light source so it won't dazzle or surprise my subject. I try to make the moment vibrate to suggest duration.

My credo: *photograph only what I can love.* Turn my gaze into that love, always and only. Of all my photography projects, the one I'm proudest of is a series of sleeping nudes called *N(o)us:* bodies of all ages, colours and sexes, obese and scrawny, smooth and wrinkly, hairless and hirsute, spotted with tattoos, birthmarks and scars, dreaming and breathing, defenceless, vulnerable, mortal, curled up in the lovely abandonment of slumber...Each and every one of them is beautiful.

Fabrice and I conceived Toussaint during one of those, shall we say, hospitable afternoons. Six weeks into the pregnancy, I started bringing in ultrasound pictures of our baby, and Fabrice pretended to confuse my amniotic liquid with a revealing bath. 'You're right, it's the same thing,' I told him. Yes, the same thrill of surprise when you see a form coalescing out of nowhere—*here it comes.* This curve, this spectrum of greys, these increasingly ramified, complex features—yes here it comes, my love, oh look, here it comes, here it is...Something is arriving, someone is here—alive, its tiny heart beating! I had the most incandescent orgasms of my life during that pregnancy. Fabrice died a few weeks before our baby was born. He'd received the kidney of a young girl who'd died in a car accident but his body had rejected the transplant. Now that body, every square centimetre of which I once licked and stroked and kissed and actively worshipped, is buried somewhere in the Cité Soleil neighbourhood of Port-au-Prince, I'm not even sure where...

Really? Subra asks, feigning surprise. You don't know where your first husband is buried?

Okay, okay, I know. He's in Montreuil cemetery.

Time to get up, for Christ's sake.

It's nearly eleven o'clock already. The hotel proprietor is conveying his annoyance by clattering the cups and saucers as loudly as he can—Enough, already! Do these Canadese think they can just sit around all day, the way they do back at home in their wigwams?

'We thought it would be a good idea to start by going for a nice walk in a park,' Ingrid says, helping Simon to his feet. 'Get some exercise to perk us up a bit. Right, Dad? We found some gardens on the map, very close by.'

They set out, but the park isn't as close by as it looks (the map doesn't show all the streets). Their nerves are rapidly frayed by the incessant, invasive noise of impatient cars revving their motors and honking their horns in the narrow streets. Simon has become hyper-sensitive to traffic noise since the City of Westmount decided to run an expressway right under the windows of their home. Remembering this, Rena begins to suffer from what she imagines to be his discomfort, and also from Ingrid's anxiety about how the noise must be bothering him; their misery compounding her own, in a state of acute distress within minutes. At the same time, she's experiencing a strange epiphany. Thanks to the birdcalls, the gradually evaporating haze, and the greenery on ochre walls, she finds herself magically lifted out of this scene and wafted back to a solitary walk she took a dozen years ago in Mumbai's Hanging Gardens.

She'd come to the city to work with women in the red-light district, but within a day or two she'd found herself overwhelmed by their sheer number—there were thousands of them, living in tiny rooms stacked like beehive cells in three- and four-storey buildings—street after street, an entire neighbourhood run by the mafia. 'Oh, there are worse places than this,' smiled Arunha, the young woman she eventually chose to photograph. 'Here, at least, we can go out in the morning, walk around, chat together, do a bit of shopping... In other neighbourhoods there are ten-year-old girls locked up in cages.' After one of these conversations, Rena had gone back to her hotel feeling suicidal. The next day, rising early, she'd walked all the way up Malabar Hill to the Hanging Gardens and been revived by their beauty. And today, even as she moves with excruciating slowness through the streets of Florence, she is unexpectedly soothed by the memory of Indian greenery and Indian haze, the mingled scent of smoke, musk and dung that hangs in the air over Indian cities.

You'll survive, Subra whispers. Tomorrow you'll rent a car and go speeding through the hills of Tuscany, the days will pass, they're already passing, this trip will end, you'll return to Paris, recover your apartment, your lover and your job, pick up where you left off... Don't worry. Every step you take in Florence is a step towards Aziz's arms.

When they reach the Via P.A. Micheli at last, it turns out that the Semplici gardens, though clearly indicated on the map, belong to the university and are not open to the public.

Through an archway, Rena glimpses flowerbeds and trimmed hedges. 'Let's give it a try,' she says.

Red light? Go for it! Subra teases her. Barrier? Plough right through.

A rigid little guard in uniform rushes up to them at once: it's obvious that no one in their trio belongs to either the faculty or the student body. 'May I help you?' the man queries aggressively in Italian.

With an apologetic smile, Rena explains that her parents are exhausted. Would it be all right if they rested for a moment on a bench?

Her smile is anything but hypocritical—to her mind, elderly

people should be allowed to rest on benches the world over, and she hopes to assist the little guard in acknowledging this simple human fact. He hesitates. On the one hand, he, too, has elderly parents; on the other, he yearns to demonstrate his power. Taking advantage of his momentary paralysis, as with the young Lubavitch from Outremont those many years ago, Rena catches his gaze and hangs on to it. A good three seconds elapse.

Hmm. Losing your touch! Subra says. What will become of you a few years down the track? Once wrinkles, bags and dark circles have done permanent damage to your lovely gaze, and the seduction techniques you've been polishing for decades no longer suffice to get you what you want, what you're so utterly accustomed to obtaining...

'No photos,' the man mutters at last, staring pointedly at the Canon between Rena's breasts.

Be my guest, she thinks. Go ahead and stare at the nipples pointing through my black T-shirt, if it makes you happy. Get an eyeful; both of us are mortal anyway.

Not much to see, if the truth be told, Subra teases her. Not exactly Fellini material...

Seated on a bench surrounded by idyllic Florentine beauty, Ingrid and Simon decide that now is a good time to fill Rena in on the details of their recent visit to Holland—the ageing, illnesses and deaths of Ingrid's siblings, the new jobs, children and divorces of her nieces and nephews...Rena nods absently, her eyes following the students and professors as they wend their way across the campus grounds.

You hate universities, don't you, Daddy? Because of that Ph.D. you never finished. The thesis on *The Origins of Consciousness*, which weighed on all our lives for ten long years. You tried so hard... When reality resisted, you struck out...mutilated...and turned away, stunned by your failure. Here in Florence—yes, such a thing truly can exist—*joia della sapienza!* Look how beautiful the buildings are, amidst sunlit greenery and flowers. Look at the warmth of their colours—ochre, yellow, beige, brown, pale pink. Look how eagerly the students run up the staircases to attend their lectures in Philosophy, History, Mathematics, Philology, and Life Sciences…Never could you have found that sort of harmony and peace of mind in the grey, glacial city of Montreal, amidst the forbidding stone buildings of McGill…All so long ago now. All so terribly too late. Come, close your eyes, relax…The origins of consciousness can wait.

Right. So…maybe we could er…*do* something with the rest of the day? Fine, no problem, we can go on avoiding the Uffici, but… couldn't we maybe take in…ah…(she checks the map)…the Archaeological Museum?

They're off.

Gatto

All of a sudden Ingrid announces that she feels thirsty and wouldn't mind stopping somewhere for a Coke.

No, thinks Rena. I will *not* scream with impatience. I will *not* rant and rave at this couple's mind-boggling force of inertia. I will *not* protest at how they keep pitilessly plunging me into banality.

On the contrary, Subra puts in, you should take advantage of this rare opportunity to study banality at close range. The tiny stuffed kitten dangling from the key to the ladies' toilet, for instance. Now, *there's* an object that unquestionably plays a minor role in the history of humanity…But since the *signora* who runs the café felt it deserved to be attached to a key, it must hold meaning for her. Did she buy it herself or receive it as a gift? Did it remind her of a cat she loved when she was little, but that unfortunately got run over by a car or savaged by a dog? You are *here*, Rena, and nowhere else. Why are you always convinced the important stuff is happening elsewhere?

Oh, poor, banal moment of my life—will no one ever sing your praises? Sitting on the toilet, Rena takes a few photos of the ridiculous stuffed kitten. That moment fades and vanishes, and the next one comes into being. It's Ingrid's turn to pee while Simon and Rena wait for her outside, leaning against the wall, side by side.

Silence between the two of them. The sun is at its zenith. Its golden rays pour down over the church steeple, warming the wall behind them. This moment she does *not* photograph—but it, too, fades and vanishes. She'll remember the stuffed kitten for the rest of her life and forget the church wall, warm and luminous.

Cartoline

Here they are in the Piazza della Santissima Annunziata, and once again—there's nothing for it—Rena seethes inwardly with rage.

Most Holy Annunciation, my eye! My ass! Mary didn't get knocked up by a whispered word from the angel Gabriel, she got knocked up by some guy's tool. Same goes for your mom—and yours—and yours!

Oh! Shocking! Subra laughs.

Enough already! When will we finally cut the bullshit? When will we stop propagating the ridiculously immature fairytale of immaculate conception, invented by Neolithic human males? Like all mothers, Mary got herself shtupped. Whether she was well or badly shtupped, whether her deflowerer was a brute or a delicate lover no one knows for sure; what we *do* know for sure is that a man came along and ploughed her furrows, so when oh *when* will we put an end to all this nonsense about virgin mothers? That's where East meets West. Pornographers want eroticism without procreation,

Talibans want procreation without eroticism; the idea of orgasmic moms is unbearable to everyone.

She hesitates. Decides to ask a passer-by.

'Excuse me, is this the Archaeological Museum?'

'No,' he says, 'this is the Hospital of the Innocents.'

'I see...'

Scratching her head, she checks it out in the guidebook.

Not half bad, either. Also designed by Brunelleschi. Painting gallery, arcades, Della Robbia medallions. Suddenly she feels dizzy. Why go here rather than there, visit this rather than that, guzzle down these facts rather than those? What is it we are hoping to see? What are we looking for in this city—and, more generally, in life?

At the thought of giving in to indifference and starting to flounder through the same fuzzy, amorphous time as Simon and Ingrid, Rena begins to panic. She clings desperately to their 'plan' (devised a mere three minutes ago) to visit the Archaeological Museum. Bravely following the passer-by's directions, they strike off down the Via della Colonna. As usual, the footpaths are too narrow for them to talk or walk together, and trucks and buses keep thundering past. As usual, her father finds any number of things worth paying attention to along the way. As usual, Rena takes the lead, walks too quickly, and has to stop every few yards to wait for them. Seeing an Italian flag up ahead, she tells herself it probably marks the museum entrance. Oh, but it's hopelessly far away, we'll never get there, ever. Might as well turn around and go back right now—first to the hotel, then to our respective countries—this whole trip is one enormous mistake...

Her mobile rings. It's Thierno.

'Hey, kid.'

'Hi, how's it going?'

'Good!'

Incredible, Rena thinks, to have this sort of laconic

exchange—'How's it going?' 'Good!'—with a person who once lived inside you and whose development you supervised for twenty years, a person you taught to speak, to whom you read a thousand bedtime stories, for whom you cooked countless meals, whose homework you helped with and whose ill health you nursed, whose problems you listened to and whose friends you welcomed into your home. Incredible to end up exchanging platitudes with your own children.

Yes, says Subra. Don't forget, though: you were terse over the phone with your own folks, when you were a teenager.

'Where are you?' she asks Thierno. (This, too, she has learned to say.)

'Still in Dakar. Quick, remind me—what are the rules for three-man crib?'

'Well, there are two schools of thought. Either you deal five cards to each player plus one to the crib and each player puts a card in the crib, or else you deal six cards like in the regular game—in which case the dealer puts two cards in his crib and the others put one in the crib and another on the bottom of the pack.'

'Which way's the most authentic?'

'The first. Your dad and I invented the other one. Generally speaking, it results in superior hands and inferior cribs.'

'Got it. Thanks, Ma. Take care.'

'Bye, my love.'

By the time Rena has finished shaking her head at the idea that this card game, originally a pastime for idle Victorian ladies, has spread all the way to Senegal via Australia, Canada and France, they find themselves at the ticket desk of the Archaeological Museum.

The minute they enter the first room, though, she feels like turning around and walking out again. Damn it all to hell, what are they doing in ancient Egypt? They've come here to see Tuscany, not ancient Egypt. They can see ancient Egypt any old day, in Boston, New York or Paris, whereas Tuscany...

Whereas Tuscany *what?* Subra queries. What would seeing Tuscany be like?

Well...I suppose we might as well take a look, since we're here.

Gold, planished 5600 years ago. One display case after another of precious stones—necklaces, bracelets, earrings—a bedazzlement. As they move through the cool calm rooms, Ingrid's voice drones on and on about Rotterdam yesterday and today, the harshness of the post-war years...*Stop it!* Rena refrains from screaming at her. What have you come here for? Do you want to see these wonders or don't you? Look—right there, before your very eyes—planished gold and precious stones from ancient Egypt! Enjoy them or I'll kill you!

Swallowing down her annoyance, she says nothing. After all, she tells herself, the Theban courtesans who wore those jewels were probably chatterboxes, too.

Yes, Subra murmurs. And moreover, they had slaves.

Romulus e Remus

On the second floor, her father suddenly tugs at her sleeve. 'Rena, look!'

She glances impatiently at what he's pointing to—a block of pink granite with a fragment of bas-relief representing a child and an animal—fine.

'What do you think that's about?'

'Frankly, Dad,' she says with condescending kindness, 'I wouldn't presume to have an opinion on the matter. Egyptologists, historians, and archaeologists have been studying these objects for centuries. They *know* the answer, so there's no point in our guessing at it. Just a sec.'

Grabbing the sheet of plasticised cardboard listing the objects in the room, she finds the granite block and reads aloud, rather haughtily: 'An extremely rare representation of the cow Hathor suckling Horemheb, the Pharaoh who came to power after Tutankhamun's death (fourteenth century B.C.).' You see, Dad? she natters on, though not out loud. No point in our having an opinion.

My own periods of lactation, she continues in an aside to Subra— and to a lesser extent, my pregnancies—were the only times I ever had breasts worthy of the name. Such an insanely erotic experience, those first months of motherhood. Deep sweet perpetual inner climax. Sheer joy of being so passionately desired and caressed, and fulfilling someone's needs so utterly. Exhilaration of having another person's body, first nestled inside your own, then perfectly fed by it: the baby's lips tugging away at one nipple while its tiny fingers play with the other, making it stiffen in pleasure. In Renaissance paintings you sometimes see baby Jesus playing with his mom's breast that way...

Yeah, Subra says, but the Madonna never seems turned on by it.

Women are right to hide that pleasure from men, Rena laughs. They'd have good reason to be jealous. Poor guys—forever at a distance, dry, tense, nervous, on their guard, never entirely convinced that they're loved, wanted, needed...

'Even so,' Simon insists, not offended by her peremptory tone of voice, 'doesn't it remind you of something?'

'What do you mean, something? Frankly, there's not much point in our...in our...Wait a minute.'

At last Rena looks. Really looks. That's all her father has been asking her to do.

A two-ton block of pink granite brought back from Egypt by the Romans...The Romans, when? Why? *Look*. Look at what the bas-relief is about: a beast suckling a boy.

Suddenly it's obvious. Blindingly clear. No doubt about it, Rena tells herself. My father is right and the specialists are a bunch of nincompoops. If the Romans dragged this monumental sculpture all the way from Egypt to Italy in the third century A.D. (and just think what that entailed: the weight...the distance...in the boats they had back then...and no Suez Canal!), it was because it spoke to them of themselves. Yes: in Horemheb they recognised Romulus; and in Hathor, the She-wolf.

One point for you, Dad.

Horemheb suckled at Hathor's breast...Romulus at the She-wolf's... Jesus at Mary's...Pico at Giulia Boiardo's...How about you, Dad? Whose nipples would you have needed to drink from, in order to become immortal?

Granny Rena's two children were born in the sinister 1930s. Years of painful exile for her, persecution and terror for all the Jews of Europe. If she nursed her children, they can only have drunk down anxiety and bitterness along with their breastmilk...

That's how destinies get forged, Subra says philosophically.

Rowan and I were Lisa's Romulus and Remus, I know that. Remus was an afterthought, a usurper, an impostor, I know that. In the first sculptures of the She-Wolf that symbolises Rome, only Romulus crouches beneath her, sucking at her teat, I know that...

Yes, I'm familiar with that scene now. Rowan told me about it last summer—first laughing, then in tears.

Tell me, Subra says.

I'd gone to Vancouver to help him celebrate his forty-ninth birthday. He didn't want to make a big deal about his fiftieth like everybody else—'Why do people always celebrate round figures?' he asked me over the phone. 'I mean, it's completely arbitrary, isn't it? I've never liked round figures and I see no reason to celebrate them. My own lucky number has always been seven, so I've decided to throw a big party for my seven-times-seventh birthday. Please try to come, Rena…' So I made the trip.

It's about eight thousand kilometres from Paris to Vancouver. I flew all that distance just to see my big brother's eyes light up—those beautiful green eyes we both inherited from our Australian mom. Some fifty friends of his—musicians and actors of both sexes, mainly gays and lesbians—had converged for the celebration, which was heavily laced with gin, cocaine and a number of other magic potions. When we finally found ourselves alone together at around three in the morning, Rowan suggested we go on celebrating for a while and I said yes, I said yes, I've always said yes to my older brother. 'For me it's already twelve noon,' I told him. 'I can't possibly be tired.' Rowan laughed. So we talked for another three hours—or rather, since gin loosens his tongue, Rowan talked for another three hours, and by the time dawn started whitening the sky he was telling me about my arrival in his life when he was four.

'You took Lisa away from me,' he said. 'One day, I remember, she was nursing you and I tried to drink from the other breast but she pushed me away. She had eyes only for you. I wanted to kill you, you know? I mean, it wasn't personal or anything,' he added, laughing. 'I had nothing against you personally. I just wanted you to disappear and for things to go back to the way they were before. Was that too much to ask—that things should go back to the way they were before? I think it was a completely reasonable thing to ask. The idea was to do it very gently. No bloodshed or anything. Just to keep you from breathing, so you'd go back to wherever you came from.' Again he laughed. 'So first I held a pillow over your face while you were asleep, but you woke up and started crying and Mommy ran in looking horrified. "What's the matter? Rowan, what's the matter? What's that pillow doing in Rena's crib? I told you babies slept without pillows, didn't I?" "Yes." "No pillows for babies. Right?" "Yes." "Will you be sure to remember that next time?" "Yes." "Rena doesn't like sleeping with a pillow, she's not big enough yet. For you it's different, you're a big boy. Do you understand?" "Yes…" So I went on to my second plan—strangulation. I fetched a scarf, slipped it around your neck, tied the two ends together and pulled with all my might…But again Mommy woke up. And what happened next was awful.'

Tears were reddening his eyes now, his cheeks were grey with stubble and his features were twisted into a grimace of pain; my usually handsome brother looked ugly at that moment, exhausted, inebriated and ugly in the pallid light of dawn. 'I'll…never…I can't ever, ever forget it. How Lisa's face came right up close to mine. Scarlet with rage. Deformed by hatred. Her mouth open, and her lips—those sensual lips I so loved to kiss—all sort of stiff and square. She was screaming at me. "Ro-o-o-o-wa-a-a-a-a-an! How could you do-o-o such a thing? Do you reali-i-i-i-ise, Rowan? Rowan, you almost killed your little sii-i-i-ister!" I couldn't stand it, so I turned off the sound. I could tell she was still screaming from the way her mouth was moving but I couldn't hear her anymore…and then…in that silence…she started strangling *me*…She probably did it…so… so…so I'd realise what I had done…so I'd see what it felt like not to be able to breathe…"But Mommy," I wanted to say to her…"But

139

Mommy, it's just because I love you so much!" What could I do to make her love me again? "I'm sorry I'm sorry I'm sorry I'm sorry I'm sorry I'm sorry I'm sorry I'm sorry I'm sorry I'm sorry I'm sorry, it's because I love you, Mommy! I'm sorry I'm sorry I'm sorry I'm sorry I'm sorry I'm sorry I'm sorry I'm sorry I'm sorry I'm sorry I'm sorry…'"

Rowan was sobbing softly, his head on the counter. I came and put an arm around his shoulders. Does he strangle his lovers, too? I wondered. Or ask them to strangle him? I'd be moved but not surprised if the answer was yes…'Hey, bro'. It's all over now…Listen, it's getting late, I'm going to put you to bed.'

At least Lisa nursed you, Subra points out.

Yeah, I was glad to learn that, says Rena. It's something, anyway, isn't it?

They move together into the hall of mummies.

Mummia

Penumbra. They're all alone in the enormous room. (The conformist crowds can *keep* the Duomo and the Uffizi!) Profound, disturbing mystery of the swaddled dead.

Oh, the Egyptians! Peerless embalmers! Unsurpassable technicians of the Passage…

As they move past the sarcophagi with their magnificent painted effigies of the departed, they notice some of them are open, their contents visible. The ancient strips of cloth, though still impeccably twined, are tainted and tattered. The presence of human corpses is palpable.

'Brrr,' says Ingrid.

And Simon: 'Do you think they really believed their slaves would go on working for them in the Great Beyond?'

And Rena (still humming her no-point-in-having-an-opinion refrain): 'I mostly think we can't project ourselves into the minds of pharaohs.'

And Simon: 'Really? Why?'

And she: 'Well, I can't, anyway. Maybe you can, because—like them—you believe in the soul's immortality.'

Though Simon Greenblatt is a scientist and a rationalist, there's a whole section of his brain set aside for metaphysical mysteries.

Tell me, Subra says.

He flabbergasted me by not laughing his head off when, in the spring of 1996, his idol Timothy Leary started making preparations for his death. First he made arrangements with a company called CryoCare to have his corpse frozen. Then, before his body rotted completely from the mind-boggling quantities of nicotine and narcotics he'd been pumping into it over six decades, he figured maybe he should commit suicide 'live' on the internet. Finally he requested that his ashes be rocketed into outer space—and his preposterous request was granted.

'Don't you think that's *bananas*, Dad?' I yelled over the phone. My tone of voice upset Thierno, who was doing his homework next to me in the living room. At twelve, Thierno was hypersensitive to conflict; the faintest stirrings of a quarrel would plunge him into a state of panic.

Maybe because you and Alioune were fighting non-stop at the time? Subra suggests.

Could be. Anyway, just as my father in Montreal said, 'Why bananas?' into my right ear, my son came over and whispered into my left ear, 'Why are you yelling at Grandad?' 'People do all sorts of things with their dead bodies,' Simon went on. 'Why is it sillier to put them into orbit around the Earth than to donate them to worms or vultures?' 'Daddy, I can't believe my ears!' I yelled. 'Are you telling me there's a little glass bottle up there in the sky with Leary's name on it, and he's counting on extraterrestrials to come and wake him up twenty million years from now, and you don't think that's bananas? Come off it!' At that point, Thierno put a hand over my mouth and I had no choice but to drop the subject.

Today in Florence, though, I suddenly feel very lonely. On their side, believing or having believed in the soul's immortality: mummies, Bach, Michelangelo, endless multitudes of human beings from that handsome hunk of Cro-Magnon down to my sweet Aziz. On my side, the materialistic side: Lucretius; maybe Shakespeare; a handful of modern miscreants.

Ah, whispers Subra. But retain this instant, in the shadowy silence. Look—two thousand years after J.C., three living people lean down over dead ones dating from two thousand years before. May they rest in peace, in peace, in peace.

Rena holds the instant...then it dissolves.

Straightening, the living leave the darkened room and move towards their own deaths.

Why hurry? Oh, whatever is the rush?

Chimera
___

Their bodies stay close together as they inch down the broad, sunlit corridor filled with Etruscan art—ah, astonishing grace in bronze, tall thin figures, leaping acrobats, funerary urns—but their thoughts scatter in all directions. Each of them mixes the museum's contents with that of his or her own brain. Facts gleaned over the years, memories, moods, associations...

Okay, Rena is telling Subra. Okay, you're right, there was no article in the *Gazette*. The stagnation of Simon's career wasn't the *Gazette*'s fault. As for 'Australia'…well, that's a figure of speech. When I say native land…When I say my mother abruptly decided to return to her native land…

'Rena, look!' Simon cries.

She whirls around and sees—right there in a glass cage, smack in the middle of the corridor—she'd missed it, moving from case to case along the walls, her mind elsewhere—a chimera. Called the *Arezzo Chimera* because it was found in the vicinity of that city, but dating from long before its foundation. Etruscan, fifth century B.C.; Greek influence? A lion is poised to leap; its tail is a snake that rears up to attack the horned antelope bursting out of its back…

Simon and Rena stand rooted to the spot, stunned by the creature's violent beauty.

'It's like a prefiguration of the Freudian psyche,' Simon says. 'Ego the lion, Id, the antelope, Superego the snake.'

Rena nods. We know all about the struggle of self against self, don't we, Daddy? You against you and me against me…

But Ingrid interrupts: 'It's five-thirty already. I'm famished!'

So they retrace their steps—bronze figurines, tattered mummies, Hathor giving suck to Horemheb, great stone staircases, ancient jewellery, and then—a mandatory stop, after the bathroom but before the exit—the postcard stand. Suspecting that Simon and Ingrid will take a while to make their choice, Rena forces herself to study the cards. Which of the objects contained in the museum will the curators have deemed worthy of reproduction?

Despite her own resolutions and Aziz's good advice, she herself is taking fewer and fewer photographs. Both her art and her eroticism wither and die in the presence of Simon and Ingrid; she's reduced to living in reality and, at the same time, deprived of what makes reality liveable for her.

143

Her eyes scan the postcards. Hey...what's this?

A smiling, perfectly preserved polychrome maidservant, forty-two centimetres high, dating from the Fifth Dynasty, kneeling on the ground and kneading dough...

Aziz's grandmother still makes bread that way, in her village in the Algerian district of Chelef: she kneels down and bends forward, almost in praying position. Aziz once told me why Muslim men and women have to pray separately: the faithful stand shoulder to shoulder, he said, to prevent the evil spirit from slipping between them. And a man wouldn't want his wife, mother or sister to rub shoulders with a male stranger, now, would he? Nor would he want male strangers in the row behind them to see their rear ends sticking up in the air as they prayed!

How did we miss that little statue? Rena thinks. And what should I do now? Rush back up to look at her this very minute, all by myself? For who knows when (or if) I'll see Florence's Archaeological Museum again?

And you *do* want to see that perfectly preserved statue of a little smiling slave, murmurs Subra. Don't you?

Feeling like a coward, Rena buys the postcard. She'll tell Aziz she saw the statue and that it reminded her of his grandmother.

What, after all, is *seeing*? she says to herself. By the time it gets projected onto our retina, even the real statue is an image. Seeing a photo of it is basically just another way of *seeing* it, right?

Subra has a good laugh.

Disputatio

They find a convivial greasy-spoon for their early dinner. Unfortunately, the only free table is right next to the toilet; there are incessant comings and goings in that corner and most of the customers forget to close the door when they come out...Still, Rena chooses this moment to return to the subject of the soul's immortality.

W.C. versus the Great Beyond? The abject versus the sublime? But that's exactly what is at stake. The very dilemma Michelangelo ran into as he prepared to paint his *Last Judgment* frescoes—what do people's bodies *look like* after resurrection?

'So tell me,' she says, stabbing at her tomato and mozzarella salad, 'just what is this belief you both believe? Can you explain it to me? You, dear Ingrid—tell me, I'm all ears. You say the soul is eternal, but...starting when?'

'Sorry?'

'Yes, when does the soul's eternity begin? At conception? At birth? Or is it *whenless*, being eternal—extending to infinity both in past and future? Before conception and after death?'

Ingrid is uncomfortable. Though raised a Protestant, she stopped attending church when she married a Jew, reassuring herself with the vague idea that they saw eye-to-eye on important things. Now, avoiding Rena's gaze, she butters a piece of bread, folds three slices of mortadella onto it and takes a big bite. 'All I know,' she says with her mouth full, 'is that I'll return to meet my Maker when I die. It's simple.'

'And...are humans beings the only ones to be so lucky? Of all the possible creatures in all the billions of constellations, we and we alone, on our tiny planet revolving around its tiny sun in the tiny Milky Way...What about you, Dad? Do you, too, think we're so unique?'

They hear the toilet flush. An old lady comes out of the bathroom and a powerful effluvium sweeps across their table.

'I can think of better places to have this conversation,' says Simon as he rises to shut the door. 'And frankly, Rena, your tone of voice is a bit offensive.'

Don't worry, says Subra. He's smiling to let you know he's proud of you just the same. You're his daughter, his disciple. He taught you philosophical fencing. He sharpened the blade you're needling his wife with right now.

'Sorry, I don't mean to be offensive. I just want to understand. Okay. Only humans, then, but…starting when? With Neanderthal? Yes? No? Or that Cro-Magnon guy we ran into the other day—was his soul immortal, too?'

'Let's drop the subject,' Ingrid splutters. 'You don't respect anything…'

'I do. I respect you, believe me. Only Homo sapiens, then, not Neanderthal. I think we can all agree on that. And not animals, of course.'

'Well, I don't know about that,' Ingrid says pensively. 'Sometimes when I look deeply into Lassie's eyes, I could swear she's got a soul… Right, Dad?'

Simon nods. Having grown up between a catatonic mother and an overworked father, he has always appreciated the company of dogs.

'Dogs, then. What about cats? And horses?'

'Yes, I would think they had souls, too,' Ingrid says, attacking a plateful of gnocchi. 'Right, Dad?'

Simon lifts a hand as if to say, why not?

'But not mosquitoes, right?'

'Rena!' Ingrid says, reddening. 'To you, everything is a joke!'

'No, she's right,' says Simon. 'I mean, we wouldn't want to itch and scratch up there in heaven, would we?'

Again the toilet flushes and a heavy-built man comes out of the bathroom, zipping up his fly. Rena thinks of all the flies she has undone in the course of her long love life, all the penises that have entered her body, here, there and everywhere, all the men who have bellowed as they poured into her what Dr Walters called their 'half-children'—yes, crying out in fear and rage and loss as they hurled themselves over the cliff's edge, tumbling head over heels into their chromosomes, thrashing about in the tangled threads of their DNA, releasing in a violent spurt the magic potion of their future, a liquid teeming with their offspring, their immortality, returning momentarily to their earlier bodies, their animal, child and savage bodies, their nothingness bodies, passing on the splash of sperm so as never to die, and dying as they do so...

'I'm not joking,' Rena tells Ingrid with an ingratiating smile. 'I'm sincerely trying to understand what a soul is, and on what condition, under what circumstances, it becomes immortal. Okay, then, not mosquitoes. Maybe the soul depends on warm blood? Sorry. All right, we can forget the whole animal issue if you like...but will it have a body?'

'What?' Ingrid says in bewilderment.

'Your soul, when it goes to meets its Maker. I mean, what does a soul actually *look* like after death? Is it a vapour, an ethereal essence, or does the flesh resuscitate as well? When you get to heaven, will you have a body and all that goes along with it—blood, lungs, tocnails, digestive tract—or will you be a pure soul?'

For once, Ingrid feels she's on firm ground. 'The Bible says we'll rise up from the dead on Judgment Day with our bodies intact. Right, Dad?'

'Absolutely.'

Snippets of Bible passages go floating through their memories.

'Ah. Now we're getting somewhere,' Rena says. 'And how old will our bodies be, in the Great Hereafter?'

'We'll rise up with our bodies in their prime,' Ingrid says jubilantly. 'It's written that the body will recover all its limbs, and that not a hair will be missing from its head. Good thing for you,

Dad—you'll get all your hair back in heaven!'

'Ha-ha-ha-ha!' Simon says, rubbing his balding pate to make sure Rena has got the joke.

'What about babies?' she asks.

'What about them?' says Ingrid, nonplussed.

'I mean, people who die as babies…Do they, too, rise up with their bodies in their prime?'

'Rena! You should be ashamed!'

The waiter brings them their desserts.

'Okay, we can forget about babies, too…to say nothing of foetuses, right? I won't even mention them. Abortions, miscarriages… down the drain. But, er…what about Hindus?'

'What about them?' Ingrid says.

'Well, you know…Hindus…Muslims…Buddhists…voodoo adepts…the billions of people who happened to be born before Christ—or afterwards, but on non-Christian soil—do they get to meet their Maker, too, or will they—'

'*Stop it!*' Livid, Ingrid sets down her spoon. 'It's impossible to have a serious conversation with you. Anyway, this place is unbearable. It spoils my appetite, it spoils—everything.'

This time they head back to the hotel in silence.

Elettrizzare

About halfway there, Rena's phone rings. Aziz's name shines up at her from the tiny screen.

'My love.'

'Rena…'

Aziz can barely speak. Rena can tell he has a lump in his throat, like when he was a kid in school and didn't know the answer to a question and was afraid the teacher would make fun of him in front of the whole class. Instantly, she knows it's serious. A matter of life and death. If the event took place in the projects around Paris and needs to be conveyed to Florence at once, someone is dead for sure.

Rena presses the phone to her ear—harder, then so hard that it hurts. As she listens to Aziz, the beautiful buildings before her eyes—Palazzo Rucellai, Palazzo Strozzi—are gradually replaced by the housing projects she knows so well, with their graffiti, satellite dishes, leprous walls, broken elevators, rat-infested cellars, young men swamped in hopelessness and rage. Running away from the police this afternoon, two teenage boys had taken refuge in a transformer and died of electrocution.

'I knew one of them,' Aziz says. 'His mother's one of my aunt's b-b-best friends…Rena, you c-c-c-an't stay away on holiday at a time like this…Shit, my work phone's ringing…I'll try and get back to you later on.'

Rena recoils as if she herself had just received the jolt of an electric shock. The hairs at the nape of her neck bristle and she feels inordinately, unpleasantly wide awake. Two young kids…*dead?* Oh God, Aziz must be grinding his teeth, smoke must be pouring out of his nostrils…She says nothing of the tragedy to Simon and Ingrid, so as not to weigh them down with it—but as they approach the hotel she can't help hastening her step. Wishes them a good night the minute they reach reception. Starts dialling Aziz's number as she goes up the stairs. Connects only with his recorded voice. Leaves him a message: 'Darling, please try to understand. Everything about this trip is slow and heavy and confusing. I still haven't had time to check the internet, or even buy a French newspaper…Believe me, I'm as upset as you are about the death of those two kids…Keep me posted, all right? I'll be waiting for your call, my love.'

When she finally falls asleep at nearly three in the morning, Aziz still hasn't called back.

SATURDAY

'I just want to stay with my eye to the keyhole forever.'

Supplizio

A man has set up a camera facing a machine. He stands in front of the machine and declares, 'No matter what you do to me, I'll never reveal the truth about…' (I forget about what). *To prove it, he climbs into the machine, lies flat on his stomach between two metal plates, hooks his left foot to the one above him so it's bent at the knee, and presses a button. The top plaque starts moving slowly downwards, crushing his leg against his back—No, no, I protest inwardly, horrified—No, stop!—but the plaque just keeps coming down and down—No, no!—down and down—NO!—eventually crushing him completely.*

Rena may have forgotten most of what she learned in her *Introduction to Psychology* class at Concordia, but she still knows one thing: all the characters in a dream are the dreamer.

So. Myself, the guy who brags about his ability to remain silent… the absurd hero who tortures himself to death. I'd rather die than tell the truth about…what?

What would I rather die than tell the truth about?

Sregolatezza

Getting out of bed, she sees bright red bloodstains on her sheets and nightgown—a shock, coming in the wake of that nightmare.

Damn it all to hell. It's not fair. I had my period only two weeks ago, in all its crimson glory. It has no right to pursue me all the way to Tuscany—I didn't pack any tampons. How dare my ovaries misbehave like this?

Not only that, but she was so busy torturing herself that she didn't hear the alarm clock go off—it's nine-thirty already and her appointment with the car rental agency is at ten. How will she manage to wash up this mess, pack her suitcase, help Simon and Ingrid carry theirs downstairs, buy a box of Tampax (Super), put them in place (two—and maybe a Kotex thrown in for good measure) and rush to the agency, all in the space of half an hour?

My periods have got pretty chaotic these past few months.

Maybe an early symptom of menopause? Subra suggests.

Yes, I suppose I'm getting there. No hot flashes so far, but plenty of night sweats…Could be one of the causes of my insomnia, come to think of it. And when I asked Kerstin how long I'd have to endure these symptoms, she said, 'Tell you the truth, I don't remember… Seven, eight years, something like that.' 'Seven, eight *years*? Are you *serious*?' 'Sure, why?' 'Come off it. You mean I'm supposed to put up with this crap for the next one hundred months and keep my mouth shut?' 'Oh, I doubt that.' 'You doubt what?' 'That you'll keep your mouth shut.'

At age twelve, I faked it…

Tell me, Subra says.

I was impatient to have my period. I figured that, by making a woman of me, it would bring me closer to my mother. So once a month I'd writhe theatrically in the throes of abominable abdominal pain (loved the way that sounded)—and it worked! Lisa would allow me to stay home from school, and she'd take care of me. Divine days of calm and clarity in my sun-filled room, snoozing in bed and gorging on Daphne Du Maurier novels (an author I worshipped because my mother's brand of cigarettes was named after her). Every couple of hours, Lisa would knock at my door and I'd put a long-suffering look on my face. She'd sit down at my bedside, stroke my hair and give me my medicine. 'It's nothing to worry about,' she'd say. 'Some women's periods are more painful than others, that's all.'

'You wouldn't believe how I found out about menstruation,' she added once. 'My mother was a prude—it embarrassed her to talk about such things, so she told me nothing at all. Then, the summer I turned twelve, a cousin of mine in Sydney—a couple of years older than me, and far more worldly-wise—told me all about it during the Christmas holidays. I thought she must be pulling my leg. Are you nuts? Blood dripping out of us once a month—nah, come off it! Just as I was about to get on the train and head back to Melbourne, she stuck a medical pamphlet under my nose and said, "Don't believe me if you don't want to, I could care less, but if by any chance you're interested, read this." Well, I read "that" on the train and it left me speechless. When I got home, I realised I still had the pamphlet in my bag—how could I get rid of it? I couldn't toss it into the wastebasket because all the wastebaskets were emptied by my mother. So I went up and hid it under a pile of old magazines in the attic, as if it was pornography or something.'

Mommy laughed and I laughed right along with her. I was grateful to her for assuming that at age twelve I knew about pornography…which I did. Thanks to the neighbourhood I walked through every week for my dance classes, a red-light district rife with strip joints, sex shops, peep shows and hostess bars, I was far more savvy about dildoes than I was about menstruation. Even as I went on playing the role of the obedient, submissive young daughter in my official life—the smooth, clean world of Westmount from which my brother had been banished—I was magnetised by the sordid scenes on Saint Catherine Street.

Lisa went on with her tale. An unusually thorough housekeeper, her mother had stumbled on the pamphlet one day as she was cleaning out the attic. 'She figured it must have been left there by former tenants and decided it would enable her to teach me about puberty without pronouncing a word. "Here, Lisa. Time you knew." And that was it.' I giggled. Mommy hugged me to her, then pressed her lips to my forehead. 'You're fine, sweet Rena. You don't have a fever. See you later!'—and she trotted off to receive her next client.

I loved it when she said 'sweet Rena'. I loved hearing her call my name from her office or the kitchen, and rushing to her side. Sometimes I'd drag my feet on purpose, just for the pleasure of hearing her call me again—'Rena!' It was marvellous. I existed. This woman was my mother, and she wanted to see me. No matter what the reason (whether to send me on an errand or to use me as a go-between in one of her quarrels with my father), when her lips formed the word 'Rena' it meant that instead of struggling for women in general, she wanted to see one woman in particular, a diminutive woman whom she held infinitely dear. Me. Her daughter.

I was so proud.

Didn't happen often, Subra remarks drily.

Stupid tears drip into the tiny bathroom sink of the absurd Room 25 in Florence's Hotel Guelfa, where Rena is feverishly rinsing bloodstains out of her nightgown. Good, good, the biggest one is gone.

Washing out menstrual blood is one of the arts of womanhood. You have to do it as swiftly as possible, preferably before the blood has had time to dry, and using lukewarm water, neither too hot nor too cold. Memories of standing at sinks early in the morning or late at night, over the course of three decades, and scrubbing away at sheets, the corners of sheets, bedspreads, sleeping bags, underwear, skirts, tights, trousers and dresses, in hotel rooms, apartments, lofts, campground bathrooms, hovels, trailers…And Samuel-the-bearded-cantor's indignation when, after our first clumsy attempt at love-making, he spotted a drop of blood on the sheet, then another on his shrivelled penis. I saw him recoil. He leaped out of bed in horror. 'Rena!' 'What's the matter?' 'You…' 'No, no, I wasn't a virgin, don't worry.' 'You've got…you've got your…' 'Yes, as you can see. It just started this morning.' 'You mean…you knew you were impure? You wilfully caused me to transgress…one of the most sacred laws of my religion?' The question went through a weird crescendo, attaining scream level by the time he reached *religion*. I still remember Samuel's wide-open mouth, his teeth and tongue visible in the middle of his beard, screaming the word *religion* at me.

Now I was genuinely pissed off. 'What do you expect?' I said with a shrug. 'Serves you right for fooling around with a…um…what's the female of goy, again? A goya? No, sorry—a shikse.' Though Samuel had deemed me shtuppable because of my Jewish name, I knew he was really attracted by my goyity. My mother was a goy so I was a goy; without admitting it even to himself, he'd wanted to go to bed with a goy. It always annoys me when love-making diminishes me instead of enhancing me—when it reduces me to one dwarfy little aspect of myself instead of multiplying me and turning me into a giant…'Listen, man, you wanna shtup a shikse, you've got to accept the quirks that go along with it. Sorry, but shikses don't feel impure when they menstruate. Now, whatever shall you do to purify yourself?' Samuel, who had been dressing hastily as I spoke, stopped and stared at me in wide-eyed disgust. 'Dip your kosher pickle in virgin donkey milk? Beg papa Abraham for forgiveness?' The cantor high-tailed it out of there.

That incident took place in my little student's studio on Maisonneuve Street. A few months later I found myself between the same pair of sheets with my French professor, a Catholic who was keen on shtupping me because I was Jewish. In the heat of the action, even as he groaned and panted, he repeated over and over, 'You're really Jewish, aren't you? How do you like my goy cock, huh? How do you like it? Jesus-Mary-Joseph I can't believe it, I'm fuckin' a fuckin' Jewess, oh, Momma, if you could see me now, oh, if you could only see me, Momma, hey you guys I'm fuckin' a fuckin' Jewess, I'm gonna come I'm gonna come I'm gonna come, aaahh good Christ it's coming, it's, aaah. Aaaaah. AAAHHH—AH!' After which, from the bathroom where he was washing his crotch with my facecloth, he made some terrible puns about foreskins and foreplay, and two weeks later I discovered I was pregnant.

Fortunately Mom was able to smuggle my Canon into the hospital. The photos I took there—clandestinely, using an 87C filter and infrared film—turned out to be my first published reportage. They created quite a stir. Curettage with no anaesthesia. Blanched faces of very young girls, grimaces of pain and fear, blood-drenched sheets, sadistic nurses. I quoted one of the latter in the text I wrote to accompany the photos: 'She had her fun, let her scream a bit. Maybe she'll think twice before she sins again.'

That's all well and good, Subra says, but shouldn't we be looking for tampons?

After slipping six carefully folded Kleenexes into her panties, Rena drags on her tightest pair of black jeans to make sure it won't even occur to the blood to go slithering down her thighs.

'So much blood!' as Lady Macbeth put it. 'So much blood!' whispered Alioune, my proud Peulh husband, who was annoyed at all the noise I had made giving birth to our son. I had whined, laughed, moaned, caterwauled, and chatted my way through the afternoon and evening, whereas a Peulh woman—to prove herself worthy of her future role as mother, enduring all sorts of suffering in stoical silence—mustn't let so much as a sigh escape her during delivery. When, after sixteen hours of labour, Thierno's head finally burst from between my thighs along with a flood of blood, plunging me into an incomparable state of ecstasy, the plenitude of absolute creation, I saw that Alioune was as white as a sheet. 'So much blood!' he said queasily. 'Stay with me, my love,' I told him. 'Don't look down there, stay up here next to my head. It's all over, Alioune, stay here, don't look at the blood…Alioune! Our son has arrived!'

But he had passed out.

Even as a child, Arbus was fascinated by menstruation, pregnancy and delivery. As a grown woman, she took delight in every facet of her femininity, refusing to shave her legs and underarms or even use deodorants. If she had her period while on an assignment for *Life* or *Vogue*, she'd boast about it to the whole crew. She insisted on having a home birth for her second child, and later described it as the most grotesque and sublime experience of her life. Few women artists—none, in fact, with the possible exception of Plath and Tsvetaeva—ever embraced maternity as wholeheartedly as she.

A pity, Subra murmurs. A pity that, one sweltering day in July 1971, she decided to add several pints of her own blood to the bathwater in her Manhattan apartment. Yeah, a real pity she wound up killing herself. Hmm, so did Plath, come to think of it. *Molto peccato.* Hmm, so did Tsvetaeva. What a coincidence.

'*Vorrei una scatoletta di Tampax, per favore...Grazie.*'

As she goes back up the hotel staircase, she passes Ingrid and Simon coming down.

'You guys packed?'

'Just about, just about. Have you had breakfast already?'

'No, I'll grab an espresso on the way to the car rental—I should be there now.'

'We'll be all set when you get back.'

Five minutes later, the absorbent cotton duly inserted into her innermost being, she emerges into the blinding light of the Florentine morning.

If the vagina were an erogenous zone we'd have heard about it by now, she says to herself. How would women be able to stuff tampons into it four times a day, six days a month, twelve months a year without feeling at least an occasional twinge of pleasure? But no. Not one of my women friends has ever blushingly confessed to getting her kicks that way...Memory of myself at fourteen, having finally reached puberty after two years of faking it, twisting and turning on the bathroom floor at my best friend Jennifer's place, legs akimbo, desperately trying to insert a tampon as Jennifer shouted advice to me from beyond the door—'Relax, Rena. You gotta relax. If you tense up, it won't go in. Don't worry, you won't lose your virginity or anything.' Naturally, I wouldn't have dreamed of enlightening her as to the state of my hymen.

The car rental is on Borgo Ognissanti, All-Saints Street—same name as Toussaint, her older son. She decides to interpret this as a good omen.

People are often puzzled that a virgophobic atheist like myself would have named her son Toussaint—but it's because my beloved Fabrice idolised Toussaint Louverture, the great leader of the Haitian Revolution in 1802, and his dying wish was that our son be named after him.

Louverture himself was anything but a saint, Subra points out.

Yeah, his folks probably just had him baptised on November 1st and gave him the name they found on the Catholic calendar that day...Could have been worse. Other kids in France's former colonies wound up with names like Epiphany or Armistice.

Here we are—Ognissanti.

Guidare

Rena fills out the necessary forms with the Auto-Escape employee. He insists on speaking French to her, and she answers him in Italian: under pretence of being deferential, both are in fact showing off. At last he entrusts her with a red Megane.

'This, madame,' he explains unnecessarily, showing her the remote control attached to the key chain, 'is for locking and unlocking the car doors. Do you understand?'

'*Si, certo, signore,*' she retorts. '*Non sono nata ieri.*'

At her first manœuvre on the Piazza Ognissanti, she manages to stall. On the verge of hysteria, she wonders if she should interpret this superstitiously, as Aziz would. Allah does not want me to rent a car; he does not want me to spend four days traipsing around Tuscany with my father and stepmother. He wants me to obey my husband's subtly expressed command: head straight for Amerigo Vespucci airport and jump on the first plane for Paris.

On her third try, unfortunately, the car takes off like a fireball and she finds herself hurtling willy-nilly through the sumptuous Renaissance city of Florence, Italy.

Reading glasses perched on her nose, Rena attempts to keep her left eye on the road while darting desperate glances with her right eye at the city map on the passenger seat, where the itinerary to Via Guelfa has been highlighted in green by Auto-Escape's elegant employee. 'Because of all the one-way streets,' the man had told her in his excellent French, 'you'll need to make a big detour—like this, see? You get on this ring road north of city centre—be careful, it has three different names—then take a right here, in Via Santa Caterina.' A piece of cake!

Sweating profusely, zooming along the Viale F. Strozzi at sixty miles per hour in bumper-to-bumper traffic, she hears her mobile ring.

Maybe it's my father…Maybe they're in some sort of trouble… Maybe someone really did make off with their precious *sacco* this time…

Digging the phone out of her jeans pocket, she tosses it onto the seat beside her and the map slides to the floor.

Oh God, it's Aziz! Heart aflutter, she leans over to make sure it really is his name on the screen; as she does so the car drifts leftward and narrowly escapes a collision.

'Aziz!' she says, clamping the telephone between her ear and shoulder.

'Yes.'

'Hang on a minute!'

'What do you mean, hang on? We haven't spoken for days, and when I finally get you on the phone you tell me to hang on?'

'Just a second, love, I'm driving…'

She slows down, setting off a cacophony of honking horns behind her. Having cut the connection with Aziz, she spews epithets in French and English at the Fiats and their impatient, aggressive macho drivers, nods perfunctorily at a giant fortress to her left and its probable thousands of dead of whom she knows nothing, and finally, perspiring and palpitating, pulls over to the kerb at the corner of Santa Caterina.

'Aziz. Sorry, love. Driving alone in a foreign city can be a little nerve-wracking.'

'Rena, you've got to come home.'

'What?'

'Drop everything and come back to Paris. Things are getting too serious.'

'You…I…Aziz…'

'Stop stammering. Are you trying to make fun of me?'

'No, of course not…Listen, I just rented a car, my father and stepmother are waiting for me in the street, I can't just leave them in the lurch…Schroeder's the one who gave me this week's holiday…'

'I'm not talking about Schroeder. Hey, Rena, listen to me, okay? I've been up here working for three days and three nights non-stop, we're trying to hold things together but the place is on the verge of exploding. The media are already rushing in to do their sensationalist crap. We need intelligent night photos for the magazine. The point of view of someone who has a little background, a minimal under-standing of what's going on, you know what I mean? I can't put it more clearly than that. Rena, get your ass back here.'

'No, I...'

'Okay, forget it.'

Aziz cuts off the connection. As she inches down the Via Santa Caterina, Rena shoves her hat back to keep the hairs on the nape of her neck from bristling.

To her surprise, Simon and Ingrid actually are standing in front of the hotel with their luggage, ready and waiting on time. They load up the car. Ingrid climbs into the back seat and Simon settles in at Rena's side; it's almost as if she had dreamed that abominable phone call.

'I'll take charge of the maps,' her father says. 'I'll be your guide.'

'Okay, look...we're right...here.'

It was your job to show me the way, Daddy. It was your job to help me. You're the one who taught me to drive. *You* weren't supposed to get hopelessly lost in life's dark labyrinths. Lousy Virgil, Daddy! Lousy Virgil...Why so tense now, sitting next to me in the car?

Tell me, Subra says.

When I was little, Simon would sometimes take me to visit his sister Deborah in the Eastern Townships. When we got onto one of those long straight roads, he'd tuck me between his thighs and let me steer. It thrilled me to think that my tiny hands were controlling the big black Volvo. Every time an oncoming truck pulled out to pass, hurtling straight at us, I'd let go of the steering-wheel and bury my face in my Daddy's chest. And he'd always make things come out all right, in a great burst of laughter. I couldn't help boasting to Lisa about it afterwards. 'I drove the car all by myself, Mommy!' Pale with rage, she'd light into Simon for having risked my life.

Where transgression was concerned, Subra says, you were always on your Daddy's side.

Yeah…sitting between his thighs, mad with excitement. Mad with excitement, sitting between his thighs…

And your father…?

Hmm. I don't recall his having given my older brother that sort of driving lesson. All I remember is that when Rowan had a minor scooter accident at age sixteen, Simon confiscated his licence for a month.

The sun beats mercilessly down on them. Aziz's last words ricochet in Rena's head: 'Okay, forget it.'

Dear Lord…if I were to lose Aziz…

Tell me, Subra says.

I fell in love with him the minute I set eyes on him. I'd come to do a reportage in the projects northeast of Paris…One day I walked into a cultural centre and there he was, tutoring a little first-grade kid from Mali. The boy was behind in learning how to read, and Aziz, sitting there next to him, bent over his textbook, was calmly showing him the letters, asking him questions, listening to his answers…I saw the kid staring up in adoration at this lovely, gentle young man and I said to myself, Wow, he's right. I think the guy's pretty amazing myself. If only he'd lean over *me* and talk to *me* like that…I didn't yet know that in addition to everything else Aziz was a poet, a songwriter and a guitarist, that he'd grown up in one of the worst projects in the area, that he was second-born in a family of eight, that his older brother was doing time for dealing, that he'd started working at fifteen, taking night jobs in factories while attending school during the day, that he had a degree from the Rue du Louvre journalism school…Then one day a miracle happened: he was hired as a reporter by *On the Fringe*, the magazine I freelance for. Our first exchanges took place during accidental meetings in the magazine offices, running into each other in the hall or in front of the coffee machine, but our handshakes rapidly became hugs, our traded jokes traded glances, our hugs kisses, our glances caresses, our coffees lunches…and by the end of the week, the office a hotel room. Though he couldn't make love to me at first, I was entranced by every square inch of this tall young Arab's magnificent body—his doe eyes, powerful hands, white teeth, muscular back, firm buttocks, to say nothing of his long, fragile, lovely penis, darker in hue than the thighs it rested on. Never could I have dreamed that this man would have so much to teach me, that I'd teach him to love a woman's body, and that one miracle would follow another until we found ourselves signing a lease together for a four-room apartment on the Rue des Envierges. Both night birds, we work together in perfect harmony— I've never known anything like it! Our marriage means the world to me, but I can't just throw up everything and fly back to Paris at the drop of a hat…

Subra nods sympathetically. She refrains from pointing out that Aziz generally spends only one or two nights a week at Rue des Envierges, and hasn't yet come to a decision about moving in with her, let alone making her his wife.

'You're not very talkative today, Rena,' says Ingrid after about an hour's drive west on the FiPiLi (Firenze, Pisa, Livorno).

'Sorry.'

To bring them up to date on what is happening in France's impoverished suburbs these days, she'd have to give them a lecture on French colonial history since 1830. Not having the strength for that, she holds her tongue.

Ingrid hums to herself to fill the silence.

Obsessed with his responsibility as guide, Simon keeps his eyes glued to the map and sees virtually nothing of the gorgeous landscape it represents.

Vinci

Lunch break. Across from their charming restaurant at the cliff's base, the Tuscan hills undulate to infinity. Grapevines, cypress trees, red roofs: the very landscape Leonardo immortalised in his *Gioconda*. Ah, ineffable harmony…

Harmonious, too, are the hues and flavours of the dishes brought by the waiters.

Among the three of them, though: nothing but false notes.

Looking at her stepmother, Rena thinks of her mother and feels anger rising within her. She is furious that it should be too late for fury, too late for anything.

Oh, Lisa! Mona Lisa! Nearly thirty years now since you effaced yourself, like Alice's Cheshire Cat. Yes, that's one way of putting it. It's as if Leonardo had rubbed out the Gioconda's hair…the contours of her forehead…her cheeks, her eyes, and finally her enigmatic smile…Now all that's left is the landscape, undulating to infinity.

She gets up and goes to the bathroom, where she changes her tampons and has a good cry. Still sitting on the toilet, she wipes her nose and crotch, then starts flipping through the *Guide bleu* to calm her nerves.

Hmm. Turns out Leonardo had not two but *five* mothers— Caterina, Albiera, Francesca, Margherita, Lucrezia. All but the first (who gave birth to him) were married to his father—successively, of course. Not simultaneously, like Fela Kuti's wives.

You see? Subra exclaims. The word 'family' has always meant *una cosa complicata*.

Yeah, you'd think people would stop acting so surprised about it. As if the norm were a stable, stainless-steel nuclear unit. Bullshit. Œdipus grew up with adoptive parents, far from his native Thebes. Kerstin's son Pierre has only a nodding acquaintance with the man who sired him; my Toussaint, Fabrice's son, was raised by Alioune, whose own father was polygamous and absent; as for Aziz, his dad died when he was four and he has no memory of him at all. Families have always been a mess, so why am I sitting here crying my eyes out in the toilet of a restaurant in Vinci?

'It's nearly three,' she says, re-entering the dining room dry-eyed and straight-backed, all her fluids under control. 'Shall we do some visiting?'

Vinci gives them the choice between two museums, the Leonardiano at the top of the hill and the Utopian Museum at the bottom. Both promise wondrous machines, models and sketches. (A wooden bridge, for instance, built without a single nail! Logs, nothing but logs, criss-crossed into a structure of mutual support—very handy, if you're an army and you run into a river...)

'Which do you prefer?'

'I'll let Dad decide.'

'Dad?'

Her father hesitates, compares, skims the brochures, dawdles, temporises, checks out the façades of church and castle, admires the panoramic view from the esplanade.

The minutes go sliding by.

Finally he makes up his mind: 'Neither...This little book will do just fine.'

The story of his life.

'Well, then, let's at least visit his birthplace—it's called Anchiano. It's just three kilometres away.'

A winding mountain road...

It was on winding roads such as this, in the Laurentians, that my father later gave me real driving lessons. Teaching me, for instance, to avoid carsickness by moving to the left of the white line as I came out of a leftward curve. I've now got that technique down pat; I wish Simon would notice it and say something about the good old days...

But her father goes on obsessively studying the maps.

Anchiano

Having dropped off the couple next to a sign pointing to the artist's birthplace, she drives on alone to the car park. When she catches up with them, they've come to a halt in front of a tree.

'What kind of tree do you think this is?' asks Ingrid, turning to her.

'It's a fig tree,' she says peremptorily, hoping to cut off idle speculations.

'Are you sure?' asks Simon.

'Sure I'm sure. Look—the leaves have five fingers, like an open hand. And here's another way of checking—crush a leaf and smell it; the scent is unmistakable.'

Exquisite memories of fig trees from the past go wafting through her mind. The heady, honeyed fragrance of the dried fig leaf Aziz handed her in the inner garden of Paris's Great Mosque, an hour after making real love to her for the first time. Walking down a fig tree-lined path as a dramatic harvest moon rose over the Black Sea and her Bulgarian lover's hand stroked the small of her back, then slipped inside her shorts and caressed her intimate flesh with such musical precision that she started to come, amazed to be able to come and walk at the same time. Toussaint and Thierno climbing into a fig tree and stuffing themselves with its fruit, one November weekend in Syracuse...

'I'm not so sure,' her father says. 'Where are the figs?'

'It's not the right time of year,' says Rena.

'Yes, it is,' he objects. (Touché!) 'Maybe Jesus struck it down in a fit of rage,' he goes on. 'You know, there's that strange passage in *Saint Matthew* where...'

'Yes, I know,' she says, cutting him off. 'I know.' What else? Fig tree, fig tree...(When did this hateful rivalry between them begin?) 'In Italian,' she says, 'the equivalent of "I don't give a damn" is "*Non me ne importa un fico*".'

'Really?' says Ingrid, to say something.

'Yes. The *fico* is a symbol of the vagina—the very epitome of worthlessness, as everyone knows.'

Ingrid blushes and turns away.

'And that's not all,' Rena insists, recalling a reportage she did long ago in the favelas of Rio. 'In Brazil, instead of giving people the finger, you give them the *fica*.'

'What's that?' her father asks.

'Uh...' she says. Oddly enough, she can't remember. Do they hold up an open hand, its five fingers symbolising the fig leaf? No, she doesn't think so...Hm. 'It'll come back to me.'

As they turn their backs on the tree at last, she brings the crushed leaf to her nostrils.

It smells of nothingness.

Two white-washed rooms, touchingly stark and spare.

Here, she thinks. Born here. Babe-in-arms here. First gaze on life here, the master of the gaze.

Ostensibly in homage to Leonardo, the first room is plastered with hideous paintings by a contemporary artist. Rena and Ingrid take one look at them, shrug and move on. The second room is filled with reproductions of the master's anatomical drawings. Studies based on corpses, the surface stunningly rendered thanks to the artist's familiarity with the depths. Bones, muscles, tendons, arteries—the intricate, secret machinery of the human body...

An hour later, they go back to join Simon, who has remained in the first room all this time, cursing the modern paintings. 'It's outrageous,' he says, as the guard announces closing time. 'I felt like slashing them!'

Yup, says Subra. That's Zeus's big problem. With great lightning bolts and deafening rolls of thunder, he has managed to destroy—not the abhorred paintings, but his own visit to Leonardo's birthplace.

Scandicci

'Maybe it's a bit late to drive all the way to Pisa?' says Simon, his nose on the map.

'It sure is,' Rena agrees. 'If we want to reach our B & B in Impruneta before nightfall.'

'Well, let's at least take the scenic route back, then. Through Pistoia.'

But an automobile race prevents them. Racing cars go zooming past them on the steep, narrow, twisting roads: heart attack after heart attack. Some villages are completely closed to traffic.

'Maybe we could take this alternate route?' Simon suggests.

But the roads grow narrower at every turn, and they end up in a farmyard.

Oh, Virgil! Rena thinks, sighing in exasperation. Can't you guide me better than this?

Suddenly the *fica* gesture comes back to her. You slip your thumb between your second and third fingers, then scornfully wave your fist in the air. But the moment to demonstrate it is past.

Well, they can drop the Pistoia idea, too, and return the way they came.

At six p.m. they find themselves back on the Florence ring road, parched, sweating and exhausted. Dazzled by the million glancing reflections of the setting sun on the chrome and glass of oncoming traffic, Rena now has a splitting headache. Simon sees an exit coming up and advises her to take it—'Yes! Here, right here! Quick!'—but it's a mistake, and they find themselves in a suburb called Scandicci. Braking angrily, Rena double-parks and goes storming into a shoe store to ask for directions. All the salespeople are busy and there's a long queue of customers at the cash register.

She studies the features of every person in the store. These people are here because they want to be—normally, naturally, as part of their daily lives. I, on the other hand, am just passing through. My presence here is as arbitrary as it was in that farmyard an hour ago, or in the Kodak shop the other day, or on Earth...

Her mobile rings.

'Rena, where are you?'

'In a shoe store in...uh...Scandicci.'

'I don't believe it. What the fuck...? My city's going up in smoke, I need you more than I've ever needed you before, and you're trying on Italian shoes?'

'I'll explain later, Aziz. I really will. Just at the moment I'm double-parked and my folks are about to pass out from dehydration. To each his emergency.'

Aziz hangs up without another word.

'*Per andare all'Impruneta, per favore...?*'

Salespeople and customers have a vast array of opinions on the subject.

Sometimes you wish you could just press stop, then fast-forward to a more bearable moment of the video of your existence. Yes, let's do that. Let's forget all about the starting and stopping, the backing up and turning around, the tension and hesitation, the sighs and silences, the petrol station restrooms, the overflowing tampons, the language barrier, the frustrating fruitless phone calls, let's forget about the groping the misery the excuses the bad smells the sordid bedrooms the sad eyes of child prostitutes in Thailand the endless heaps of garbage along the roads north of Dakar the despicable behaviour of the customs officials in Algiers who, to welcome Aziz on his first visit to his parents' native land (the year was 1993, he'd just turned eighteen), opened his suitcase, dumped his carefully folded clothes on the floor and told him to pick them up, the homeless kids in Durban who sniff glue and sleep in highway tunnels at night, the chaos of our lives whose stories we try to tell coherently so they'll seem to fit into some sort of pattern, make some sort of sense, let's just forget it, all of it, as we go along...

Impruneta

As they accept second helpings of her delicious *zucchini frittati*, Gaia (the gracious, sexagenarian owner of the B & B they eventually did manage to find) tells them first about her husband who committed suicide, then about her architect lover who designed this house, built it with his own hands, and died of cancer three short months after its completion.

How do people go on? How do they manage? How does Gaia get through the day? She chops up zucchini and onions, fries them golden, beats a few eggs, stirs in heavy cream, parmesan cheese, thyme and a little salt (not too much because the parmesan is already salty), pours the mixture into a buttered pan and slips it into the oven.

Then she sets the table, embellishes it with a vase of hand-picked flowers, lights a candle and opens a bottle of wine. She does not spend her days screaming My love my love where are you and how am I supposed to go on living without you, sixty-six years old but still beautiful still alive and sensuous and palpitating with desire?

A bit like Kerstin Matheron, Subra puts in.

You're right, Rena agrees. Kerstin found herself similarly at a loss after her husband Edmond's death. She told me about it one evening as I was making prints in my darkroom. She finds it easier to confide in me when she thinks my mind is otherwise occupied and in fact I have no trouble listening to her as I work; the two activities take place in different parts of my brain. 'I think I must envy you a bit,' she said to me that night with a little laugh. 'All your sexual adventures...I haven't made love in ages...almost seven years.' 'Because of Edmond's illness?' I asked. 'Not only that. Not only that. What happened was...He sort of...ah...well, you see...a few years before his illness, he sort of left me, actually. He fell head over heels in love with one of his patients, a poetess named Alix. She was only twenty-nine at the time, whereas he was pushing sixty. Alix had everything. She was brilliant, beautiful—and so very *young*. Edmond told me he was thrilled by the smoothness and firmness of her skin. And how could Alix be anything but flattered by the attentions of a distinguished, cultivated doctor like my husband? He didn't move out, but he stopped touching me and my life sort of imploded. As long as he had loved me, I'd sort of muddled through the years thinking, well, so far so good—but now, looking in the mirror, I saw, really *saw* for the first time, the wrinkles on my face and the spots on my hands, the flabbiness of the flesh on my upper arms, the serious beginnings of a double chin...' 'Stop it, Kerstin! Stop it right this minute. I refuse to hear my best friend slandered like that.'

'Oh, Rena...All of a sudden I couldn't stand being my body.

Things were bad that year. Then they got worse. Edmond started complaining about fatigue. He went in for tests and they found he had an extremely rare form of blood cancer. The illness evolved slowly but cruelly, attacking not only his body but his mind. Destroying his beauty, his fine intelligence, his humour, his personality. One day—he'd been hospitalised by this time and was already unable to walk—I ran into Alix at his bedside and discovered she was a lovely person. Of course I'd made her out to be a scheming conniving witch, but that's because I was jealous. So as the weeks went by we started getting together to comfort each other. God knows we needed it: before our very eyes, the man we both loved was turning into an incontinent, deranged, obstreperous monster. He refused to see anyone but the two of us. He was ashamed...He'd been so proud of his looks, and now they were gone for good...It was a shock, Rena, to go to the hospital and find our Edmond surrounded by a bunch of obscene, paranoid, loudly abusive old men...Oh, we'd tell ourselves, but deep down he's not like the others. With him it's only temporary; he'll soon be his old self again—but we knew the other visitors were thinking the same thing about *their* men. They, too, had once been young and debonair, maybe even incomparable lovers...Every time our paths crossed in the hospital corridor, Alix and I hugged each other desperately, not wanting to let go because we knew the only place to go from here was down. We wanted time to stop. Then it was the other way around—we wanted it to speed up. We longed for the end of this slow, sadistic, relentless destruction of the man we both loved.

The night before Edmond died, I spent four hours at his bedside, holding and kissing his hands. He had such beautiful hands, Rena, I'd been in love with them for thirty-five years and they'd hardly changed, they were as slim and strong as ever. Strangely enough, at that moment, I felt *the rightness of it all.*'

Long silence. I was flooding my prints with water, holding them up to the light, setting aside the ones I liked. 'I hope you know how beautiful you are, Kerstin,' I murmured at last. 'Thanks. Oh, I was pretty pretty once…It doesn't matter anymore.' 'Don't say that. You are truly, right now, with no reservations or qualifications whatsoever, an incredibly beautiful woman.'

I meant it. But not for a second did I imagine the effect my words would have on Kerstin Matheron…

Gaia keeps refilling their wine glasses and chattering up a storm. Rena listens and nods, weak with relief not to have to make a single decision until the next day.

Simon and Ingrid retire early—annoyed at being excluded from the conversation in Italian, or dead tired, or both. As she helps Gaia do the washing-up, Rena strives to preserve her hostess's illusion that she understands at least half of what she's saying.

Having guessed that Ingrid is not her mother, Gaia asks the dreaded question in a gentle voice, '*Dov'è la sua vera madre?*'

It knocks the wind out of her. Unable to form a phrase in Italian, she answers simply, '*Partita.*'

Not bad, crows Subra. It suits Ms Lisa Heyward to be described as a piece of music.

More than half asleep herself, Rena wishes her hostess goodnight and goes up an elegant wooden staircase that comes out across from the bathroom on the second floor. The two bedrooms are on either side of the landing and, because of this architectural choice made by Gaia's dead lover—because of her fatigue, and the stress of the trip, and her boss's anger, and the two electrocuted kids, and Aziz's strange new aggressiveness, but especially because of the bathroom being directly across from the staircase, with one bedroom to the right and another to the left—the scene bursts into her brain.

It was summertime, the month of June. Rowan's school had finished a week before mine and he'd returned to Montreal. He was back in his old room again just as if nothing had changed, but I was ill at ease. I didn't recognise my brother. It was like a science fiction movie—as if there were an inhuman soul living in his body and transforming it according to its needs. His height had increased by six inches in the course of the school year, the soft blond fuzz on his upper lip had turned dark, and his hair was cut very short...But it wasn't only that; the changes weren't only physical; there was a new jerkiness to his movements and his eyes no longer met mine. He made fun of me every chance he got, calling me tattle-tale, birdbrain, goody-goody.

'No, Rowan,' I protested in panic. 'I'm *not* a goody-goody, I just pretend to be one! Deep down I'm still bad and dirty, I haven't changed, I swear!' 'Prove it. You don't even know what you're talking about. Poor little innocent girl.' 'Well, then teach me. Please don't reject me. All you have to do is teach me. I've always been a good student.' 'Get the fuck out of my room. Did I give you permission to come into my room?' 'No, but...' 'Did you so much as knock?' 'No, but I didn't used to have to knock.' 'I didn't used to have to knock!' (Sarcastic imitation.) 'You may not be aware of this, Rena, but things change. Learn the new rules. You fucking well have to knock now. Got that?' 'Sure, Rowan. I won't forget.' 'Okay. See you later.'

But since my cheeks were aflame with the rage of rejection, and since Rowan was sitting at his desk with his back to me, I couldn't resist the temptation of snitching his miniature transistor as I went past his dresser.

The next memory is slapped up against that one as if it came right afterwards, whereas several hours must have elapsed because the sky had changed colour in the meantime. Night was falling...it must have been about nine p.m. Where were our parents? I don't know. Oddly enough, Lucille wasn't home either; Rowan and I were alone in the house.

You weren't little anymore, Subra gently points out. Rowan was fifteen and you were eleven. You didn't need babysitters anymore.

Yeah, that must be it...I was already in my pyjamas, doing my homework and listening to *Sweet Emotion*, I'd practically forgotten about the theft of the transistor, when suddenly I heard Rowan coming up the stairs. I knew he was furious because his step was light and swift—if he'd been faking it, he would have come upstairs with heavy plodding giant steps: 'Okay, now you're in for it!' Suddenly I was electrified by fear. My heart started hammering in my chest. He'll kill me, he'll kill me...I decided to take refuge in the only room with a lock—the bathroom. I dived into it just as Rowan reached the top of the stairs and managed to slam the door in his face, but before I could lock it he started throwing his whole body against it like a mad bull. He'll come in and murder me, my parents will find me lying here in the morning, bathed in my own blood...

I pushed against the door with all my strength but I could feel Rowan's greater strength pushing on the other side, my slippers were sliding on the tiling and the door kept coming open...Icy with fear I pleaded with him—'Please, please, Rowan!'—no, I *tried* to plead with him but I'd lost my voice, fear had frozen my vocal chords and my throat emitted nothing but a series of rusty croaks. I kept striving to calm my heart, clear my throat and articulate the words clearly, 'Please, I'm sorry! I apologise! I'll do whatever you say! Please!' but all that came out was an absurd whisper and Rowan, in silent, furious determination, kept crashing into the door with monstrous thumps of his shoulder. Finally the weakness and impotence of my vocal chords spread throughout my body and I gave up, gave in, the door burst open, inwards, knocking me flat, Rowan grabbed me by the hair and dragged me across the tiles, my head banged up against the toilet bowl, and he said, 'Now I'll teach you, you asked for it.' I kept pleading with him, saying, 'No, no, please, Rowan!' over and over again—that is to say, my lips shaped the words, the air passed through my throat, but not a word came out of my mouth and my body didn't put up even the semblance of a struggle. All this was in semi-darkness, it was late evening and there was almost no light coming from outside, just a single streak of orange along the top of the blue-black rectangle of sky framed by the bathroom window as seen from the floor, interrupted by the jagged black silhouettes of three pine trees, the sentries of our back yard.

When his spasms had abated, Rowan glued his sweating body to my back and I felt a fraternal tear run down my neck. Then, getting to his feet and adjusting his clothes, he said in a voice so low as to be all but inaudible, 'Remember when you were little you always wanted me to teach you what I'd learned at school?' His voice broke then and I had to strain to hear what followed—'Well, now you know... what I've been learning...in that goddamn fucking school I got sent to...because of you.'

Rena takes a Noctran and a half before slipping into Gaia's large soft bed. Impeccably washed and ironed, the white linen sheets are redolent of lavender.

SUNDAY

'The principle of photography…secrets no one knows.'

Doing a reportage with Aziz in a foreign city—we're in a bus but we forget to ring the bell and the bus goes hurtling past our stop—by the time we lurch to the front to ask the driver to let us off, the bus is already beyond the city limits. Getting off at last, we find ourselves in an unbelievably beautiful landscape—bright sunlight, clouds scudding across the sky, trees waving in the wind—'Look!' I exclaim. 'It's pure Stieglitz!' Glancing around, I see some enormous animals in the field right next to us. 'Look, Aziz! What are they? Oh, my God...they're gorillas!' There are several of them, circling one another and emitting angry cries, clearly about to start fighting...I see lions as well, and other wild animals roaming free—there's no barrier of any kind between them and us. 'I'm scared, Aziz,' I say. 'Let's get out of here.' A bit farther down the road, a wildcat has escaped and a woman farmer is running after it...'Oh my God, Aziz,' I keep repeating. 'Oh my God!'

Maybe your own wildness trying to escape? Subra suggests.

Strange how I kept saying *Oh my God* in the dream—an expression that never crosses my lips in real life. *Fermata* means stop—a bus stop, for instance, except that the bus doesn't stop, it goes hurtling past the city limits and plunges us into savagery, the woman farmer in my dream is desperately trying to catch the wild animals and lock them up on her farm, just as I was trying to do by firmly closing the door behind me, yes, *firm farm fermata*, you want to lock things out but sometimes you just can't, and if the truth be told I wasn't wearing a blindfold that day, Dr Walters had contented himself with binding me hand and foot, and though my bonds prevented me from moving freely I did catch a glimpse of my father as he burst into Room 416 wearing a bathrobe which, being wide open, gave me some idea of what had been going on in Room 418...Yes, you, dear Commander! Poor tottering, detumescent, living statue, reaching to tear the whip out of Don Juan's hands in a trance of fury and indignation—*What is the meaning of this, sir? With my daughter? How dare you?*—and punish him for the same infamies you were committing with another man's daughter in the next room, thus revealing the depth of the complicity between you, revolving around your irresponsible cocks. Commanders in bathrobes, dads as pals, shrinks as lovers—none of this fatally confusing mess should ever have existed.

She drifts back to sleep.

Domenica campagnola

She is wakened by silence—the silence of a Sunday morning in the country. Its purity is almost disturbing, after the hustle-bustle of Florence's Via Guelfa with its honking horns and revving motors...

She opens her eyes and stretches luxuriously, revelling in the charm of her room and the perspective of the relatively low-stress day ahead of them. San Gimignano in the morning, Volterra in the afternoon, after which they'll come back to Impruneta and spend a second night here at Gaia's.

The bathroom is flooded with sunlight. An enchanting order reigns in this house; everything bears the precise and colourful imprint of their hostess—towels in different shades of green, small bouquets of dried flowers, copies of Etruscan statuettes, scented soaps in the shower stall...Even the hills seem to have been carefully arranged by Gaia and her architect lover so as to offer a pleasant view from the bathroom window.

As she splashes her body with warm water, Rena realises she's in an excellent mood.

All is well, Subra says. You've passed the halfway point of the trip and so far no one has murdered anyone; there'll definitely be an *afterwards*.

A moment later, she turns off the hair-dryer and stands looking at her naked body in the wardrobe mirror, first from the front then from the back. Still passable. Peaceable. Impassive. Straight, discreet lines. No one would ever guess what it's been through.

For all that, I didn't become allergic to sodomy.

I should hope not! exclaims Subra, who is also in an excellent mood this morning. If you had to give up everything you learned in discomfort, what would you have left, right? There'd be no reading, no eating, no playing the violin…

The first time I suggested to Alioune that he take me that way, he responded with indignation, disgust and a firm religious condemnation. Gradually the idea grew on him, though, and within a few months he'd mastered the technique of relaxing me without resorting to gadgets or vaseline, preparing me only with his fingers, tongue and words. Once he got the hang of it, he could impale me almost surreptitiously, so to speak, as I was negotiating a photo fee with Schroeder over the telephone…or hanging up the laundry in the bathroom…or even (once, unforgettably) out of doors—in July 1998, on the Dakar cliff road overhanging the ocean, while the entire population of the city was engrossed in a World Cup soccer final on TV. He even became a little more tolerant of gays.

Our marriage began to disintegrate when he found out my wanderings weren't only geographical. For my part, I'd accepted his numerous affairs without batting an eyelid, asking only that he give me the same freedom in return. As a lawyer, Alioune could see my attitude was logical, but as an African male—or a male *tout court*—he was eaten away by jealousy. Like his father, his grandfather and all his Peulh ancestors before him, he considered polygamy to be natural and polyandry inadmissible. In nature, as he told me one day with a straight face, ewes live together peacefully, but you put two rams in the same field and they'll fight to the death. 'Bullshit!' I retorted. 'In our species, males are the ones who band together. Maybe because most women are mothers, they don't need to keep rubbing up against each other, jostling and measuring and competing with each other just to feel they're alive...' 'Oh yeah?' snarled Alioune. 'Then how come you're never around, *mother*? How come you're always galli-vanting off to the four corners of the earth? Our sons suffer from your absences!' That hit home, as Alioune had known it would—and as Aziz knows it does now—because of my own mother's absences. I must admit I'd got into the habit of hiring one or more 'Lucilles' to manage the household while I was away. And I worried about the fact that Thierno, then four or five, had started tying his GI-Joes to every chair in the house...Would he tie up his mistresses later on, as Josh Walters had tied me up? Or as I myself had threatened to tie up poor, autistic Matthew Varick?

What are all these ropes about? Subra asks rhetorically, giving Rena her cue.

Oh the incredible refinement of Araki's smooth, slender, lovely models, artistically bound and strung up in trees to be photographed. He set up this series entitled *Sentimental Journey* with the utmost care. The girl is horizontally suspended from a branch; ropes circle her breasts and come up in a *V* around her neck, forming slipknots at her chest, waist and thigh. Her arms are tightly squeezed against her body; her head dangles backwards and downwards; her face is concealed by a black cloth. All the women thus bound and photo-graphed by Araki were consenting, they may even have been content; as usual, no mention is made of the fact that they were also *paid*. The photos are contemporary echos of *kinbaku*, an ancient Japanese rite which entailed stringing a woman up in a tree next to a Buddhist temple for the monks' contemplation. What had the woman done to deserve such treatment? Oh, no, nothing, the monks just wanted to contemplate her, that's all...with one hand, perhaps. Yes, as they sat there meditating in their solitary cells, listening to the gongs that marked off the hours of the day, they must have derived a certain pleasure from thinking about life's transience, the crudely material, ephemeral and ultimately meaningless nature of human existence, admirably illustrated by the woman that hung day and night from a tree in front of their window, twisting, wailing, moaning, then falling silent, then starting to rot in the wind and rain as the ropes gradually sawed into her flesh. You can't fool me: that woman was mommy as well. All tied-up women are mummy.

To get back to Alioune…Subra prods.

In the final years of our marriage, Alioune became jealous of everything. Not just my trips and lovers abroad but my success, my notoriety, my every phone call…Hmm…Don't want to spoil this lovely Tuscan day by thinking about the dark rain of violence in the eyes of my handsome Senegalese…his fits of rage gradually making me blind and impotent, unable to work…my Canon locked away in its case for months on end…my darkroom deserted…our two sons desperately clinging to two foundering adults…the terror that came into their faces, Thierno's especially, whenever we raised our voices…my own terror at realising, in the midst of a quarrel, that my adolescent sons in the next room were enduring exactly what I'd endured as an adolescent, and vowed never to inflict on my kids…

The situation worsened with every passing day. Alioune began to drink, and I met the Mr Hyde of his Dr Jekyll. On bad nights, as of the second drink, I could almost see his white teeth turn into fangs and hair sprout from his handsome face. He'd wait for some pretext to come along, then turn and pounce on me, roar at me, crush me beneath the weight of his scorn. Appalled to find myself still vulnerable to the female atavism I most abhorred, that awful paralysis of will which makes us murmur *Yes, master* when confronted with a male who's mad with rage or just plain mad—I finally walked out on him. 'Behave like a Cro-Magnon if you feel like it—but without me.' That's when I cut my hair cut short.

Maybe this is as good a time as any to change the subject? Subra suggests.

Right. Mustn't ever forget that shred of wisdom gleaned long ago on LSD: hell is only one of the countless rooms in the Versailles palace of the brain; you can always close the door on that room and walk into another. I can choose, for instance, to relive the divine love-making of my first years with Alioune. Waking up in the morning, I'd feel his hardened cock against my thigh, he'd slip into me and not move, I'd close my eyes and pretend to be drifting innocently back to sleep whereas in fact I was squeezing him inwardly with all my might, skilfully massaging his sex with the contractions of my own. Then he'd start to move inside me, as gently as in a dream. At first I'd keep my pleasure at bay, purposely remaining above or outside of it, but before long the weakness would become irresistible—a *thing* I could feel expanding within me, slowly invading my whole body, turning it inside out, and when I came it was like weeping. Afterwards Alioune and I could touch each other in any way at all— I could press my head against the inside of his thigh, for instance, near the top—and we'd be happy just like that. It's incredible how happy you can be sometimes for no reason at all. Is it possible I'll never know that kind of happiness again?

Hmm, murmurs Subra. Maybe we shouldn't hang around in that room, either.

So go back to the night we came home from a party at three in the morning and, having put on a Susanne Abbuehl record, I let Alioune slowly peel off my clothes and carry me to the bed, my loins draped in a scarf of turquoise silk. Giving myself up to Abbuehl's voice singing e.e. cummings and the warmth pulsing through my body, I released an interminable cry of joy as his tongue caressed the very point of my being and then, after the convulsions, first mine then his then mine again, I remained curled up in the disorder of the sheets as the after-tremors of my body gradually spaced themselves out and subsided, melting into the final poignant chords of *somewhere I have never travelled, gladly beyond*...But Alioune, who spoke not a word of English, jolted me out of my reverie by exclaiming, 'Boy, what syrupy music!'...

Rena finishes dressing, impatient to go down to the kitchen and let Gaia's chatter deliver her from her demons. When she gets to the landing halfway down the wooden staircase, however, her mobile rings.

'Alioune! Incredible! I was thinking about you just a minute ago!'

'Is that so unusual?'

'No, what's unusual is for you to call me.'

'How are things with you?'

Ah, yes. Ritual greetings. Rena loves ritual greetings. The first time Alioune took her to Senegal with him, just before their wedding, she thought people were having her on. '*Salaamaalekum!*—*Maalekum Salaam!*' But no, they weren't. Ritual greetings are taken very seriously in Africa. And now she misses them. Not easy, afterwards, to readjust to the rude and rapid manners of Parisians.

'Just fine, thanks...How have you been doing?'

'I'm fine, too. I heard you were in Italy?'

'You heard right.'

'How's your father doing? Is he in good health?'

'Not bad, not bad at all.'

'And your stepmother—is she well?'

'Hanging in there. What about your own folks?'

'They're fine, *inch'Allah*.'

'I'm glad to hear it.'

Even when he was pleading in court, Alioune never spoke fast. He refused to be rushed—whether he was eating, walking, reading or making love. The first time they found themselves alone together in a bedroom, Rena was blown away by his consummate calm and self-confidence. He taught her the African tempo.

Tell me, Subra says.

Not many men are so utterly devoid of impatience, so gifted at eliciting desire. Alioune would lie down on me, naked, his sex would approach mine and he'd watch me start to tremble…Oh the beauty of that indefinite moment when, though hard, a man hesitates at the entrance to your body, playing and rubbing and teasing and pretending to wonder if you want him to come in whereas he knows you're dying for it, yes, when you know for sure he'll enter you but he wants to keep you guessing as to when…and then he enters you…only slightly at first, to prolong your exquisite torment of knowing he'll move in further…then he moves in further… suddenly plunging in up to the hilt, and the cry which then rips from your throat is one you didn't know you contained, a cry of liberation in crescendo…Other times, with me on top, Alioune would guide my body down at a particular angle that made me swoon at every thrust, at, every, thrust, swoon, swoon, close my eyes and give myself up to pure sensation, the infra-infra-infrared of longed-for warmth beyond visibility, oh yes that man certainly did know how to elicit, prolong and intensify my body's vibrato, quivers becoming tremors, tectonic plates sliding, the earth opening up, boulders cracking, cascades tumbling, volcanoes erupting…Sometimes, when we were already well launched into this mad affair, our bodies would suddenly stop moving and we'd hang there suspended on the crest of an intense, all but motionless thrum—just as a warbler sits frozen on its branch, only the ripple at its throat revealing its lifesong—until at last, far from exploding, we'd slide endlessly down and down together, cascading in slow motion into the abyss...

Ah, Subra sighs, you've certainly lost that African tempo since your break-up with Alioune.

La nonna

'Which way's the wind blowing, Alioune?'

'Oh, the best possible way.'

'Must be a trade wind, then.'

She sees the two of them one evening, strolling through the fortress ruins at the top of Goree, caressing each other amidst the caresses of that divinely cool Atlantic breeze.

'A trade wind, exactly. And along with my voice, Rena, it brings some marvellous news.'

'What news, Alioune?'

'We're going to be grandparents.'

She swerves to study the hills framed by the six small rectangular windows in Gaia's front door. A double triptych of photographs. You could shift the images around, she thinks, changing their order, putting the sky beneath the hills...Everything is photography, when you think about it. All of us are constantly framing and reframing, zooming in and out, freezing and retouching the instants of our lives—the better to preserve them, protect them, prevent them from being whooshed away by Time's mighty current...

'Are you there, Rena? Jasmine is pregnant.'

Objectively speaking, her legs don't have a lot of weight to carry, but suddenly they can't carry it anymore. Of its own volition, her body sinks onto Gaia's leather couch, which is almost the same reddish-purple as the hills framed by the windowpanes.

When Toussaint was little, he liked playing in the bath so much that he never wanted to get out. So I'd spread a large, sand-coloured towel on the bathroom floor and say, 'Now the famous explorer has to make an emergency landing in the desert!' Toussaint would turn to me and stretch out his tiny arms, I'd pick him up by the underarms and lift his small body out of the tub, shake him slightly so the excess water would run off, see his diminutive cock and balls jiggling, set him on the towel that was desert sand, then wrap it round him... How many times did we act out that little play together? Hundreds of times, and then...

Finished, Subra chimes in, always happy to sing a refrain she knows by heart.

When you're a mother, you touch your newborn baby boy's penis and testicles with respect; they're soft and strange and fragile, sometimes the penis hardens slightly when you graze it and you smile. You wipe your baby's anus, change his diapers, oversee the cycle, certain liquids and solids going in at the top, others coming out down below. You clean the boy's penis; later you teach him how to hold and aim it when he pees, whether in the toilet bowl or at the side of a highway...and then...that's over and done with.

The main reason I decided not to marry Xavier, my handsome French art collector and connoisseur, is that we couldn't agree on the subject of our future son's penis. Our worst fight broke out one day in the Louvre. One minute we were standing in front of a seventeenth-century painting of baby Jesus amidst a swirling group of rabbis in coloured robes, one of whom was brandishing a knife; the next minute we were screaming at each other about whether or not to circumcise our son, not yet conceived. 'No!' I said. 'It's a barbaric practice dating from another age.' 'Yes!' said Xavier. 'To me it's a symbol of his connection to the Jewish people. I want my son to feel he belongs to something—a lineage, a history. Even if other customs and rituals have died out, it matters to me that this one be preserved.' 'No way!' I retorted. 'Customs *evolve*. You don't have to go on blindly repeating them, you're allowed to change them or chuck them. Men have stopped dragging women by the hair, shrinking their enemies' heads, slitting oxen's throats at the altar—they can also stop mutilating their children, whether boys or girls. Cut up your own body if you feel like it; no one's going to damage the physical integrity of my kids.' 'How American can you get?' said Xavier, who knew how much Canadians dislike being assimilated to their neighbours from the south. 'You have the Americans' silly naiveté, their arrogant ignorance, their lack of culture, history, and depth—in a word, their superficiality. If you'd read up on the subject, you'd know that circumcision is basically a measure of hygiene. Statistics show that circumcised men are much less vulnerable to STDs.' Then he added, shouting so loudly that half a dozen Guadeloupian museum attendants moved across the room to shush us, 'I can't *believe* how uneducated you are!' 'Uneducated yourself!' I screamed back at him. 'Ha! You don't even know that until recently, all male children born in North America were circumcised.' There was no way our relationship could have worked out. A few years later, Alioune and I were at each other's throats over the same issue: only one fight, but a monumental one. 'No matter what his religion,' thundered Alioune, 'a non-circumcised African male is not human.' This time, though, it occurred to me that my older son could protect his younger brother. For how could we justify circumcising little Thierno and leaving Toussaint intact?

Mother and son, Subra murmurs. Go on.

After two years or so, you stop wiping his bottom and holding his penis to help him pee because he's learned to do it by himself. He'll do it by himself for a few decades, after which (as was the case with Kerstin's husband, Edmond) he might need help again—but by that time you, his mother, won't be around anymore…Yes, you stop touching and looking at your son's genitals, and supervising his peeing and pooping. You leave him alone, move away, avert your eyes, give him room to grow—this is indispensable. (It's hilarious, in a way, to think of all the perverts who, generation after generation in bordellos the world over, reinvent the scatological wheel…and all the whores who, half docile and half despairing, shrug their shoulders, roll their eyes heavenwards and, for a fee, go on playing Mommy to those big fat babies.) Your little boy grows and…and then…of course, it's only natural…You know his genitals have been growing along with the rest of his body…his cock and balls have become those of an adolescent…Without giving it much thought, you assume dark hair has sprouted in that area of his body you used to attend to and no longer attend to, used to wash and no longer wash…You surmise that, like all pubescent boys, he's started getting hard-ons, fantasising and masturbating…When you launder his sheets, you're not surprised to catch an occasional glimpse of what the French call a map of France; you wonder whether the Chinese call it a map of China and the Russians a map of Russia and the Canadians a map of Canada; you sort of doubt the Japanese call it a map of Japan—lots of little islands everywhere—or the Chileans, a map of Chile, one long narrow streak…You abstain from speculating about your son's sexual fantasies. You have no idea whether they're homo, hetero, zoo-o, scato or necro. His desire is none of your business so you avert your eyes and avoid thinking about it. That distance is sacred: never again must you be involved with your son's genitals, the engendering part of his body, the part that will turn him into a father. Yet it's dizzying to think that the lips which so recently drew milk through your nipples are now teasing and sucking on another woman's nipples, that the body you once held in your arms is now rising in lovely virile violence above another woman's body, that the

191

boy who once inhabited your womb is now spurting his seed into another woman's womb...Then one day a line gets drawn beneath your children's generation—and, twenty-five rungs farther down the ladder of your life, another generation bursts into bloom, reshuffling all the roles for a new deal. One day you wake up to discover that the grandfather has become a great-grandfather, the mother a grandmother, and the son a father.

'Rena? Are you there, Rena?'

'I just can't...Why didn't...'

'Why didn't he call you himself?'

'Yes...'

'Well, I think he's a bit intimidated...He sent you an email three days ago and it worried him when you didn't answer.'

'Ah. I admit I've been a bit cut off these past few days. I'm somewhere...uh, in the middle of the fifteenth century.'

'You do know what's going on in France, though?'

'You mean the death of those two boys?'

'That was just the beginning. The young people in the projects are up in arms. The proverbial shit is going to hit the fan, Rena—there'll be riots any minute now. I've been thinking of you. It's the sort of subject you usually cover.'

'Yeah, well, unfortunately, Alioune, I still haven't learned how to be in two places at once.'

'Hey!'

'Sorry. I'll be back in three days' time. Don't worry, I'll catch up.'

'I never worry about you, Rena.'

'Tell Toussaint I'll...Tell him I...'

'Sure. I'll pass your congratulations on to him. Give my best regards to Simon and Ingrid.'

Gaia is waiting for her in the kitchen, an apron tied around her waist and a smile on her lips. 'Did you have a good sleep?'

Yes, she had a good sleep…even if the universe has shifted since.

Gaia pours her coffee and introduces her to the various jams and jellies on the breakfast table. 'Everything is homemade,' she says. 'Even the bread.'

I admire the way this person turns domesticity into one of the fine arts, she tells Subra. Leading the sort of woman's life that has always been a mystery to me, mothering everyone who crosses her threshold, planting and picking flowers and fruit to make bouquets and jams, taking pleasure in the simple joys she bestows upon her clients. She must be about Ingrid's age.

Also the age Lisa would be now, Subra points out, if she hadn't effaced herself at thirty-seven.

True. It's weird being older than one's own mother—do you realise you're my little sister now, Ma?

'Do you have any children?' Rena asks out loud.

'Just one daughter, in Milan,' Gaia says. 'But three grandchildren,' she adds, pointing to their snapshots on the fridge door. 'What about you?'

'Two sons. Also grown.'

But no, no photos. I, the professional photographer, have always eschewed carrying around photos of my sons. I wonder why?

You avoid simple happiness, Subra clowns, imitating Ingrid's voice.

Yet I'd give anything to be able to show Gaia what Toussaint and Thierno looked like last summer, and no longer look like, and tell her that Toussaint teaches children with learning difficulties, lives with a vivacious young colleague of his, named Jasmine, and will soon be a father…

Instead she says nothing. Contents herself with nodding as she listens to her hostess's patter and samples her delectable homemade jams.

After a while, Gaia turns on the radio and starts washing the dishes. A Bach cantata comes to an end and is replaced by the heavy, monotonous drone of a man's voice.

Rena tenses up at once. 'Mind if we change stations?'

'*Ma perché?*' Gaia says.

'I have a thing about preachers…'

Seeing her hostess's eyebrows knit in incomprehension, Rena catches herself in time and banishes the words she was about to utter—Oh, men's voices! Men's voices! They have the right to harangue us, harass us, boom at us at all hours of the day and night from balconies, pulpits and minarets the world over; do they have to invade our kitchens, too?—and replaces them with 'I prefer Bach.'

Wisely, Gaia switches off the radio, goes into the living room and puts on a recording of Bach's *Brandenburg Concertos*. Then, untying her apron, she dons a pert blue hat and announces in Italian, 'I'm off to town for ten o'clock mass. I should be back at around noon—will you still be here?'

'Oh, no, definitely not. *Spero di no!*'

So Gaia hands her a bunch of keys—this one's for the door to the driveway, these two are for the house—flashes a bright smile at her, and vanishes.

Good thing my anticlericalism didn't alter her kindness.

Bach…

No, all right, she concedes to Subra, who has been frowning at her sceptically for the past half hour. I didn't leave Alioune, Alioune left me.

For once I'd made an exception and agreed to see one of my lovers in Paris. Yasu was a photographer. I'd first met him in a gallery on top of Tokyo's Mori Tower. He's my twin! I breathed in astonishment the minute I set eyes on him. Young, slender and androgynous, with black hair and dark eyes, dressed in black from head to toe, he was utterly engrossed in the photos he was taking. At first I mistook him for a woman. I *wanted* him to be a woman; I would have liked for a woman to be engrossed in her work to the point of not even noticing my existence, and when I realised he was a man I wanted to *be* him—or, failing that, to be one with him. When that dream came true within the hour, I learned that he had delicate hands, long sinewy limbs, hairless, amber-coloured skin and an incomparably graceful body, but that he was a twisted, perverted little prince. Apart from himself, Yasu loved no one but his dog—a young pedigree bitch named Isolde. As for women, he made love to them only to keep them at bay, took them to bed with him only to icily reject them afterwards. His photos were as cold, beautiful and frightening as he was—either inhuman urban landscapes with sharp angles and starkly alternating light and shadow, or ultra-refined pornography.

Sometimes one is magnetically attracted to one's opposite, one's nightmare, one's antithesis—that's what happened to me with Yasu. So when he called to say he was in Paris for one night only, and asked me to join him in his hotel room a few hours before his opening, I broke my own rule about Parisian monogamy and rushed to obey. And as we busied ourselves with a number of (to my mind) rather depressing gadgets on the super-king-sized bed in his five-star hotel room, the bitch Isolde, in a fit of jealousy that would later give me food for thought, methodically chewed holes in every single piece of my clothing scattered on the floor, leaving her master's clothes intact.

What was I to do? It was five o'clock and I had an appointment with Thierno and his school counsellor at five-thirty. And. So. Well. Hastily donning Yasu's elegant black suit, which he needed for his seven o'clock opening, I rushed to the Monoprix next door, bought myself a new set of clothes, raced to Thierno's school, attended the meeting, then raced back to the hotel—yes, son in tow, I had no choice—to give my lover back his suit, at which point the bitch Isolde could think of nothing better to do than leap on my son and sink her savage teeth into his thigh. And that is how my third marriage came to an end.

Sitting at the coffee table, Rena flips through the past week's newspapers. The events in France are mentioned only briefly, on inside pages.

Aziz, Aziz, where are you? *What's going on?*

She dials his number and gets his answering machine. 'It's me, love,' she says…and, not knowing what to add, hangs up.

Disturbed by the memory of Yasu, she tries to imagine the church service Gaia is attending right now. This stirs memories of all the religious ceremonies she has sat in on—forever an outsider—in Durban, Mumbai, Port-au-Prince, New Orleans, Ouro Preto or Dublin, moved in spite of herself by the beauty, solemnity and power of these collective rituals. She replaces Bach with Pergolesi on the sound system, all the while pursuing a futile argument with Gaia in her brain—Yes, I *do* have the right to love this music, she insists defensively, even if I reject the church that gave rise to it…

The morning is melting away like snow in springtime.

At ten-thirty, Ingrid comes down alone and announces, 'Dad's not feeling well.'

'Oh? What's wrong?'

'Nothing, he's just having a hard time emerging, that's all. It happens more and more often.'

'It does?'

'Yes.'

Rena wonders if she detects a note of reproach in Ingrid's voice—but no, only worry.

'But…will he be getting up?'

'Oh, he's up.'

'And is he planning on coming down?'

'Yes. He told me to tell you he'd be right down.'

She serves Ingrid her breakfast, desperately trying to be as sweet and gentle as Gaia…but it's no use, she feels sullen and mean. Doesn't want to share with Ingrid the good news that wafted in on Alioune's trade wind this morning. Everything feels 'off'.

Heavy silence between them.

Simon, at last.

Ingrid and she, in chorus: 'Are you all right, Dad?'

He grunts his assent, smiles to dispel their fears, and breakfasts royally.

Then he says, 'Can we sit down in the living room and talk things over for a while?'

Scartoffie

Rena looks at the perfect Sunday morning around her. Out of doors: calm, sunlight, the marvellous Chianti hills—*gold!* Oh, gold of grapevines, red of October maples, mauve of heather and lavender, a landscape copied from Leonardo's paintings…And indoors: elegant burnished furniture, books serried on shelves, the neat stacks of Gaia's dead lover's architectural magazines, ceramic bowls… Every thing in its place. All the day's possibilities converging here and now…And her father wants to talk things over.

'When I retired five years ago and we had the house in Westmount renovated,' he begins, 'I had a sort of dream. Or, let's say, a hope. I hoped we'd be able to entertain more often…And now I see that dream's just not coming true...maybe because when you invite people over, they feel obliged to invite you back...or because... I don't know...the food shopping is getting to be a burden on Ingrid...'

Rena sees Ingrid hesitate, gather her courage, hesitate again, then decide to speak up. 'I don't want to sound critical, Dad,' she says, on the verge of tears, 'but how can we entertain when the dining-room table is stacked high with all your papers?'

Dante neither saw nor foresaw the circle of Hell to which my father seems condemned for all eternity.

'I'm getting old,' Simon says, looking steadily at Rena, 'and my concentration is not what it used to be. I only have an hour a two a day of mental clarity—if I'm lucky! If I've had a good sleep, and if my medication hasn't made me lethargic. So when, by miracle, I do get a bit of clarity, rather than squandering it on practical chores like tidying up my study, I prefer to use it for something, uh, let's say, well...creative.'

It's eleven-thirty. Soon Gaia will be home, and they won't have budged. Oh, well. They can give up the idea of Volterra and settle for San Gimignano; what difference will that make?

In Ravenna, Dante sat down at his desk, took out a sheet of paper and a pen, allowed the images to well up in his mind, and transcribed them word by word.

Same thing when I enter my darkroom and close the door behind me: the space is orderly, the surfaces clean and bare. I prepare the baths, measuring one part substance to nine parts water, dust my negatives with a tiny paintbrush and slip them (shiny side up) into the enlarger, choose my filters and paper, peer through the grain magnifier at the arrangement of the tiny grains of silver halide, those molecules informed by light. When at last everything is ready, when the silence is ready, I turn off the lights and start exposing.

Calm, concentrated, absent, I count off the seconds of exposure, work, rework, improve, stay there, expose, count the seconds, study the grain...

It's all about *framing*. You've got to keep some things outside the frame. You've got to exclude. Only God can get away with embracing everything.

Impossible—such is his hell—to set a sheet of paper on my father's desk. It vanished years ago, beneath a Himalaya of inextricably miscellaneous papers. On its surface, the urgent and the futile writhe together like the snakes of Laocoon; the future is blocked off by perpetual, guilt-inducing calls from the past. Every surface in his study literally overflows with ancient invitations, leaflets, newspaper clippings, magazines, advertisements, concert programmes, scribbled chemical formulae, snapshots, to say nothing of the report cards of children long grown and gone...The painful grimace of an African woman dying of AIDS overlaps with the benevolent smile of a Buddhist monk; the photocopy of an old Leonard Cohen poem finds itself face-to-face with the latest treacly letter from Simon's sister Deborah (turned Zionist and pious in her old age); hip X-rays are interleaved with outdated issues of *Brain* magazine. Sufferings jostle and jive, memories vie for attention, reminders from the tax office scream their impatience...

Simon Greenblatt's papers slide off the table, line up on the floor in military formation, march out of his study in Montreal, cross the Atlantic Ocean and invade Impruneta. A triumphant army of ancient papers overwhelms Gaia's living room, wrenching Rena's guts, causing tears to well up in her stepmother's eyes, obstructing their bronchial tubes, clogging their arteries, blocking the circulation of blood and meaning, drowning out the music in their ears, cutting off their view of the Chianti hills, darkening the delightful Tuscan sun, and striking their perfect Sunday morning dead.

'Daddy! Stop it!' That's Rena screaming at the top of her lungs. 'Stop it! Stop it!' She seems unable to find a more subtle way of putting it. 'STOP IT!'

She flees.

Lombaggine

Head awhirl, she runs up to her bedroom.

The clay-footed ogre pursues me by not moving. His torpor strikes terror into my heart, breathes down my neck. *Oh, Daddy! Daddy! Save me from the ogre who is you!* If I don't run as fast as I can, panting and sweating, he'll catch up with me and throttle all my hopes—gloop, gloop. Engulfed by his misery, I'll disappear forever. Look at Horemheb, he says. Look at Romulus. Look at the soul's immortality. No, Daddy, no!—I need to run and run and keep on running—to escape your immobility!

Though it must be eighty degrees in her room beneath the roof, she's shivering; her hands are freezing; and when she takes out her mobile to call Kerstin, she misdials three times in a row.

'Dr Matheron's office.'

'Kerstin!'

'Rena! How marvellous to hear your voice. Tell me! How's the Tuscan trek?'

'You first—how have you been? How's your lumbago?'

Rena feels a bit responsible for that lumbago. Shortly after their fateful conversation in her darkroom, when she'd told Kerstin how gorgeous and sexy she still was, that stoical widow (whose erotic experience up until then had been limited to three or four impatient deflowerers, a fine husband lost to illness and an endless desert of abstinence), had shyly sat down at her computer.

Tell me, Subra says.

It wasn't easy for her. It meant choosing a pseudonym, then learning to filter out weirdos, psychos, phallocrats...Still, the pickings have been excellent, overall. Between the ages of fifty-five and sixty, Kerstin has had a good dozen lovers and the things they've done together sound intriguing not to say extraordinary, even to my jaded ears. The men are almost all married, between forty and sixty. They confide in her after the love-making. They tell her their problems and listen to hers, make her laugh, shower her with compliments, tenderness and flowers. 'You were right,' Kerstin told me, after a few months of assiduous experimentation. 'As long as you keep away from intellectuals, Frenchmen are remarkable lovers. They've got all sorts of qualities—curiosity, delicacy, boyishness, a sense of humour, a taste for vice...I can hardly believe my luck! I'm having a ball and I don't plan to stop any time soon. God bless the internet!' One day she confessed to a weakness for whippings and thrashings, probably dating back to the spankings her severe Protestant Swede of a father regularly inflicted on her plump pink bottom. She recently made the acquaintance of a young man in the Auvergne region who showed himself willing to punish her in all the ways she'd ever dreamed of, and many that had never occurred to her. 'It's pure theatre,' Kerstin assured me. Though I don't object to this sort of *mise en scène* on moral grounds (every true erotic encounter, be it with a...member of the other sex or of one's own, with a broomstick or a mere fleeting image, opens our bodies onto the void that surrounds us and revives the violence of brute animal infantile life—a life that emerges from matter is destined to return to it), I admit I feared for my friend's safety. So when she was struck down by a lumbago attack, following a strange excursion to the Auvergne last summer for a *rendez-vous* with the whipping man, I interpreted it as a wise warning from her body.

'Better. A little better, these past few days.'

'What does "a little better" mean?'

'Well, I'm not about to go schlepping through the Afghan mountains with a sixty-pound back pack, but I do manage to get out of bed now and then. So I'm making progress. How about you? Oh… my darling Rena…are you crying?'

Absurdly, Rena nods.

'So you're having a rough time? As rough as you feared?'

She nods again, squeaking out a yes between sobs.

'Dear heart. Come on, now, take a few deep breaths the way I taught you…'

'Thanks, Kerstin.'

'What about Aziz?'

'That's part of it. I haven't heard from him for two days.'

'The magazine's probably making him work around the clock, don't you think? Because of the events?'

'Yeah.'

'Don't worry, dear one. It's just a bad patch, you'll see. You'll pull through. Everything will turn out all right.'

L'amore

Car tyres crunch on gravel—Gaia is back.

Rena comes out of her room. 'So what do you guys feel like doing?'

As traumatised by her outburst as if he were a little boy and she his mother, Simon answers in a low voice that he plans to spend the day here. She and Ingrid are welcome to go sightseeing wherever they want.

'No problem,' says Rena.

'No, Dad,' Ingrid protests. 'I'll stay here with you. It's a good idea to rest up a bit. We've been running around so much these past few days.'

'No problem,' says Rena.

Fine. So they'll see neither Volterra nor San Gimignano; they'll go nowhere. What difference does it make?

Gaia's cheerful voice wafts up to them from downstairs: '*Tutto bene?*'

'*Sì, sì. Molto bene!*' Rena replies.

And the day goes by.

Rena settles down with a book beneath the open dormer windows of her bedroom. As the afternoon sun crosses the sky, snatches of the couple's gentle madness come floating up to her ears.

'We haven't had the time to write a single postcard. If we don't do it now, we'll get to Montreal before they do.'

'Good idea. Where did you put them?'

'I thought you had them. Wait a minute, I'll check…Our bags need repacking anyway…'

'Where should we sit? Cold in the shade, hot in the sun…'

'Forgot my hat.'

'Shall I fetch it?'

'No, no, let's sit in the shade.'

'Which ones do you want?…Okay, I'll take the others.'

'So where should we start?'

'Let's make a list.'

'The children, of course…and the grandchildren.'

'But it's the same address. No point in wasting stamps.'

'Just as you like…'

'Deborah…No, I'll do hers later.'

'My stomach's growling.'

'Hey, I'm getting hungry, too.'

'Maybe we could ask Gaia to make us a snack and bring it out here.'

'Sure. She could set up another table, it shouldn't be a problem.'

'Wait, I'll ask…What a talker that woman is! She's coming, though.'

'So you write to David, okay?'

'No, go ahead, you do it. Here, take Michelangelo's *David.* The complete view, eh? Not the close-up of his thingamajig. Ha ha!'

'Know his address?'

'Not off the top of my head.'

'Too bad. We'll have to give him the card when we get back.'

'And Whosit's Campanile—should we send that to Freda?'

'Sure thing. I wonder how she's doing…Hope her medicine has kicked in by now.'

'Speaking of which…what about Marcy's operation?'

'You're right, it was scheduled for last week. We should have given her a call.'

'Oh, she knows it's not easy to telephone from overseas…'

'Aren't those hills just beautiful?'

'Mm-hmm! The foliage back home must be looking great, too.'

'Should I take a picture?'

'Why not?'

'Where's the camera?'

'Upstairs in the red bag.'

'I'll get it—tell the sun not to move!'

'Could you bring a sweater down for me, too?'

'Are you cold?'

'Just a little.'

'Maybe we should go inside.'

'Okay. I'll bring the tray.'

'Careful of that step!'

'Oops! Just in time!'

…They love each other.

Where is Aziz?

Grabbing her Canon, Rena joins Gaia outside in the garden and starts taking photos. She photographs everything she likes, and she likes everything. One photo after another: Gaia herself—a marvellous woman, radiant despite mourning and solitude. Her hazel trees and fig trees, her vegetable garden, her autumn flowers. All in black in white. An orgy of greys.

Gaia talks and talks, smiling, seeming to understand her.

She'd understand, Rena says inwardly to Subra, if I could tell her, if I could make it clear to her, if my Italian were better than it is, I'm sure Gaia would understand that *the words escaped me*. I didn't mean to say them. *The* word, rather, a single word, the word Sylvie, the name Sylvie, such a lovely name, meaning forest or glade… 'What?' my mother said. 'What are you talking about? Sylvie wasn't with you in London!' And my silence then my silence then my silence then…I'm sure Gaia would believe me if I told her I didn't do it on purpose; the word came out all by itself. Three months after the trip to London, I was chattering about flea markets with my mother who adored flea markets, I was telling her about the Portobello Market and how much fun Sylvie and I had had trying on vintage dresses there…'What?' Silence. 'Sorry, no, of course she wasn't there…' Cringing, blushing, stammering…I saw the dawning of catastrophe in Ms Lisa Heyward's eyes. I didn't mean to, I swear. I didn't do it on purpose, it was a simple mistake, not a Freudian slip, just a mistake, people do make plain ordinary mistakes sometimes, don't they, Gaia? I'm the one who…it's my fault that…no way of unsaying it, taking it back…undoing the damage…The word *Sylvie* irreparably destroyed…

It's six o'clock. Sweetly, with a sharp, burning sweetness, dusk arrives. Rena has taken a hundred photos. Simon and Ingrid get up from their nap. All they need to do now is invent an evening for this day…

'I don't want you to cook for us again,' Rena tells Gaia. 'We'll find ourselves a restaurant in town.'

'Yes,' she replies. 'I'm afraid I won't be able to make dinner for you tonight, I'm having friends over.'

'Ah. *Benissimo.*'

She's having friends over, thinks Rena. Maybe that's how the whole thing all started: waking up this morning, Simon must have sensed this was a house in which it was possible to entertain.

As Rena heads for the staircase, Gaia turns on the TV to catch the evening news. '*Dio mio*, look!' she exclaims suddenly. 'It's about your country. *La Francia.*'

Rena covers the six yards between the staircase and the TV set in zero seconds.

Scenes of chaos. A doorway, with choking men and billows of smoke pouring out of it. Thunderstruck, Rena recognises the little mosque—part of the same building as the Turkish baths she visited with Aicha. From inside the baths, she recalls, the women could hear the men praying; other days of the week it was no doubt the other way around. She recognises the men, too. Not the individuals but the type. Modest, humble. Not young. Not proud. Bruised and battered by life. All-enduring. 'What's going on?' she asks Gaia, because the Italian anchorman is speaking much too fast for her to understand.

Even when Gaia repeats what he's saying at a slower speed she doesn't understand it, and even if Gaia were to translate it into French or English she wouldn't understand it, because what he is saying is incomprehensible. The police, it would seem, tossed, it would seem, a tear bomb, it would seem, into the mosque, it would seem, during the evening prayer service. The two women sit there and watch the coughing, weeping, spitting men pour out of the building. Then the camera jumps to another scene—crowds of young men shouting and throwing stones—'It looks like the Intifada!' says Gaia (and Rena is reminded of an elderly Jewish couple she met in Haifa, Argentine-born but living in Israel since the 1950s, shocked to hear she planned to visit the Palestinian Territories as well, asking her if she took her Canadian friends to visit Sarcelles when they came to Paris; Rena had been disconcerted by the comparison—quite an admission, when you thought about it)...Violent clashes between the young men and the riot police, cars burning, women's faces convulsed with rage, more cars burning, and she realises Aziz must be on the spot. Of course he's there, either in the middle of the crowd or right next to it, covering the event for *On the Fringe*, maybe if she looks at the TV screen hard enough she'll catch sight of him and be able to say to Gaia, Look, that's my husband— the one over there, see? Do you see the one I mean? The tall thin young Arab with the high cheekbones. Yes, him, him! Isn't he just so beautiful you could weep? That's him, I swear! We've been working together for two years and living together since last summer. He's a real hero...He learned early on how to turn sadness into energy and bitterness into creativity. A poor student in grade school, he got turned around by a wonderful teacher in eighth grade and made it through to his baccalaureate, and it didn't take long after that for the fast-talker to turn into a reporter. Today he's one of France's few bicultural journalists, capable of bridging the gap between the nervous, touchy, overcautious old-stock popula-tion of France's city centres and the boiling cauldron of the suburbs with their hundred nationalities, seventy languages, fifteen religions and two million problems...True, he's younger than I am, indeed closer to my sons' ages than to mine (it wasn't easy for them to accept this new stepfather), but all is well now, Gaia, I can hardly believe my luck...

Rena says none of these things because the cameras have long since moved away from the projects, impatient to highlight other suppurating sores of the planet—interspersed, naturally, with advertisements. When she goes upstairs to dress for dinner, she can hear Simon and Ingrid getting ready in their room.

The storm will have blown over by tomorrow, Subra tells her, and you'll all get off to a new start. You'll be on the last leg of your journey.

Right, Rena says. Cool it.

In the restaurant, they alternate between clumsy attempts at conversation, embarrassed silences and contrite smiles.

Early to bed.

Vast hiatus between lights out and sleep.

MONDAY

'I want to do something unfathomable like the family.'

France is in ruins—a landscape like Baghdad or Mogadishu—heaps of rubble, wandering shadows—scenes of unspeakable horror…Right afterwards, I'm supposed to give birth to a baby—apparently a boy. His mother(??) gave him to me and asked me to do this as a favour to her. The delivery itself is swift and easy—but the child comes out motionless and caked in fat, looking like a lump of duck conserve—not only that, but it's in two pieces. Horrified at having given birth to a stillborn baby, I call Alioune. He joins me…'No,' he says, picking up the larger of the two pieces and gently unfolding it. 'No, look. The baby's alive, it's magnificent!' I take the tiny boy in my arms. He's beautiful indeed. He smiles up at me, staring straight into my eyes…Then I have to run and find the mother, to tell her that her baby is born and that everything went fine—it was an incredibly easy delivery, I didn't suffer at all—ah!—compared to the birth of my own children! Alioune and I are amazed at the baby's innate capacity to smile. We're so happy…Then, just as we're preparing to leave, I remember that the country is war torn…

No problem interpreting France as a country at war—the images I saw last night more than suffice. But the baby. Who is that baby? Myself? 'Apparently a boy.' Half dead. The dream doesn't say what happens to the other half, the part no one bothers to unfold or take in their arms, the part no one smiles at. *It's there, too, though.* I mean, we can't just toss it onto the garbage heap. Why does the mother take no interest in it?

Who is that mother? asks Subra.

Parting the bedroom curtains, Rena sees that Sunday's limpid brilliance has given way to a chilly, steel-grey Monday—as if the Creator himself were reluctant to head back to work after His day of rest. A thick fog has invaded Chianti, narrowing the universe, effacing the distant hills and blurring even the contours of the garden. Only nearby objects are visible, and even they look dull and lustreless.

It's only eight o'clock but Gaia has told them she needs to lock up the house by nine-thirty at the latest. How will they ever manage to extricate themselves in time?

Determined not to go stir-crazy waiting for Simon and Ingrid, Rena flips through the beautiful edition of *The Divine Comedy* in Gaia's library, admiring Gustave Doré's illustrations, and stumbles on a passage about bodies metamorphosing...

The two heads were by now to one comprest,
When there before our eyes two forms begin
To mix in one where neither could be traced.
Two arms were made where the four bands had been;
The belly and chest and with the legs the thighs
Became such members as were never seen...

Hard to believe this passage was written seven centuries before movie cameras were invented, Rena says to herself. You'd think it was describing special effects for the next *Harry Potter* film.

This house is so lovely...

Still no sign of Simon and Ingrid. Maybe when they come down she'll tell them to take the Megane and continue the trip without her; she's decided to stay here. She wants to live with Gaia until the end of her days, absorbing her wisdom, making fruit jam, drying flowers, planting vegetables in the earth...

Her mobile rings. It's Schroeder.

'Patrice! How are you?'

'I'm not calling to make small talk, Rena.'

'I'm listening.'

'I don't know if you've been keeping abreast of...'

'Yes, I finally caught some footage last night. It's...'

'What about this morning?'

A wave of fear washes through her.

'Not yet. Is there…'

'Rena, listen. There's a civil war going on here. Aziz tells me he asked you to cut your holiday short and you said no. Don't you think you're going a bit far? I mean, you're not Salgado, you know? You're replaceable. I'm sorry to put it so bluntly, but I want to be sure you understand. Rena, you've got to come back today. That's an ultimatum. If you decide not to, I won't be able to renew your contract.'

'Is Aziz with you?'

'Did you hear me? *On the Fringe* won't be able to publish your photos anymore.'

'Could you put him on? I'll talk to you again right afterwards.'

A silence. Her brain is shrouded in the same fog as the landscape.

'Yeah.'

Aziz. His bad-day voice.

'What's going on, love? What have I done to deserve this over-dose of silence?'

No, that's not the right approach—she shouldn't force him to discuss their love life in front of their boss. It will only make him feel trapped, cornered, tricked. But she can't help it.

'*You're* thinking about replacing me, too, is that it?'

What a stupid thing to say. The worst possible tactic. She can practically see his shoulders shrugging to shake her off.

Schroeder has taken the phone back.

'Well, Rena. What's your decision?'

'*Ciao*, Patrice.'

There. I've lost my job. Good start to the day. Let's see what else can happen before the sun goes down.

Going upstairs to pack, she passes Ingrid coming down for breakfast. Simon isn't hungry, she informs Rena. But they're almost ready...

Rena brings down her suitcase, moves the car to the doorstep, and settles down to wait in the living room with Gaia.

The minutes inch by like slobbery, amorphous slugs. They swell up into obese quarter-hours, ugly and useless as gobs of saliva.

Gaia puts a sympathetic arm around her shoulders and tells her in a low voice that her father was depressive, too. So many failed Galileos! So many immature Zeuses! So many Commanders in bathrobes! Why did no one warn us about this?

Using hand gestures and her modicum of Italian, Rena conveys to her hostess that the little mice are fed up with tiptoeing around their big, depressed lion-daddies. Gaia bursts out laughing.

At long last, Ingrid comes down and tells her they're all set. Rena goes up to help Simon with their suitcases...But first he wants to carry down the plates, glasses, cups and saucers Gaia brought them for their various snacks.

'Leave it, Daddy, please. Don't worry, Gaia will take care of it. It's her job.'

Simon thinks it would be more polite, more generous, indeed, more feminist of them to take care of it themselves. The debate goes on for a good five minutes; downstairs, Gaia must be losing patience. Rena gives in and carries down the tray.

The car is waiting at the doorstep; the luggage is in the trunk; *now* what's holding them up?

Oh, right. Life.

Simon has come to a halt in the middle of the living room. A step. A pause. A question—insoluble, as always. A sigh. Encroaching darkness. His hands go up to cover his face. Blackout. Endgame.

They'll go nowhere. They've been struck motionless, like the party guests in Sleeping Beauty's castle.

Finally Gaia breaks the spell. Striding across the room, she kindly, smilingly—'*Arrivederci*'—but firmly—'*Ciao! Ciao!*'—kicks them out of her house.

God bless her—if, that is, He's still able to lift a finger.

They're off. Naturally, though, their troubles are far from over.

'Looks like we took a wrong turn,' Rena says after a while, braking gently. 'We're headed for the highway, not the Chiantigiana.'

Simon studies the little map Gaia sketched for them. 'Okay,' he says. 'But if we keep on going, I think we can catch up with it a bit further on.'

'I don't think so,' says Rena, stopping at the side of the road to make a U-turn.

'Fine!' Simon says, slamming his palms down onto the open map of Tuscany on his lap. 'No point in my reading the maps, then—just do as you please!'

Zeus does the Zeus thing, Subra says. What do you expect? He rants, raves, and thunders, reducing all to ash.

Listen, Zeus, I'm fed up to the teeth with your temper tantrums, do you hear me? You'd better watch out or I'll warm your bum!

Rena forces herself to take a deep breath, behave like an adult, control her voice. 'Okay, show me.'

Trembling with the same contained rage, the two of them study the map together. Rena is right. She turns around and drives back through the invisible hills at top speed.

A while later, on the Chiantigiana, she feels suddenly euphoric.

When you come right down to it, she says to herself, I'm a manic-depressive with ultra-short phases.

When they reach Siena at morning's end, she parks in the Via Curtatone near San Domenico's—illegally, but only slightly so—and the three of them start wandering through the lovely streets of the old city, feeling perfectly miserable. Neither Ingrid nor Simon have said a word since the altercation at the side of the road. Rena banishes from her brain the images of herself as a young woman discovering Siena at Xavier's side—tired old memories that are now stretching their limbs and rubbing their eyes, trying to wake up…Don't bother, she tells them. Go back to sleep, I don't need you. I prefer to create new memories!

A bit farther on, Simon tugs at her sleeve—'Rena, look.'

His voice is low, his tone ominous. It startles her.

Turning, she sees a newspaper stand and the headlines leap out at her, silently shouting the same thing in a dozen different languages: *France, France, France,* they say. *Paris, Paris, Paris. Fire, fire, fire.* She sees photographs. Chaotic crowds of teenage boys, ranks of anti-riot police. Flames. Helmets. Shields. Stones. Flames. Riots spreading. Three hundred cars burned. Her Canon dangles uselessly between her breasts.

'I know,' she says lamely to Simon.

He purchases some newspapers in English and starts flipping through them as they walk. 'Hey,' he mutters in a worried voice. 'Isn't that the place Aziz comes from?'

'Yes, it is,' she says. 'It's also where Victor Hugo wrote *Les Misérables.*'

'Oh, *Les Misérables!*' exclaims Ingrid. 'We saw the musical comedy at the Place des Arts a few years ago. It was terrific, wasn't it, Dad?'

'Well, it's been playing non-stop in that city for the past hundred and fifty years,' Rena says. 'Thousands of Jean Valjeans have been locked up for stealing a loaf of bread, or for less.'

She doesn't tell them how many times Aziz has been held in custody overnight, or that his brother has spent the past eighteen months in the Villepinte penitentiary...Knowing that Ingrid thinks her native Rotterdam is in the process of becoming a second Kabul, she has no wish to get her started on the subject of the Muslim threat.

Instead, feigning gaiety, she chirps, 'Why don't we check out the cathedral?'

Duomo

Their disappointment is instantaneous.

The façade is under renovation, concealed beneath a tarpaulin on which its red, white and black striped marble has been painted in trompe-l'œil.

'Hey!' says Simon. 'That almost looks like a copy!'

He's not joking. Afflicted with near-sightedness, far-sightedness and perhaps a bit of astigmatism as well, he's convinced he's looking at the real thing, sun-flattened. *Those who tourists do become...* This time Ingrid goes about unfooling her husband's eye.

They file slowly across the threshold, into the penumbra of the enormous cathedral. Seeing their twin fedoras, an employee gestures to Simon to take his off (in places of Catholic worship, as everyone knows, women's heads should be covered and men's uncovered). Without missing a beat—condensing humour and insolence, obedience and insult into a single act, eliciting Rena's reluctant admiration and the employee's acute annoyance—Simon removes his hat and plunks it on his wife's head.

Unlike San Lorenzo in Florence, the space here is crowded, congested, fairly dripping with hybrid decoration. Fearing they'll be overwhelmed, they decide to concentrate on the coloured marble pavements—twenty-five thousand square feet of Biblical scenes. Despite this restriction, Rena soon finds herself in the grip of familiar anxiety: how much should I try to understand? How can I be *here*, truly here and now—for it's today, not tomorrow, that we're visiting the cathedral of Siena? Determined to engrave the floor mosaics in her memory once and for all, she moves a little ahead of the others.

Here is *The Slaughter of the Innocents*...How many times, in paintings, drawings, photos, movies or documentaries, have we seen the emblematic image of a mother screaming as she struggles to wrest her living baby from a man bent on killing it, or wailing in despair as she holds up her dead baby?

What about you? whispers Subra. The dead half-baby in your dream...who will weep for you?

Just last April, fourteen people, including an old woman and two little girls, were massacred at a false roadblock near Larbaa. Over the past few years, more than one hundred and fifty thousand people have been murdered in Algeria, Aziz's parents' native land. And who are the assassins, if not our own sons? Yes, our boys—forever marching off to war, eager to suffer and spill rivers of blood, dying, killing, screaming, hating, marching, singing, putting on uniforms, saluting, seeking unison, destroying the bodies of other mothers' sons with daggers, lances, swords, bombs, bullets, poisons and laser rays...

Feeling a sudden vibration on her left thigh, she starts as if a stranger had just pinched her.

No. Her mobile. A phone call.

Digging the phone (Aziz?) out of her tight jeans (Aziz?) with some difficulty (Aziz?), she glances at the screen. No, it's Kerstin.

'How are you doing?' she whispers, heading for the cathedral door.

'What about you—still kicking?'

'Barely.'

'I've got some bad news.'

'Ah.'

'Bad for me, anyway.'

'Then it is for me, too.'

'Well...even for me, it's not *that* bad, but...'

'Cut the suspense. Who's dead?'

'Alain-Marie.'

'Oh.'

'Heart attack—bang, gone. Yesterday. His sister called to tell me. Since then I've talked to a number of his friends and learned the details...He was with a young woman...'

'Twenty-four?'

'Something like that. And...don't laugh, Rena...'

'Oh, no, let me guess...An overdose of Viagra?'

'Isn't that awful? He was just my age, sixty-one. It's so weird, you know? The veterans of May '68 are starting to die...Weirder still, Pierre is devastated. He says I prevented him from getting to know his real father. He wants to learn all he can about Alain-Marie; he's even composing piano music for his funer—'

As if in imitation of Alain-Marie's heart attack, Rena's mobile emits a series of panicky beeps and suddenly the screen goes blank. Silence. Even though Siena's cathedral was wired with electricity in the late nineteenth century, she doubts they'd let her use it to recharge her phone battery.

She goes back to join the others.

They're seated on a bench across from an enormous fresco. Ingrid is leaning forward to rub her ankles; Simon's eyes are closed. Standing next to them are four tall, blond individuals dressed in white: clearly a happy, closely knit Scandinavian family. The mother is analysing the painting; the father is nodding his interest; their teenage son and daughter are asking intelligent questions.

In desperation, Rena opens the *Guide bleu*. What can she tell Simon and Ingrid about this cathedral that will bring it alive for them?

You're not the only one, Father, to have had your plans thwarted and your dreams defeated by the ups and downs of fate...Look at Siena! The original project was to build the biggest church in the world right on this spot (the present Duomo was just the transept!). In 1348, however, construction ground to a halt as the city's population was reduced by two-thirds. Mounds and mounds of dead bodies. Disgusting, purulent, stinking corpses. Black buboes, people moaning, women screaming in agony, babies tossed at random into common graves...The whole European continent writhing in the same pestilence...There...That make you feel better?

Naturally, she holds her tongue.

Kannon

The minute they leave the Duomo, Ingrid begs for a lunch break— yes, now, in the first café they come upon. Hoping to find a terrace in the sunlight, Rena convinces her to wait a bit—and suddenly they find themselves in Il Campo. Ah yes: she remembers this splendid, scallop-shell-shaped square, each of whose nine pavements represents one of the communes that made up the independent republic of Siena in the twelfth century, before it became the Ghibelline enemy of Guelfan Florence. Something like that, yes, something along those lines. They find restaurant tables on the sunny side of the square, and, preoccupied not with Siena's heroic past but with their own petty problems, just as the inhabitants of twelfth-century Siena were preoccupied with theirs, and so it goes, they order sandwiches, salads, *acqua gassata*.

A self-styled clown is circulating among the tables, heckling the customers, offering to imitate them. Finding him unpleasantly reminiscent of the other night's dictator in Florence, Rena brushes him off unceremoniously: '*Non voglio niente, niente!*' Ingrid stares at her, eyebrows raised, taken aback by her violence.

Relax, little one, Subra murmurs in her head. Look around you, take a deep breath, calm down. Life is lovely.

'You look lovely today,' says Simon out of the blue. Rena jumps at the coincidence between his actual utterance of the word and Subra's imaginary one. 'Can I take your photo?'

'You haven't been taking many pictures, Rena,' Ingrid points out, as Rena hands the camera to her father.

'Hard to compete with the postcards,' she mutters sarcastically. 'True.'

Rena finds it troubling to see the Canon in her father's age-speckled hands. It's as if he were holding one of her own limbs, a detached but living part of her body. After examining it with great care, he positions it, aims it, and presses the shutter. Once, twice...

'Don't you want to smile, Rena?' asks Ingrid.

'Not particularly. Do I have to?'

'No,' says Simon. 'You're fine just as you are. With your dark glasses, fedora hat and leather jacket, you look like a movie star incognito.'

'Movie stars aren't what they used to be,' says Ingrid.

Rena shouts with laughter. Ingrid hesitates, then joins in.

You're the exact opposite of Marilyn Monroe, teases Subra. She was happy only when looked at; and you, only when looking.

Their orders arrive, and Simon passes the camera back to her with a flourish. 'Do you know who Canon cameras are named after?' he asks.

'Jimmy Canon, the sworn enemy of Bill Kodak and Bob Nikon? No, I have no idea.'

'K-A-N-N-O-N,' Simon spells out. 'An exceeding strange Japanese bodhisattva.'

'Why strange?' queries Rena, stabbing a number of aqueous little shrimps with her fork and slipping them into her mouth.

'Because the Japanese made a woman of her, whereas in India she was a man. And not just any man: Guanyin, the most popular bodhisattva of the Great Vehicle. I happened to see an article about it a while ago...'

'Really?' Rena says in surprise. So her father is still interested in Buddhism? 'And what is Kannon's specialty?'

'Compassion. She's the...hang on a sec, I jotted it down somewhere...'

Her surprise turning to stupefaction, Rena watches as her father riffles through his wallet and comes up with the appropriate scrap of paper in less than five minutes.

'"She who listens to and receives the pain of whole world,"' he reads aloud, '"and responds to it with one giant word of compassion that encompasses all in an ocean of infinite joy."'

'A bit like the Virgin of Divine Mercy?' suggests Ingrid.

'You don't know how right you are,' Simon nods. 'Japanese Christians bow down before statues they call Maria Kannon. Isn't that incredible? And Canon, the Japanese company, was named after

221

that very bodhisattva. You remind me of her.'

'A goddess of compassion,' Rena grumbles. 'What next?' Tears fill her eyes, fortunately concealed by her dark glasses.

'Seriously. We went to your *Misteries* show last April…'

'You did?' She feels dizzy.

'Do you think our daughter could have a show in Montreal without our going to see it? It made a big impression on us.'

'Yes, it was interesting,' Ingrid concedes, 'although I keep hoping you'll eventually choose a more—'

'I found it admirable,' Simon says, interrupting his wife. 'Not just because you'd obviously put years of work into it, but because…to open up their private lives to you like that, to allow you to get so close to them, those men had to feel you really accepted them…Kannon, see what I mean? A strong show indeed,' he concludes.

'I would have seduced Bin Laden,' says Rena, to lighten the atmosphere.

'I'll bet you would!' Simon laughs.

'I would have seduced the Pope.'

'Rena!' Ingrid says.

'Sorry. Er…would you believe…the Great Rabbi of Jerusalem?'

A silence ensues, in the course of which Rena directs her full attention to making sure the little beasties of her *insalata di mare* stay on her fork.

As they're having coffee a while later, Simon glances through the newspapers he purchased earlier. 'Wow. Looks as if sparks are flying in France!'

'Of course sparks are flying. What do you expect? Two kids get their brains fried and the government contents itself with saying they deserve it. I should hope sparks would fly!'

The clown she rebuffed earlier comes up to her. '*Grazie mille, signora, per il vostro spettacolo,*' he says in a loud voice. '*Era veramente meraviglioso! Formidabile! Stupendo!*' So saying, he slips a fifty-centime piece into her palm.

'You guys feel up to visiting the Museo Civico?' she says, pocketing the coin.

'Sure thing!' Simon and Ingrid crow in unison.

What's going on? wonders Rena. You'd think we loved each other or something.

Dolore

White, nude, gigantic, marble hand pressed to marble brow, looking like a Rodin *Thinker* who swapped meditation for despair, the man on the museum's ground floor stares transfixed at the source of his pain. No: the word pain being masculine in Italian, it's not what he is enduring, it's what he is.

I'm not saying it's you, Daddy, I'm not saying it's you.

In fact the statue reminds her of Gérard, a former prison inmate whom she had decided not to include in *Misteries*, after an afternoon spent talking with him in his twentieth-arrondissement squat.

His shame at living in such poor surroundings, his stilted conversation, his complete lack of emotion when he took his childhood photos out of an old shoe box to show them to me…Those should all have been warning signs, but somehow I didn't pick up on them.

Tell me, Subra says.

Gérard had been sentenced to—and done—ten years for the hard-porn films he'd produced and posted on the net in the mid-nineties. Because they were banned, those films are worth a mint today. He had hired the best lawyers in Paris to draw up a contract for him, and convinced a dozen young women to sign it. *I agree*, the contract said in substance, *to remain naked in front of a camera for two hours and let two men do whatever they want to me*. 'The films really got interesting, Rena,' Gérard told me, 'when the girls changed their minds.' He didn't offer and I didn't request details as to the reason for this reversal. With a firm contract, Gérard knew he was legally covered, so he paid no attention when the women begged him to call the whole thing off. Staring at the man's handsome face just a few inches from my own, I realised I'd have to renounce taking his picture. Gérard is one of the few people I've been unable to photograph—that is, to love. He was beyond the pale.

Never could he have told me what was done to *him*, long ago. Forever obliterated, the memory of his mother—a young, exhausted single woman, her nerves on edge—teasing and mocking him when he was a boy of two, making him sob, then hitting him to make him sob louder—Hey Gérard, stop crying you little baby, you little asshole, you little cocksucker—slapping his face, then really getting into it, raining blows down on his head, giddy with the possibility of killing him—you little asshole—and he, Gérard, so tiny, helpless, utterly at her mercy. The more he begged her to stop, the more she felt like bullying him, breaking him. The more ear-shattering his cries grew, the more she wanted to get rid of him. They were alone in the apartment—just as, later on, Gérard would be alone in a soundproofed basement of Paris's ninth arrondissement with the beautiful, reckless, masochistic, penniless young women who, for money, had agreed to take off their clothes in front of a camera. It excited him to have them at his mercy, just as children are at their mothers' mercy. When they sobbed he felt a rush of euphoria, and when they begged him to stop he motioned to the cameraman to keep shooting: that was when the very best scenes got shot, the ones that caused the most sperm and money to flow. Men who hate themselves—and they are legion, as Gérard well knew—are more than willing to pay to ejaculate. The more they pay, the more they feel they're worth. In Washington, Moscow,

Paris, and Tokyo, big shots who are still little boys deep down are prepared to part with ten thousand dollars for a single coitus with a call-girl; they're sure to come then, because they've paid a fortune to do so.

Back when Gérard was producing those films, his wife had guessed he must be involved in something fishy because suddenly they were rolling in it—but, happy to be able to buy mink coats and go on holidays in Majorca, she hadn't asked too many questions. Then everything fell apart. Of the dozen young women Gérard had paid to be savagely raped in front of a camera, four decided to sue.

Just the sort of case Ms Lisa Heyward might have handled, Subra puts in.

True...Gérard was sent to prison, and his wife left him. *Dolore, dolore,* he lost everything. 'I'll never understand, Rena,' he told me, at least fifteen times in the three hours we spent together. 'I didn't break a single law!' Like Eichmann's, his incomprehension was sincere. I'll bet anything Eichmann's mother tortured *him*, too. Impossible to understand your punishment, afterwards. What little boy would ever dream of dragging his mom to court?

They ascend the grand staircase together.

Buon Governo

Still radiant from their recent exchange over the shrimp, they stand side by side in front of the famous Ambrogio Lorenzetti frescoes. Next to them, an elderly Englishwoman is giving explanations to a young man, probably her son.

My sons! Where are my sons? Suddenly Rena misses Toussaint and Thierno terribly. If I take a trip with them a quarter of a century down the line, when *I'm* seventy years old, will they be as tormented by guilt, impatience and fury as I've been with my father over the past few days?

'What are the prerequisites of *Good Government*?' asks the pedagogical Brit. 'Reading the painting as if it were a book, from left to right and from top to bottom, you can find the answer. There have to be strong bonds, first between heavenly angels and Lady Justice, then between Lady Justice and Lady Concord. Concord goes on to weave those bonds into a rope and the rope gets passed from one burgher to the next, eventually coming out over here, where it moves upwards to become a sceptre...'

'...in the hands of the king!' the young man guesses.

'No,' his mother corrects him gently. 'He's not a king, that's what's so amazing. For the space of seventy years, in the twelfth century, Siena wasn't a monarchy at all, but a republic. So this man is the governor.'

'Still, the republic wasn't exactly a bowl of cherries,' Ingrid whispers. 'Look over there, in the bottom right-hand corner: men in chains. Prisoners-of-war. I wonder where *they* come from!'

'Good question,' concedes Rena. Again she remembers Jean Valjean condemned to the galleys, and the fury that overcomes Aziz every time the police make him pull over because he looks like an Arab. 'Shut up, turn around, hands on the boot of the car.' 'Hey, what's up? What did you stop me for?' 'Are you resisting arrest, you little prick? Just wait, you'll be sorry...' And they take him in and lock him up and frisk him. They make him strip, squat down in front of them and cough three times, ostensibly to check for dope in his anus but really just to humiliate him and make sure he knows who's in charge. He comes home from those nights pale with rage, a little more deeply wounded every time...

Turning to the wall on their right, they study *The Effects of Good Government*: flourishing countryside, graceful women dancing, students listening to their professor. Work and rest, order and joy, prosperity and peace. On the wall to their left, on the other hand, are *The Effects of Bad Government*: the beautiful statue of Justice toppled and smashed, cities burned, fields gone sterile, distress and disorder, violence running amok. That fresco, moreover, is less well preserved than the other—as if the citizens' misdeeds had corroded the very wall on which they were painted.

To the right, murmurs Subra, the landscape you've been traipsing through with Simon and Ingrid. To the left: Aziz's universe, teetering on the brink of an abyss. These days you're split between the two—your body here, your mind over there.

You said it, Rena sighs. My holiday was badly timed, as it turns out. I'm only beginning to realise what it's going to cost me.

Motorini

Back in Il Campo, she unfolds the map of Siena and spreads it out in front of Ingrid. 'You wanted to see the ramparts? I suggest we head up this way, then along from here to there, then here, and come back around to the car like this. What do you think?'

'I didn't bring my glasses,' Ingrid answers, 'but I trust you. Fine, Let's go.'

The two women strike out, with Simon close behind. But the hills are steeper than they had expected; the narrow streets twist and turn, stubbornly refusing to lead them to the ramparts.

When they reach the barrier called San Lorenzo (him again!), Ingrid tells her they have to stop off at a pharmacy. Simon has a headache. He wants to buy…no, not aspirin, he's not allowed to take aspirin, but some sort of analgesic.

'Look,' he says, drawing an empty vial out of his pants pocket.

The pharmacist sets about translating the English label into Italian.

Ingrid has glimpsed a post office across the street. 'Rena, would you mind buying us some stamps while we're busy in here?'

Yes, I would mind, thinks Rena. I don't feel like either buying stamps or translating labels. I want Aziz, I want Aziz, I want Aziz.

She exits the pharmacy, slamming the door behind her.

If I can't remember the word for stamps, I refuse to ask for them. What's the point in buying stamps for postcards that haven't been written yet?

Of their own volition, her feet cross the street. Of its own volition, her brain rummages around in its darkest depths. And Rena finds herself standing at the counter like a normal human being, smiling and murmuring, '*Francobolli, per favore!*'

The medical parenthesis lasts and lasts, drawn out by her father's indecision. Rena waits for Simon and Ingrid outside, determined not to explode with impatience. Kicking her heels at the corner of the Via Garibaldi, she absent-mindedly reads the plaque recounting the Italian patriot's heroic deeds in Siena…then forgets them at once.

When the couple emerges some thirty-five minutes later, the afternoon turns into a nightmare. In the steep hilly streets near Porta d'Ovile, motor-scooters with no mufflers zoom past them one after another. How can a bunch of pimply teenagers be allowed to inflict such violence on their ears and souls? Forgotten, the bonds woven by Lady Concord! Night is falling and Simon is furious with her for having read the Garibaldi plaque without him…A thick cloud layer has swallowed up the sun…The air is heavy with a thousand human exhalations: poisonous gases, failed aspirations and petty quarrels… Rena's Canon bangs relentlessly against her solar plexus. Why aren't you working? it needles her. Why have you stopped looking? Don't you want me to help you see things anymore? They get lost, wandering at length and at random through smelly Siena. And when at last they find their car: a parking ticket.

A plague upon the planet!

As they head towards their B & B on the outskirts of the city, the silence in the car becomes so charged that Rena turns on the radio for the first time and stumbles upon a world news bulletin in Italian. The riots in France are now breaking news. The announcer runs through the statistics at top speed, citing the number of *macchine bruciate, carabinieri feriti* and *ragazzi arrestati* in one city after another. Rena doesn't get it all, but her heartbeat speeds up uncontrollably. Wiped out, Simon and Ingrid sit in the back seat saying nothing.

A bucolic residential suburb. This time they have no trouble finding the place, but (alas!) no Gaia awaits them there. The owner is a young, blonde, and appallingly efficient mother of three. Sure, that'll be fine, thank you...Shower's in the hallway...Perfect.

They go back out an hour later. Admire the purity of the full moon (almost full, almost pure—above the Ponte Vecchio—was a century ago). Bundle back into the car to search for a restaurant.

Here? No...There? No...Over there, maybe? U-turn...Hey, there's one!...Quick, quick, turn left!

The young man on the pedestrian crossing jumps, hastens his step.

'Don't *do* that,' Simon mutters to Rena. 'I hate people who do that!'

The phrase hits a nerve. (Flashback to 1975: 'You hate me!' 'No, I don't. It's not you I hate, it's your lies. I hate to see you stealing things, skipping school, lying to me and your mother. Rena, I really think you should see a professional. I have a friend who could at least refer us to someone...' Simon and I have been at loggerheads for three full decades...)

'Sorry, Dad,' she retorts. 'But I'm driving an unfamiliar car in an unfamiliar city'—guided, moreover, she manages to refrain from saying, by a lousy Virgil...

Simon apologises in turn. He's getting old, he tells her, and cars often force him to speed up when he's crossing the street.

Father and daughter are both contrite, and mad as hell.

At last Rena parks and the couple gets out of the car. A few seconds later, Ingrid taps on her window: 'You can't park here, Rena, it's a bus stop. If you get two parking tickets on the same day, they're liable to press charges.'

Simon points to a spot across the street. Impossible (illegal) to make a U-turn. Rena tries to nose her way around the small square, but far too many cars are parked there and she gets stuck. Instantly, a dozen men rush over and surround the Megane, shouting advice at her in Italian. Flustered, she turns the steering wheel the wrong way as she backs up, grazing the fender of an Audi and eliciting even louder shouts from the men. They sense that she's a foreigner and start haranguing her in English. This is the last straw: she rolls her window down and makes a most unladylike gesture in their direction.

Having extricated the car from that mess at last, she drives half a mile before finding a place to turn around. Her right leg is shaking so badly that the pressure on the accelerator is spasmodic and the car moves forward in fits and starts. Her chest slams up against the steering wheel, and an electronic beep berates her for not having attached her seatbelt. By the time she finally glides into the parking spot her father has been saving for her, she's on the verge of a nervous breakdown.

'You could have stayed right where you were,' he tells her, smiling, as she locks the car. 'Turns out the buses stop at eight.'

Nothing has happened, nothing. Yet she wants to scream, beat this old man over the head, clasp him to her, tell him off, shake him so hard that his teeth fall out, collapse on the ground at his feet.

They embark on a lengthy examination of the menu, including the conversion of euros into Canadian dollars and an etymological discussion, possibly the three hundredth of Rena's life, of the misleading word *pepperoni*, a type of sausage in North America and a vegetable in Italy. Somehow they manage to place their order.

Suddenly Simon turns to her and says, 'That's a lovely scarf!'

Rena freezes. Blanches. Lowers her eyes and murmurs, 'Thank you—I like it, too…' The conversation picks up where it left off.

He gave it to you, murmurs Subra. That beautiful velvet scarf in shimmering red and mauve and blue…

Yes, a good ten years ago. He chose it especially for me, wrapped it and mailed it overseas—accompanied, like all his gifts over the years, by a carefully chosen birthday card. Then he waited for my response. In vain. Hurt, he brought it up a few months later: 'Didn't you like the scarf?' 'What do you mean?' I protested. 'I loved it! Didn't you get my thank you note?' 'No…' His expression made it clear he didn't believe I'd sent one. Since then, every time I wear this scarf, it brings back not my father's generosity but his mistrust. I decided to wear it tonight for our last meal in Siena, and now… he's forgotten it ever existed!

Their pizzas arrive and the conversation grows animated. Perspiring, Rena takes off the scarf.

Back in their B & B—panic. No scarf—must have left it behind in the restaurant. No, I don't believe it!

Rushes to the car, drives like a madwoman, bursts into the restaurant—'Did you by any chance see…?'

Finds it, heads back towards the car, and bursts into tears.

Not tears of relief. No, not exactly.

She waves the remote control in the car's direction…hmm. Instead of clicking, the car blinks at her.

She seizes up in silly fear.

Stop it, Subra tells her. Too many emotions. Obviously, in your haste, your forgot to lock the car doors two minutes ago.

That must be it, Rena nods. And she opens the door to the driver's seat.

But. Wait. But. Wait. Stop it. Stop it. No. Think. No. Where's my bag, what happened to my bag, what the fuck did I do with my backpack?

Rena, calm down, Subra says firmly. You wouldn't have left it in an unlocked car. It's in your room.

No, it isn't. I brought it with me.

Then it's in the restaurant.

Right. A fair exchange: the waiter gives me my scarf, and to show my gratitude I give him my backpack. No…what the fuck did I do with it?

Long pause, in the course of which her brain is forced to admit the truth.

Did I really do that?

Looks like it, little one, says Subra. After travelling to seventy-five different countries including Pakistan, Afghanistan, Sudan, and the Democratic Republic of Congo without losing so much as a hairpin, you've actually managed to get your backpack ripped off in Siena.

It's past midnight. Rena glances around the small square. Clusters of men stand chatting and smoking between parked cars and in front of the two or three cafés still open. Among them, probably, a few of the guys who yelled at her earlier, and in whose direction she made her eloquent gesture.

Now what? she thinks. I can hardly go over to them and say, 'Uh, did you by any chance notice…?'

If they wanted to tell her, they'd have told her by now.

Okay, Subra says. It's neither the plague nor the slaughter of the innocents. Think. What was in the bag?

Canon. Notebook. Wallet containing cash, credit card, ID, driver's licence. *Guide bleu*. Comb. Condoms. Tampax. Kleenex. Camels.

Is that all?

Yes. No. Mobile.

Okay. Is that all?

Yes, I think so. Not my passport, not my plane ticket, not the keys to Rue des Envierges. All that's in an inside pocket of my suitcase. Just: Canon, wallet, guide, notebook, mobile.

Not a bad haul.

Rena sits at the wheel, dazed and motionless.

Quick, Subra says: your Visa card. Call to cancel.

My phone's gone. And the number's in the notebook.

She goes back to the restaurant, which is about to close. Intercepts the look in the waiter's eyes when he sees her again: What does that old biddy want *now*? (Until recently it had been unthinkable for a young man to look at her that way.)

No, the waiter tells her. No, there are no police stations in the neighbourhood. She'd have go to Siena.

You're going drive back to Siena *now*? Subra asks. At midnight? Alone? And wander around looking for a police station? Without a driver's licence?

No, I'm not, Rena says. I'm just going to…um…get some sleep, that's it. Tomorrow's another day. Maybe it will all turn out to be a bad dream.

As she drives back to the B & B at a snail's pace, Subra runs through the pros and cons of the *furto*.

Aziz won't be able to reach you anymore...But then, neither will your sons...But then, neither will Schroeder...Between now and tomorrow morning, the thief can reduce your meagre savings to naught...

But I have my ticket and my passport! Rena says. I'll take off from Amerigo Vespucci Airport the day after tomorrow, that's all that matters. The rest...well, the rest will sort itself out.

Notturno

Aziz no not Aziz Paris no not Paris her job no she doesn't have a job anymore Toussaint oh my god Toussaint is going to be a father, he's only twenty-six, that's too young to be a father, well, everything is relative, Simon had his two children at twenty-one and twenty-five...Help, Kerstin! Deliver me from my thoughts! A bit of cerebral acupuncture, I beg of you! Two days left. Just two more days. Wait for me, Aziz, I'm coming home to you, I swear. As soon as I get back, we'll do a reportage together on the situation in France's impoverished suburbs and sell it, not to *On the Fringe*, but to the best magazines in the world. That might seem hard to believe, seen from this bedroom on the outskirts of Siena, but...but...

She stretches out on her bed and looks up at the high, slanting mauve ceilings.

I'm attending an opera in an outdoor theatre, a bit like the Baths of Caracalla in Rome. In the middle of the soprano's most famous solo, I suddenly get up and start hitting the other members of the audience over the head, as hard as I can...

234

She wakes up. Gets out of bed. Goes over to the window. Stands there, naked.

Mist. A still, silent world. Not even a dog barking. Beneath her window, scarcely visible in the ghostly fog: a vegetable garden. Infrared photo? No. Camera gone.

She stands there. Frozen.

Some days (it was before you came along, Subra), the sun would vanish without warning.

'I love you, Rowan.' 'Shut up, you nobody. You crumb. Just shut your face and leave me alone.' 'But you promised to help me with my multiplication tables!' 'Poor little idiot. She's nine years old and she still doesn't know her multiplication tables. How dumb can you get?' 'Show me, I can learn. Please, Rowan. Please show me!' 'Get the fuck out of my room. Can't you see I'm busy?'

And the next day: 'I apologise for bothering you yesterday. Do you forgive me, Rowan? Can I come in? Do you forgive me?' 'Are you really sorry?' 'Yes.' 'What will you do to prove it?' 'Anything you say.' 'Okay, give me your hand. Close your eyes…Come on… follow me…'

The garage again. But this time it was the month of January and the temperature, both out of doors and inside the garage, was twenty below. Our breath visible as steam in the semi-darkness. 'Take off your clothes.' I peeled off my coat; then, very slowly, my sweater. 'Come on, keep going.' 'It's freezing in here, Rowan.' 'Is that how weak your love is? It comes to an abrupt halt after a few shivers? I did hear you correctly, didn't I? You did say you apologised and were eager to prove how much you loved your master, didn't you?' 'Yes, but…' 'Then you have to obey him.' 'Yes, but what if Mommy or Daddy…?' 'They're both busy. They won't come out here.' 'I'm scared, Rowan.' 'Jesus, what a scaredy-cat. You'll never amount to anything.' 'Don't say that!' 'Well, make it snappy.' 'Okay…'

Numb fingers fumbling with buttons and zips. At last I was naked, crouching, shivering violently, awed at the greyish-green hue of my own skin in the half-light, skinny arms circling skinny legs in an attempt to conjure up warmth. Fully dressed, Rowan stood there staring down at me. 'Okay, now lie down.' Shoulder blades on icy cement floor. 'Get up…Lie down…Get up, I told you…What are you doing standing up? I told you to lie down.' 'Rowan, I'm freezing to death. Please…' 'Jesus H. Christ! Talk about the princess and the pea! Well, I guess we'll just have to build a fire to keep my little princess warm, now, won't we?'

He lights a cigarette and inhales. When he exhales, the smoke gets mixed with the white steam of his breath. I start to cry, but stop at once because the tears freeze on my cheeks. 'Cry-baby,' says Rowan. 'Grow up. Aww, will you just grow up?' I fight back the tears and my chest convulses in great, wrenching sobs. 'Come over here, Rena. Come to your big brother.' I move into his outstretched arms. He embraces me, clasps me to him, comforts and rocks me, gently blowing the warmth from his mouth and throat onto my neck—then, squeezing harder, imprisoning me, he applies the burning tip of his cigarette to my back. Once…twice…three times. Three screams. 'Shut the fuck up,' he says, slapping a hand over my mouth. 'Hey. Are you going to stop screaming?' I nod wildly and clench my jaws as hard I can. He shoves me away from him. 'Are you going to stop blubbering, you cry-baby?' I nod again, then wipe my nose on my naked arm and watch the mucus freeze. 'It's all right, Rena. Everything's all right. It's all over now. It was just a test to see if you really loved me. You've passed the test and now you can put your clothes back on. Now we're really in it together, aren't we?' 'Yes.' 'You'll be rewarded for your obedience. Are you glad?' 'Yes.' 'Are you proud?' 'Yes.' 'And you'll never breathe a word to anyone about what just happened?' 'No, Rowan, of course not.' 'You swear?' 'I swear.'

But Lucille saw the triangle of angry red welts on my back that evening, when she carried an armful of ironed clothes into my room. She drew up short. 'What's that?' A reverse echo-chamber, the question growing louder each time it was repeated instead of softer—not fading away, not attenuating and disappearing but rising, rising in crescendo. 'What's that? Rena, what's that?' 'They look like burns, madame.' 'Rena, who did this to you? Simon! Come and look at this!' 'What's that?' 'Rena, what happened to you?' 'Darling, you have to tell us. Who did this to you?' 'Who burned you?' 'Did Rowan do this?' 'Did Rowan burn you?' 'Did he?' 'Did he?'

Not a word passed my lips. When I bowed my head, it was neither an acquiescence nor an avowal, simply a way of cowering, shrinking away, trying to disappear…But Rowan was kicked out of the house the very next day.

Double Noctran.

TUESDAY

'To have believed in both the guilt and innocence of photographing…'

No dreams, thanks to the sleeping-pills.

Lying in bed, Rena calculates how long it will be until her plane lands in Paris. Only twenty-seven hours to go...

Aziz was supposed to come and meet her at Roissy...but with everything that's going on in France, will he be able to?

It's past nine by the time she walks into the breakfast room. The minute they set eyes on her, Ingrid and Simon can tell something is off.

'You're white as a sheet,' Ingrid says in a worried voice. 'Didn't you sleep well?'

She tells them.

'Oh, you poor thing!' her stepmother exclaims. 'Look: here's the number to block your Visa card. Quick! Go ask if you can use their phone; it's a free call.'

Five minutes later, it's taken care of.

'You're right not to have gone to the police,' says Simon. 'Given car theft statistics in Italy, it's probably not even worth filing a complaint. It would only mean endless paperwork, with no real hope of finding the culprits.'

'But how will we get back to Florence?' Rena says. 'You haven't driven since your cataract operation, isn't that right?'

'Yes, but my dear wife can drive.'

Rena turns to Ingrid. 'Do you have your licence with you?'

'Of course. Wouldn't be caught dead without it.'

'Oh.' (Why hadn't it occurred to Rena to ask Ingrid if she wanted to drive?) 'And you're not afraid of dealing with Italian driver machismo?'

'Not to worry. An hour and a half on the highway should be

do-able. And since we didn't put a second driver's name on the contract, I'll pass the wheel back to you just before we get to the agency.'

Rena stares at Ingrid in amazement. Does she always think of everything?

'The worst loss by far,' says Simon, 'is your Canon.'

'Not to worry,' says Rena in turn. 'I can always buy another one. No, the worst loss is what was *in* it—your photos of me.'

It's ten o'clock. The blonde, efficient young owner comes over and starts clearing away their breakfast things.

'Well,' says Rena. 'Shall we be off?'

'Wait,' says Simon. 'Why don't you come up to our room so we can talk over our plans for the day?'

The question kills her. (*Life? Oh, that was what / went by while we were busy / making all those plans.* A haiku written by Simon himself, long years ago.) Even if they leave right this minute, Rena doesn't see how they can possibly squeeze in everything they're supposed to do today: drive back to Florence, return the car, schlep their luggage over to the hotel…and they wanted to spend at least a few minutes at the Uffizi, failing which they can scarcely claim to have visited Florence. Right now, they're not even packed, so if they have to sit down and discuss plans…No, thinks Rena. No, time will stop, I'll never see Aziz or Kerstin, Toussaint or Thierno again. I'll be stuck here forever in a B & B on the outskirts of Siena, with my father… his wife…his confusion…and his love…

'Coming, Rena?' says Ingrid.

She comes, and her pointy little ass barely touches the windowsill as she sits down.

Methodically, Simon goes about removing maps, clothing and books from the room's only chair.

'Have a chair,' he says. (Need me.)

'I'm fine, Dad. Don't bother.' (I'd sooner die!)

'But you'll be cold, so close to the window.' (Let me love you!)

'I'm forty-five years old, Dad. I know whether I'm cold or not. Trust me.' (Leave me alone!)

'But you're my guest, I want to make you comfortable.' (Whatever happened to my loving little girl?)

'Dad, how long do you plan to push me around on pretext of making me comfortable?' (Get off my back!)

Everything goes smoothly.

They speed across the Tuscan countryside, Ingrid driving masterfully. At last Rena can credit the idea that this ordeal might actually come to an end.

So this is…this was…this will have been…it?

Ingrid chirps and warbles as she drives. 'Isn't it a gorgeous day? Oh…I hope that car theft won't spoil your whole memory of the trip. You've given us such a marvellous holiday…Right, Dad?'

'I should say so!' Simon says. 'From now on, I'm going to turn seventy every year.'

They talk of going to Rome the next time around. Greece, too— oh, yes! Some other year…They talk and talk, believing not a word of what they say.

When they reach Florence's ring road, Ingrid stops at a petrol station, fills up, and passes the wheel to Rena. Putting on her glasses, she guides her stepdaughter skilfully through the one-way streets around the Piazza Ognissanti.

The agency's elegant Francophile comes out to check the car.

'I hope everything went well, ladies and gentlemen?' he asks them in French.

'*Si, si, grazie, naturalmente,*' Rena says, handing him the keys.

The rental was prepaid; it's all over. Rena feels free, light-hearted, almost giddy.

That theft was basically a stroke of luck, Subra tells her. Look at all the things you don't have to feel guilty about anymore! Not taking pictures, not calling your son who's soon to be a father... Even Aziz's silence has stopped torturing you: he might be trying to reach you, but you have no way of knowing it. So it's not your fault: you're innocent, completely innocent! Nothing to *do* with Beatrice Cenci, I tell you!

On the way to the Hotel Guelfa in a taxi, Simon startles them by telling the driver to stop. At once, car horns start honking indignantly.

'What's up, Dad?' asks Ingrid.

Without a word, he gets out of the car and disappears into a shop. Craning her neck, Rena sees it's an international bookshop. Incensed, she launches into a series of rhetorical questions: 'Is this the right time to buy a book? Does he think this is the right time to buy a book?'

Her father comes out of the store a few moments later. 'Got a little something for you', he says, handing her a plastic bag. She peeps into it: he has replaced her *Guide bleu: Italie du nord et du centre*.

Drago

Though the sour-tempered proprietor seems less than overjoyed to see them again, checking into their old rooms at the Guelfa feels almost like a homecoming. Ah, that adorable Room 25! So narrow, so original...

It's past two o'clock; they're starved.

They stride familiarly down Via Guelfa until its name changes to Via degli Alfani, then turn right into Via dei Servi. Soon come to an end, this perpetual searching for restaurants.

'This one look all right?'

'No, the music's too loud.'

'What about this one?'

'Nope. Too bad; they've stopped serving lunch.'

'Look—over here!'

Sudden perfection. A secret alleyway. A terrace. Sunlight. Lunch tables set up just opposite a tiny twelfth-century basilica. A smiling young waitress comes and goes, bringing them food.

But when Ingrid turns to Rena and asks if Aziz deals with her absences better than Alioune used to—shaken, perhaps, by the loss of all her identities—Rena doesn't appreciate it.

'He deals with them,' she says. And lights up a cigarette in the middle of the meal, knowing how much Ingrid detests cigarette smoke.

'Uncanny,' Simon breathes, 'the way you blew your smoke out through your nostrils just now, dragon-style…Your mother used to do that. For a minute, you looked exactly like her.'

'What's so uncanny about it?' Rena retort. 'Does it bother you that I resemble my mother in some ways? Who knows, maybe I inherited a few of my traits from her! My hand gestures…my green eyes…my ability to carry projects through to completion? Is that a flaw, in your opinion?'

'Rena!' says Ingrid.

'Yes, I did have a mother once, in case you've forgotten…And I don't have one anymore. And you have the nerve to ask me about *my* absences, when…when…' She doesn't know when what.

'For heaven's sake, Rena,' Ingrid says in a louder voice. 'Don't spoil our lovely holiday by dredging up all those old accusations…'

The more her stepmother raises her voice, the more Rena lowers hers.

'Who's making accusations?' she says in a whisper. 'Is someone making accusations?'

Suddenly overwhelmed by memories, Simon sets down his fork and weeps.

Whose fault was it? Mine? Rena asks Subra in despair.

No, not yours, Subra murmurs soothingly.

I mean, all right, Rena goes on, I'm the one who pronounced the words Portobello Road and Sylvie and vintage dresses and London, I don't deny it, the words slipped through my lips and no one else's—but the *facts*—the facts, Daddy—who was responsible for the facts? Me? I was sixteen and you were forty…I was alone with my mother that day, and when the words escaped me I saw your marriage of twenty years—everything you'd built together, a complex construction she still believed in, despite your money problems and your quarrels—slowly and spectacularly collapse. Yes, I saw the catastrophe in her green eyes…not because her husband had been unfaithful to her—that was banal—but because…because of me…because of the complicity between her husband and her daughter…their silence against her…the enormity and the duration of their betrayal…and then…even as my words went on exploding in different parts of her brain like tracer bullets, skewing her judgment, freezing her limbs, blurring her vision, confusing her thoughts, accelerating her heartbeat, Lisa went storming out of the house…She got into her car, that day, in the state she was in, and turned on the ignition…

San Lorenzo Secondo

Rena shoves her plate away, unable to swallow another bite.

And then…the speeding car…the pounding of her heart…the strangeness of her body…the sense of lightness in her head…the coldness of her hands…the speed…the bridge…her right leg shaking so badly that the car advanced by fits and starts...my words...the car...the bridge...my green eyes...you're the one who taught me... her green eyes...how to drive, Daddy, and...sinking...my mother... those words...down...speeding...to the bottom...heartbeats...of the river...its waters...icy in that...Saint-Lawrence...season...San Lorenzo...him again...

What is old? This waitress has been around for twenty years, my pain for nearly thirty, the ivy-chewed bricks for eight hundred, the sun for four billion...yet all of it is now. New. Raw.

'No, Rowan, no, it's not my fault, I swear...' 'Whose fault is it, then? Why did you tell her? Couldn't you keep your big mouth shut? Why did you denounce our father?' At twenty, my brother, comfortably ensconced in his gay lifestyle on the West coast, had already made a name for himself as a jazz violinist even as he finished up a brilliant course of studies at the Conservatory. He never touched me anymore; only his words fire-branded me now. 'She was *my* mother, too, Rena...And you started taking her away from me the minute you were born. She was *my* mother, too, and you killed her...' 'No, Rowan, don't say that. Don't say that...' 'I only say it because it's true...' 'No, it's *not* true—she had an accident!' 'The accident was *you*, Rena! You're the only accident our mother ever had.'

Looking around at the other customers on the terrace, Rena soberly reminds herself that each and every one of them contains a Thebes, a Troy, a Jerusalem...How do we manage to go on putting one foot ahead of the other, smiling, shopping for food, not dying from the pain?

Having licked her plate clean, Ingrid pats Rena on the hand with which she has just stubbed out her cigarette. 'Don't you think we should drop the subject? Let bygones be bygones. Look, it's already quarter to four. If we want to see the Uffizi, we should be on our way. I'll go take care of the bill and pay my little visit to the ladies' room...' She enters the restaurant.

Simon, his eyes red with tears, seeks out Rena's gaze behind the dark glasses she stubbornly refuses to remove. But when he stretches both hands out to her over the remains of their meal, she gives him hers, and he squeezes them so hard it hurts.

'Daddy...'

'I'm sorry, little one. I'm so sorry.'

She pulls her hands away and tries to smile, hiding her embarrassment by drawing out the *Guide bleu* he just bought for her.

'The place is humungous,' she mutters. 'We should choose which galleries we want to visit...'

'*Oïe vey,*' Simon says. 'I'm not sure I've got the strength to deal with the Uffizi.'

'Okay,' Rena laughs. 'To hell with the Uffizi!'

San Marco

Ingrid returns. 'The restrooms are impeccably clean here,' she announces. 'Everything's taken care of. We can go.'

'Just a second,' Simon says. 'Rena's looking for something less exhausting than the Uffizi.'

'Oh...' Ingrid says, crestfallen. 'So many of my friends told me it was a must.'

'Listen to this,' says Rena, reading aloud from the guide. 'San Marco: impossible not to be spellbound by the atmosphere of the place. The Dominican monastery which houses the museum is one of Tuscany's finest architectural jewels.'

'That sounds perfect!' says Simon.

'And it's close by,' Rena adds, 'whereas the Uffizi is a good twenty minutes' walk away.'

That clinches it for Ingrid; she gives in and their wobbly procession starts off again.

Rena goes on reading from the guide as they advance towards the Via C. Battisti. 'Monks' cells decorated with frescoes by Fra Angelico...a library built for Cosimo the Elder by Michelozzo... to say nothing of Fra Bartolomeo's famous portrait of Savonarola!'

'Who's that?' Ingrid asks.

'You know,' Simon says. 'The fanatical prior we mentioned the other day. Railer and reviler, impassioned orator, demented igniter of bonfires of the vanities...'

'Oh, yes,' mutters Ingrid. 'I remember now.'

'When he arrived at the Duomo for his sermon,' Simon goes on, 'the crowds of the faithful would drop to their knees and chant, *Mea culpa, mea culpa, mea maxima culpa.* A thousand foreheads would hit the floor at the same time. Imagine!'

'Protestants don't do that,' Ingrid says.

'See?' says Rena, pointing. 'It's right over there. We just have to cross the square...'

But no. As they step up from street to kerb on the Piazza San Marco esplanade, Simon stumbles.

Not to worry, thinks Rena. He'll catch his balance.

But no. Before her very eyes, he plummets earthward.

Not to worry, thinks Rena. He'll use his arms to break his fall.

But no. His arms buckle uselessly beneath him.

Not to worry, thinks Rena. His fat tummy will absorb the shock.

But no. As she watches, aghast, Simon hits the ground with his forehead.

It's not: *his forehead hits the ground.* No, it's: *he hits the ground with his forehead.*

As if, on this very spot, straddling the centuries, Savonarola had forced him to confess his crime.

Grande problema

So much for San Marco.

Now what. Now what do we do? Rena asks her Special Friend, but Subra has no answer.

Simon is lying on the ground, his forehead spurting blood. At once, half a dozen passers-by rush over to help him to his feet. Luckily there's a bench on the esplanade, just a few steps away. Ingrid sits down on it next to her husband, deeply shaken.

Maybe she'll faint, too, Rena thinks—why not? Anything can happen. But I'll be on that plane tomorrow morning, nothing in the world can prevent me, I'll be on it. Drawing a tissue from her pocket, she starts dabbing at the blood on her father's forehead.

'*Ghiacchio!*' a young man exclaims.

Yes, of course. That's what we need. Ice. She crosses the avenue and walks into a fancy coffee shop—gleaming chrome, towering chocolate layer cakes, elegant customers milling about. '*Ghiacchio?*' she says to a young waitress. Even as she performs a pantomime of her father's accident, she registers every detail of the girl's appearance: carefully made-up face, well-cut uniform, pink ruffles on her apron, mauve ribbons in her hair, purple polish on her fingernails... Ah, thinks Rena, what wouldn't I give to have this girl as a model...a friend...a hostage...

Now the waitress is handing her a crackly cellophane bag chock-full of tiny white ice cubes. '*Grazie, grazie!*' Rena feels like kissing her full on the lips.

She goes back outside and sizes up their new situation from afar: Tourists; spot of bother. An old man slumped on a bench, forehead bloodied; his wife muttering and fluttering around him. Called back to their respective pressing obligations, the helpful passers-by have vanished. Resolutely, Rena goes over to include herself in the tourists-spot-of-bother group. Yes, that is correct, I am the man's daughter and this is what my life is about just at the moment—this, and nothing else. Not the riots in France, not the Dominican monks' cells; this. Here's the ice, Daddy. I love you…

Simon's eyes are closed.

'You okay?'

'Sure, sure.'

'Rena,' Ingrid says feverishly, 'several people told me we should find an ambulance and take him to the hospital.'

'Did they say it in English?'

'In English, in Italian, what does it matter? They made themselves clear. They said it several times. But your father doesn't want to go.'

'There's no need,' says Simon with a wave of hand. 'I'll be fine.'

'Here,' says Rena, handing Ingrid the ice cubes. 'Can I take a look?'

Ingrid parts the tissue papers with which she's been staunching the blood. Since Rena left, the bump has risen spectacularly and is now the size of a large egg. The sight of the raw flesh makes her shudder.

'Hmm,' she says. 'I don't know, maybe they're right. Maybe we should go to a hospital and ask a doctor to check it, if only to set our minds at rest.'

'What do you say, Dad?'

'Not in an ambulance, anyhow,' Simon says. 'I wouldn't want to take an ambulance away from someone who really needs it.'

'Well, let's take a taxi, then,' Ingrid says. 'I'm sure the taxi drivers know all the hospitals.'

'Have you got enough cash?' Rena looks at her.

'Sure, I've got plenty of euros. Everyone has been so kind to us on this trip, I haven't been able to spend anything.'

When they help Simon to his feet, he reels. It's a dream. Rena hails a cab. It slows down as it approaches...but takes off again, tyres screeching, when the driver glimpses the blood on the tissue papers.

'We'd better put his hat back on,' Rena tells Ingrid, 'or else no taxi will take us.'

'Can we do that, Dad?'

'Gently, gently...'

Eventually, another cab draws up. It takes them several minutes to settle into the back seat. The driver fidgets with impatience.

Just as *you* used to, says Subra.

No reason to fidget, sir. No reason at all. Your meter is ticking, believe me. You wouldn't want it to tick any faster. Why hurry to reach the day when, like my father, you'll fall and break your head open on the Piazza San Marco? That day will come soon enough. Believe me, sir, there's no rush at all.

'*Ospedale*,' she says out loud, feeling an almost maternal benevolence for the impatient young idiot.

'*Spedale degli Innocenti?*' he asks, meeting her eyes in the rear-view mirror.

And though it would be perfectly plausible for a group of tourists to wish to be driven to that sumptuous art gallery, she bursts out laughing. No, no, I'm not innocent, no one is innocent, I mean everyone is innocent, I'm not Beatrice Cenci...

'No,' she says out loud, stifling her incongruous mirth as best she can. '*Un ospedale vero.*'

'*Il quale?*' the young man asks in exasperation.

'*Non lo so, non me ne importa un fico!*'

'*Signora!*'

'*Il più grande, il migliore, ma, per favore, subito presto!*'

It's rush hour, and traffic is at a standstill in the Via Nazionale. Squashed into the back seat on either side of the wounded man, Ingrid and Rena each take one of his hands.

'I'm fine, I'm just fine,' Simon murmurs, eyes closed, gently tapping their hands with his.

Voices and music blare from the radio in a non-stop jingle. It's impossible to tell advertisements from regular programmes; it all sounds equally imbecilic and hysterical. Other anguished car rides well up to the surface of Rena's mind: her two deliveries (her waters broke in the taxi on the way to the hospital to give birth to Toussaint, and the driver made her sign a paper promising to pay to have his upholstery cleaned)...various planes she all but missed, fearing for her life as taxi-drivers honk-honked their way through traffic in cities like Jaipur or Cairo, where the highway code is replaced by the notion of destiny...mad scrambles to get Alioune to Orly Airport on time when he had to take over for a colleague in Dakar at the drop of a hat...rushing to meet Thierno at the Montparnasse train station when he came back to Paris, depressed and angry, from school outings to ski resorts...It seems as if she has spent half her life stuck in traffic, glancing at her watch and swallowing exhaust fumes. All those marvellous inventions of the Renaissance—clockwork, machines, the harnessing of natural forces by man—have converged to produce this moment: a medical emergency at a standstill, amidst ten thousand aggressive vehicles that sit there revving their motors, spewing chemical poisons into the air, eating away at the ozone layer...

'*Ecco*,' says the driver at last, and Ingrid hands him the correct money.

'Hey, Dad,' she cries a moment later, once they're all back on the footpath. 'Look where we are! Over there…look, the cathedral! We never got to visit that, either!'

Indeed, they are but a stone's throw from the Duomo Santa Maria del Fiore, and *this* impressive building is none other than the Arcispedale di Santa Maria Nuova. Well, how about that! An archi-hospital!

'I'm fine. There's nothing wrong with me,' mutters Simon as they move through a swinging door marked PRONTO SOCCORSO.

They're taken in charge at once.

It has to be a dream…Memories of endless hours spent in the emergency rooms of various hospitals in Paris, surrounded by dozens of other panic-stricken parents with whimpering babies in their arms or glassy-eyed toddlers on their laps—waiting, filling out forms, waiting, more formalities, waiting, insurance papers, waiting. The smell of urine and disinfectant, Nescafé and shit, dried sweat, and despair…

Nothing of the sort here. Nothing but polite receptionists, reassuring nurses and sympathetic doctors…Within five minutes Simon is being wheeled away on a gurney for X-rays. How civilised can you get?

Aspetto Primo

In the waiting room, the two women settle calmly into armchairs.

'We made the right decision,' Ingrid says.

'Sure we did.'

'Everything will be all right now.'

'Of course it will, Ingrid. You've been terrific.'

'Me? I haven't done a thing. You're the one who's handled things beautifully. But that's only natural; you're a much more seasoned traveller than I am.'

Silence.

Then Ingrid asks, 'What time is your flight tomorrow?'

'Eight a.m. I should be at the airport by seven. What about yours?'

'Not until eleven. We have a stopover in Paris. It's silly—we should have arranged to take the same plane.'

'You'll have to lend me a little money for cab fare...'

'No problem. But we'll come with you to the airport. It'll mean getting up early but that's okay, we can catch up on our sleep during the flight.'

'That's sweet of you. Who's meeting you at Mirabel?'

'David...And you? Aziz?'

'Theoretically. That was the plan, yes...but given all that's been happening in the meantime, I don't know. He must be swamped...'

'Why don't you call him?'

'Very funny. I don't have a phone.'

'Take my Visa card. Go ahead, give him a ring...If you want to, of course.'

Illogically, Rena glances at her watch. Having no choice in the matter, the watch tells her what it has been programmed to tell her. ('Years, months and days are natural,' Simon had explained to her when she was little, 'but weeks, hours and minutes are man-made.' 'What about seconds?' she had asked. 'Are they woman-made?' 'Ha, ha, ha!')

Cifre

She borrows Ingrid's Visa card. Knees quaking, she walks down a long, dark corridor, at the far end of which is a payphone.

Maybe it only accepts local phone cards, whispers Subra.

You're right, I sort of hope so...Nope, no such luck. This payphone is a whore; it takes anything and everything.

Weird, isn't it? says Subra. No one ever suggests that, deep down, payphones *enjoy* their customers' calls. No, you put your money in the slot and they do what they've been paid for, period.

Rena slips the Visa card into the telephone.

We've invented so many things, she says to herself, slowly dialling Aziz's number. It shouldn't be possible to take a piece of plastic decorated with letters and numerals in bas relief, press a series of metallic buttons to dial a fifteen-figure number which is stored in one's memory along with dozens of other numbers corresponding to various facets of one's identity (telephone, bank account, social security, licence plate, postal code, bank code, door code), then lift a black Bakelite cradle to your ear and hear, encoded and decoded by twelve hundred miles of copper wire, the voice of the person you love.

Niente

'Aziz speaking.'

Ah. So her man answers his mobile when an unfamiliar number flashes onto the screen. *Rena*, no; *Not Known*, yes.

'It's me, love...' All that comes out of her throat is a pathetic croak.

'Hello?'

She clears her throat. 'It's me. It's Rena.'

The answer to that is silence.

'Aziz, are you okay? Are you there?'

'I'm here, but...'

'Listen, love, so much has happened...in France, I know... but here, too...You wouldn't believe it. It'll take us weeks to catch up…We'll start tomorrow…Are you still planning to pick me up at Roissy?'

More silence. What the hell is going on?

'It doesn't matter,' she babbles. 'I can take a cab, no hassle. I mean, I'm sure you've got better things to do at ten a.m. I'll have to borrow some money from Ingrid, though, because…'

'Rena.'

'What?'

More silence.

'What, Aziz? Tell me. Are you mad because I couldn't come home any soon—'

'Rena…we're not t-t-to…'

Oh-oh, thinks Rena. If he's stammering, something is really wrong.

'…gether anymore. I've d-d-decided not to move into the Rue des Envierges.'

'When?'

What a stupid question: when? Aziz doesn't answer it.

'But…why? What's going on? I adore you, Aziz. Living with you is the thing I care about most in the world.'

Silence.

'It's because I'm Jewish, is that it? Did Aicha finally convince you…'

'No, Rena, it's not b-b-b-because you're Jewish…It's because you're nothing. See? That's all. That's why. B-b-b-because you're nothing, Rena. I'm something. And just now…I have to give that something all my attention.'

'I haven't got the slightest idea what you're talking about.'

'Sorry if I'm c-c-c-causing you pain.'

The connection is cut off.

If you're causing me pain? Sorry *if* you're causing me pain? Rena repeats incredulously to herself as she walks down the long, dark corridor in the other direction. That's hilarious. *If* you're causing me pain…

Incapable of facing Ingrid right away, she stops off in the *Bagni Signore*. Pays no attention to the other women milling around in there. Walks straight to the farthest sink and plants herself in front of the mirror.

Tutto

Aziz's 'You're nothing' scared her so badly that she almost expects the mirror to reflect only the white tiling behind her. But no, it frames a face. She studies the face with a professional eye, trying to get behind it and see what makes it tick.

The last photos of Arbus, taken just before her suicide in July 1971, show her looking thin, tense and uncertain. She's dressed in black leather pants, her hair is cut short and there are dark shadows under her eyes…Where did her stubborn neutrality come from? Rena suddenly wonders. Her refusal to find one thing better than another? Her blindness in the face of injustice? Arbus was interested only in the particular: each, each, each.

She said yes to everyone, Subra puts in. Just like the payphone.

Right. Accepting other people to the point of non-existence. Diane *diaphanes*, a transparent film that allows light to pass through it. 'I just want to stay with my eye to the keyhole forever,' she once wrote to a friend.

What had that Maisie seen? What had she endured as a little girl, growing up in New York in that wealthy Jewish family whose privileges she detested? What evil had she been forced to construe as good, so irrevocably that she would spend the rest of her life blurring the nuances between the two?

I, too, Aziz, am something.

She bends over the sink and splashes her face with cold water, scattering droplets in all directions.

All right, so you've lost your boyfriend, whispers Subra, forever loyal. But you've found your Dad again. And the minute you get back to Paris, you'll buy a new camera…

Aspetto Secondo

It's eight p.m. by the time she re-enters the waiting room. She sees Ingrid sitting there, not flipping through a magazine, just waiting, handbag on lap, hands folded on handbag. Determined to imitate her, she goes over and sits down next to her. No longer having a bag, she sets her hands directly on her knees.

'No news?' she asks.

'Not yet. Don't you think it's a bit strange? They took him away two hours ago.'

'You're right, it is strange. Maybe there was a queue in the X-ray room. People with more serious problems that had to be seen to first.'

'Maybe. What about you? Everything A-OK in Paris?'

'Mmm…No.'

'Oh, Rena…'

Without warning, Rena turns to her stepmother and bursts into tears.

'Rena. Oh, my poor dear,' Ingrid says, stroking her stepdaughter's hair as she sobs on her shoulder. 'Look!' Rummaging in her bag, she pulls out a Kleenex and two fifty-euro bills. 'This is for your runny nose, and this is for your little expenses when you get back to Paris—don't get them mixed up now! Come on, give us a smile.'

Her attempt at humour is so puerile that Rena can't help laughing as she blows her nose.

'Maybe you could ask them what's going on? You speak Italian…'

'Okay,' Rena says, borrowing a second tissue to wipe her eyes with. 'Sure. I'll go ask.'

The receptionist at PRONTO SOCCORSO knows nothing.

'Couldn't you try to get in touch with the doctor who's looking after Mr Greenblatt?' asks Rena.

'No, we can't bother the doctors. Wait, though—I can check with the nurses on that floor. He's in radiology, you said?'

The woman puts the call through. Rena savours the music of their patronym pronounced in Italian. She observes this exhausted-looking woman who keeps tapping her pencil nervously on the desk as she waits for the answer to her question. Fiftyish, probably attractive when young, she wears reading glasses and presses her lips together far too often. Though her eyes stare up at the high window on the wall across from her desk, it's clear she sees neither the evening sky outside (deep violet) nor the sixteenth-century moulding (black with dust); her mind is on her own troubles, which have dug deep creases in her brow…Is she aware that Timothy Leary is still up there, revolving around the Earth? Has she heard Leonard Cohen's new album? Would she be interested to know that my brother Rowan Greenblatt is a peerless jazz violinist, a true genius of improvisation?

'*Signora.*'

'*Sì.*'

'They tell me to tell you to wait.'

'But we've already waited two hours! What's going on?'

'Madame. They're looking after your father. He needed some extra tests.'

'What kind of tests?'

'They didn't tell me anything else. They said only that they will do more tests over the next few hours, and can you please be patient. You have time to go out for dinner.'

'We have time to go out for dinner?'

'Yes, it will take some time. There. That is all I can tell you.'

Aspetto Terzo

This time when she enters the waiting room her step must be different, for Ingrid's eyes leap at her the minute she crosses the threshold. Rena puts an arm around the older woman's shoulders, repeats what she has just been told...and feels her stepmother's body seize up in shock.

'What does that mean?'

Over the ensuing hours, they will reiterate countless variants of that question. ('What's going on?' 'Why are they keeping him?' 'What gives them the right...?' 'What are they doing to him?' 'Did she tell you what they were doing to him?' 'What can it possibly mean?') Every once in a while they make an enormous effort to change the subject ('Isn't Italy beautiful?' 'Gorgeous!') but it swiftly peters out and they go back to the old refrain. ('Everything will turn out all right.' 'Of course it will.' 'But what are they doing to him?')

Rena drifts off to sleep.

I'm in a large café somewhere, seated at a table with a dozen strangers. Among them I suddenly recognise the famous Hollywood producer Sam Goldwyn. Though he doesn't actually look like Goldwyn—he's tall, thin, greying and alcoholic, a sort of ageing beau—I know it's him. He insults me a little, to sound me out, and I answer sweetly and humorously, thinking, Boy, if he knew who he was talking to...He asks me to dance and gradually we start to pick up each other's signals. Rubbing up against me, he finds me pliable and malleable, I receive his body totally, perfectly, melting at his touch. He picks me up and spins me around in the air. I'm careful to conceal my 'true' identity from him so that he'll go on desiring me and playing with me—oh, this is paradise, I feel light, weightless—I wish it would never end...

Waking up with a start, Rena instantly recognises the 'famous' man's initials.

Ingrid hasn't slept a wink.

At eleven p.m., they force themselves to go down the hallway and purchase sandwiches from a machine. Each of them is now mothering both the other and herself: mothers know you can't think clearly on an empty stomach. You get nervous and irritable when you're hungry; you overreact.

The sandwiches stick in their throats. They wash them down with water.

'Go out and have a cigarette if you feel like it,' Ingrid says, 'I'll tell you the minute somebody comes.'

'Thanks,' Rena answers, 'but I'm not going anywhere.'

Puma

At midnight, having dragged its heels unbearably all evening, time suddenly pounces on them, the way a puma pounces on a gazelle.

A doctor sticks his head through the door and motions Rena to join him in the hall. He prefers to talk to her, he says, because his French is better than his English. He can't fool her, though: the truth is that he dreads the wife's reaction more than the daughter's.

'What happened is this,' he says. 'We started off with an X-ray... just a routine thing, you know...your father's injury isn't serious...I mean, it's always impressive to see a big bump like that...but it'll go away in a few days, it's nothing at all...Anyway, what happened is this...' The man is in his early sixties; his tone is calm and professional. Rena can tell he has fulfilled this obligation countless times in the past and learned to keep his voice low, firm, and especially continuous. Yes, it's of the utmost importance that he keep talking: his voice is like a rope the patient's loved ones have to be able to hang onto and follow, step by step, with crystal-clear logic, from start to finish. 'We noticed something else on the X-ray—a shadow. You never know, it might have been simply a light effect, but we figured it was worth putting him through a few other tests in case it was something more serious. Your father had his insurance papers on him and he signed all the authorisations, so we went ahead and did a TDM and then an MRI. The results just came back and... well, unfortunately, madame, to put it as simply and directly as possible, unfortunately, madame, we were right: it was serious. We discovered a glioma in your father's brain, a sort of primitive tumour of the nervous system. I'm very sorry to have such bad news for you. For the time being, we've told him nothing, naturally. He's resting up. Your father is a very nice man. A very nice man indeed.'

Rena forgets. She doesn't know how. She doesn't speak French anymore, or any other language. Subra, too: struck dumb.

The doctor feeds her rope for a while longer. He tells her that, in his opinion, it wouldn't be a good idea for Mr Greenblatt to take a trans-Atlantic flight in the morning as planned. It would be better to keep him under observation for a day or two—and organise his transfer to a hospital immediately upon his return to Montreal.

Rena is hardly listening anymore. Her thoughts are rushing around in all directions like panicked mice, flashing at top speed and in random order through the images of the Tuscany trip, stopping at one only to seize up in terror and dart off to another. Her father stumbling on the Piazza San Marco...dozing off on twenty different benches...lousy Virgil...sitting on the floor in the History of Science Museum...standing in Gaia's living room, head in hands...complaining of migraine headaches...forgetting the scarf he'd given her... All this not symptomatic, as it turns out, of bad faith or bad will or bad mood, not at all—but rather, since the outset, since day one, no, since before that, maybe long before that, no one knows since when...

The third time she re-enters the waiting room, Ingrid leaps across the room and grabs her by the arm.

'Is he all right?' she asks.

'He's resting. The doctor says he's such a nice man that they want to keep him a little longer. Let's go out for a drink, hey? We deserve one. Let's get soused.'

But Ingrid cannot be fooled—not even by Rena Greenblatt, that inveterate liar. She sees right through her. Grasps the fact that the two of them are the gazelle, and that the puma has just ripped their throat open.

'Rena! Tell me.'

'Let's go, Ingrid.'

Rena virtually drags her stepmother to the desk, where the exhausted middle-aged receptionist has been replaced by a cute young redhead.

'*Prego, signorina,* are there any cafés open at this time of night?'

'Everything's closed in the neighbourhood, *signora*. Except maybe at the train station. Yes, you might try the train station—I think there's a coffee-shop there that stays open all night.'

Thus it is that Ingrid and Rena spend the night at the Stazione Santa Maria Novella, side by side not to say intertwined on a worn red-leather wall seat. This means that the following morning, just as Rena's plane is taking off for Paris from Amerigo Vespucci Airport, they have top-notch seats for the TV news headlines that flash onto the screen in flaming red letters: 'France declares a state of emergency'.

Outside, it looks as if it's going to be a beautiful day. A church bell clangs, and, capturing the first rays of the rising sun, the Tuscan capital's ancient bricks and roof tiles begin to smoulder.

NOTES

The quotes on chapter title pages are from Diane Arbus's correspondence, excerpts of which are published in *Revelations*, Random House, New York, 2003.

The translation of Dante's *Inferno* is by Laurence Binyon.

p. 26, Beckett's description of Perugino's *Lamentation over the Dead Christ* is from a letter to his friend William McGreevy.

p. 44, Pico della Mirandola quotes are from Catherine David, *L'homme qui savait trop*, Seuil, 2001, p. 125, translated by the author.

p. 52–3, the dialogue with Galileo paraphrases one of Dava Sobel's paragraphs on the subject in her book, *Galileo's Daughter*, Fourth Estate, London, 1999, p.44.

p. 53, 'Some men really deserve...' is from *Galileo's Daughter*, ibid, pp 152–3, from Galileo Galilei's *Dialogue Concerning the Two Chief World Systems*. Translated by Stillman Drake. Berkeley, University of California Press, 1967, p. 59.

pp. 79–80, 'Woe! Woe is me!' lines are from a sonnet by Michelangelo, in Nadine Sautel's *Michel-Ange*, Gallimard, Folio, 2006, p.28; the line 'Painting and sculpture have been my downfall' is quoted on p. 77 of the same work. Translations by the author.

p. 103, 'that much attention' from the notes of a student who attended Arbus's photography class at Westbeth in July 1971, quoted in the film *Going Where I've Never Been*.

On *kinbaku*, the custom of tying up women for the pleasure of monks, as well the characteristics of the Buddhist deity Kannon, cf. Philippe Forest, *Araki enfin: l'homme qui ne vécut que pour aimer*, Gallimard, 2008.

p. 123, 'because, quite simply...', interview from Jean-Pierre Krief's film *Nobuyoshi Araki*, La Sept/Arte.

My heartfelt thanks to Séverine Auffret, Mihai Mangiulea, John Stewart, Fred Le Van and Tamia Valmont.